STEPHANIE'S PLEASURE

By the same author:

STEPHANIE
STEPHANIE'S CASTLE
STEPHANIE'S DOMAIN
STEPHANIE'S REVENGE
STEPHANIE'S TRIAL

MELINDA AND THE MASTER
MELINDA AND ESMERALDA

STEPHANIE'S PLEASURE

Susanna Hughes

This book is a work of fiction.
In real life, make sure you practise safe sex.

First published in 1994 by
Nexus
332 Ladbroke Grove
London W10 5AH

Reprinted 1995

Typeset by TW Typesetting, Plymouth, Devon
Printed and bound in Great Britain by
Cox & Wyman Ltd, Reading, Berkshire

ISBN 0 352 32947 5

STEPHANIE'S PLEASURE

Chapter One

A faint knock on her bedroom door broke the silence. Stephanie was already awake, though she had made no attempt to get up; instead, she lay gazing out at the view of the lake through her terrace windows, her long black hair spread out on the white linen pillowcase like a mantle. Though it was late autumn and there was a distinct chill in the air, the sun still shone over Lake Trasimeno and this morning the sky was blue and cloudless.

'Come in,' Stephanie said, sitting up and propping herself against the headboard of the large bed. She was wearing a pure silk and lace nightdress coloured the subtlest shade of cream, its neckline a plunging V, her firm breasts cupped by the lace's intricate webbing.

Venetia opened the bedroom door a little awkwardly, her hands grasping Stephanie's breakfast tray, then came over to the bed and set the tray over Stephanie's lap.

'Good morning, glorious morning,' she said.

'I've just been looking at it. What's this? Personal service? You didn't need to do this!'

'It's my last morning. Special treat.'

'For you or for me?' Stephanie smiled, looking up into Venetia's beautiful face: her perfectly proportioned nose, her high cheekbones, and her large, fleshy lips. Her long fair hair was brushed out and fell over her shoulders. It made her look younger. She was wearing a peachy coloured silk negligee over a matching nightdress; the nightdress was short and, with the negligee open, revealed most of Venetia's long, finely contoured thighs.

Without answering her question, Venetia poured them both coffee from the Georgian silver coffee pot. She sat on the edge of the bed while Stephanie tore a piece off the lightly warmed croissant and chewed it enthusiastically before dunking a second piece in her coffee cup.

'So you're really going?' Stephanie said.

'Yes.'

'I'll miss you.'

'You'll see me in London.'

'I know. It won't be the same . . .'

'What, you mean now I'm not your slave any more?' Venetia said it with no anger. She was smiling.

Stephanie laughed. 'In that respect it will be better, won't it?'

'Well, different anyway.'

'Devlin's done what he promised?'

'Everything he promised. I've got my own business now. Free and clear.'

If it hadn't been for Venetia, Stephanie mused, it was likely that she would not have been seeing the sun rise over the lake. She would still have been down in the cells, chained to the stone floor, at the mercy of her slaves.

Most of the prisoners in the castle had entered willingly. After all, they had committed crimes – fraud, embezzlement, theft – against the business empire of Stephanie's associate and lover, Devlin. If they did not accept punishment at the castle, they faced prosecution in the courts. But some could not bear the prolonged discipline and sexual humiliation, least of all Andrew Harlock, the man who had recently led a rebellion against the castle's keepers.

'You deserve it,' Stephanie said.

'The plane's coming for me in an hour,' Venetia said, looking at her watch. It was a Cartier, another present from the grateful Devlin.

'The plane can always be made to wait,' Stephanie said. That was the advantage of private jets.

'I thought . . .' Venetia said hesitantly.

'Thought what? That I wouldn't want to say goodbye properly?'

'After what happened . . .'

'That's all over now, Venetia. Forgotten. Andrew will have to pay the price. I'll see to that. But it doesn't mean . . .'

Stephanie stroked the silk of the negligee on Venetia's shoulder. It felt incredibly soft against the tips of her fingers and she could feel the warmth of Venetia's body underneath.

'Take the tray away,' she said, then corrected herself. 'Sorry, old habits . . .' Venetia wasn't her servant any more. She had to remember that. She quickly got out of bed herself and put the tray aside.

'I'd have done it –' Venetia said.

'I know you would.'

The V of lace that formed the neckline of the cream nightdress was repeated lower down, another wide V sewn into the silk in such a way that its apex matched exactly the apex of Stephanie's belly underneath. It revealed the thick black curls on Stephanie's mons.

'One last time, as equals,' Stephanie said, feeling her body pulsing with anticipation. Venetia had been the first woman to teach her the delights of lesbian love; the first woman to touch her and move her and use her body to achieve pleasures she would never have dreamt she could enjoy. She had experienced other women since, but looking at Venetia, being with Venetia was always going to be special.

'Not the last time – just the last time for now,' Venetia corrected.

'Yes. That's what I meant.'

Stephanie slipped the wide lace shoulder strap of the nightdress off. It fell over her upper arm. Slowly she flicked the other strap aside and the nightdress slid off her body, the silk whispering against her flesh, the material cascading to the floor and blossoming outwards. Stephanie put her hand to her left breast. Her nipple was dark in contrast to the lighter brown of her areola. With the very tip of her middle finger she circled the little bud of flesh and immediately felt it pucker and send tiny sensual signals through her nerves. She raised her right hand to her right breast and repeated the process so that both nipples vied with each other: a competition to see which was the most sensitive.

She saw Venetia's eyes roaming her naked body, looking at her breasts, her slim waist, the way her hips flared out from her middle and, most of all, the triangle of her belly where, even with her legs closed, there was a diamond of space between her thighs and under her labia.

'You're beautiful,' Venetia said quietly.

'So are you.'

Stephanie stepped out of the circle of silk the nightdress had formed but did not pick it up. She came closer to the bed, within inches of Venetia, and put out her hand to stroke her long hair. Venetia's hair was as soft as the silk of her negligee. Stephanie stroked from the crown of her head down to her shoulders and down again. With her other hand she ran the tips of her own fingers over her belly, her fingers aimed at the very apex of her thighs. Combing through her thick pubic hair she found the furrow of her sex, her labia plump and spongy. As her finger nudged against the nut of her clitoris she felt an electric thrill course through her body. She looked down at Venetia and saw her eyes riveted to what she was doing. She stroked Venetia's hair and the long furrow of her sex with the same rhythm. She felt the sticky sap leaking from deep inside her.

Venetia got up. She pulled the negligee from her shoulders. The silk nightdress she was wearing barely covered the tops of her thighs. Supported by long thin spaghetti straps on her shoulders, the material rose to accommodate Venetia's big round breasts. Her nipples were clearly outlined under the peachy silk.

'You're turning me on,' she said.

'That was the idea,' Stephanie replied, climbing on to the bed and lying on her back.

Venetia did not take off the nightdress. As she got up on to the bed to kneel beside Stephanie the material seemed to float over her body like gossamer, caressing her rich curves. Stephanie glimpsed Venetia's belly and the plain of her sex, so sparsely covered with fair short hair that every detail of her labia, every crease and cranny, was open and exposed.

Venetia leant forward, her ripe breasts almost escaping their silky confinement, and put her lips to Stephanie's thighs. As delicately as possible she kissed the creamy soft flesh from knee to belly and back again, her tongue occasionally darting out to lick, just as lightly, between the kisses. Stephanie moaned as the mouth moved to her other thigh, awakening all the nerves there as they had on the first. As her mouth slid up and down, Venetia extended her hand to Stephanie's breasts, one after the other. It concentrated on the nipples, touching them as though her finger was a feather, scaling the firm flesh from one side up to the summit of the nipple then down the other.

There was no hurry. Both women felt their bodies pulsing with sensual delight but neither wanted to begin the rhythms that would, once started, only be stopped by the inevitable climax of orgasm.

Venetia's hands gently parted Stephanie's thighs, so her mouth could work along the inner surface where the skin was softest of all. Again she moved from the knee upwards until her lips were tickled by Stephanie's pubic hair and she could see the labia glistening with the sap oozing from her body. But though the temptation to kiss Stephanie's nether mouth was strong, the desire to plant her lips firmly there and delve inside with her tongue, she did not. Instead, she moved down along the other thigh back to the knee.

Stephanie ran her hand along Venetia's back, feeling the softness of the skin covering her long spine. She moved her hand to Venetia's buttocks, feeling the roundness and subtleness of their shape, before burrowing deeper into the cleft that divided her cheeks. There, as Venetia eased her knees apart to allow her access, she found her treasure: the almost hairless labia, throbbing and hot and already moistened by excitement. Stephanie stroked gently, as gently as Venetia was kissing her, letting one finger just graze the long furrow from one side to the other, feeling it pulse, feeling its heat and wetness. Like Venetia,

Stephanie was tempted too; tempted to drive into the dark wet cavern with two fingers, then three, as she had done so many times before; tempted to plunge in and out wildly and take her friend down the long road to absolute pleasure.

But she didn't. She waited, just as Venetia waited, letting the anticipation build up in their bodies, letting their nerves tingle with pleasure, letting the sensuous energy accumulate in their minds until it became irresistible. They stroked each other in tandem, the rhythm of Venetia's mouth on Stephanie's satin-soft thighs the same as that of Stephanie's fingers brushing the margins of Venetia's sex.

Without disturbing Venetia's rhythm, or her own, Stephanie sat up and used her other hand to slide the spaghetti strap of the nightdress off Venetia's shoulder. Immediately, the silk spilt one of her large spherical breasts from its confines. Venetia's breasts, though full and luxuriant, did not sag; in fact, they were so proud on her chest that her nipples pointed upward. It was the nipple that was Stephanie's target. She licked her finger and used her saliva to make the contact between her fingertip and Venetia's hard corrugated nipple frictionless. Venetia moaned as Stephanie circled the button of flesh, still stroking her labia relentlessly.

Like a barrel of water under a tap, the pool of their sexual desire was filling rapidly now, up to the point where only surface tension prevented the water from gushing over the edge. Stephanie stopped the progress of her fingers as Venetia's mouth once again reached the top of her thigh and she could feel the hot breath against her sex. With the tip of one finger, wet from Venetia's own moistness, she positioned herself at the crater of Venetia's rear, then pushed forward until her finger was buried to the first joint. It was enough: enough to send the water flowing over the side.

Venetia centred her mouth between Stephanie's labia and pushed her tongue out to lap at her juices. It snaked higher, until she could feel the tiny knot of Stephanie's clitoris throbbing under the tip of her tongue. She circled it, licked it, nudged at it, as she felt Stephanie's finger penetrate her further.

They had both started now, the mainspring of their orgasm beginning its slow but inevitable winding up, the tension slowly increasing.

Stephanie lay back on the bed, pulled Venetia's thigh gently to one side and inserted her head under the short tent of peachy silk until her mouth was below the wide plain of Venetia's sex. She could see the silk floating out from her body too, front and back, and the flatness of Venetia's navel in such rich contrast to the swell of her buttocks.

As Venetia's tongue probed the centre of her sexual being, she lowered herself on to Stephanie's willing mouth. She did it slowly, agonisingly slowly. Stephanie could see every detail, the pinkness of her clitoris, the puffy crinkled outer lips, the delicate inner ones, and the puckered roundness of her rear. What she saw was a perfect accompaniment to what she felt; the waves of sensation Venetia's tongue was whipping up in her body matched the beauty she saw with her eyes.

Opening her mouth, Stephanie pushed out her tongue to meet the descending sex. Almost immediately she tasted Venetia's juices: a taste she knew so well. As Venetia rested herself on Stephanie's mouth, her tongue sought out the clitoris and found it instantly, knowing as she did all the contours of her lover's most intimate parts.

And then they were joined. A harmony building to a crescendo. Each feeling, each breathtaking sensation mirrored exactly in the other's body. The feel of one mouth on the other's sex exactly the same for both of them. They took the same rhythm, made the same movements, each tongue circling the tiny mountain of sensitivity then dipping lower to tongue the portals of the inner sheath. They moaned together, hot air expelled in synchronised passion, making them shiver and tremble and spasm.

Stephanie worked her fingers around the back of Venetia's thighs until her fingertips could touch her labia on either side, pulled them apart, spread them open so her mouth could stretch wider and her tongue could plunge in deeper. Venetia did the same.

So close were they, so together that Stephanie was not sure whether the first hard throb of orgasm belonged to her or to Venetia. She felt it in her own sex at exactly the same moment as she felt it in Venetia's. The soft, satiny labia were vibrating. To Stephanie it felt like a butterfly flapping against her mouth and she knew Venetia was feeling the same thing because she could feel her own sex trembling too. But they did not break their rhythms or their pattern; their tongues circled then dipped, pushing deeper into the dark caverns now that they were spread open.

The waves gathered, each wave bigger than the last, the gaps between them longer as they took time to build higher and higher. At exactly the same moment the biggest wave yet broke on the shore of both of their mouths and they stopped, unable to do anything but feel. Suddenly they were engulfed, washed up in the undertow, dragged back helplessly like driftwood, unable to resist. They felt themselves being collected up into another big wave, floated higher and higher until it crashed down again, and the process began anew. They were both whimpering, moaning, making little animal noises against each other's sex. It went on and on and on. It was like an orgasm that had been doubled, doubled because they could hardly distinguish between what they felt themselves and what the other felt. Even their nipples, pressed into each other's bodies, seemed to throb in unison.

Eventually it was over, though little ripples of delicious shock still tingled in their bodies as Venetia rolled off Stephanie and came round to kiss her mouth. They wanted that: to taste themselves on the other's mouth. It was a long time before the kiss was broken, before they finished savouring the delicious taste of sex.

'I shall miss you,' Stephanie said at last, getting off the bed to sip at the orange juice on the breakfast tray. 'I owe you a lot, Venetia.'

'Because I helped with Andrew?'

'No. No. You've taught me what it could be like with a woman. I'd never had a woman before you – well, not on my own . . .'

'I know.'

'I never thought it would be like this. I mean, I'd fantasised about it. But I didn't think it would feel like this.'

'You're a very good lover.'

'You've taught me.'

'No, you just had all the right instincts.'

It was true. Stephanie had been thrilled by her experiences with Venetia right from the beginning. And subsequently, her experiences with other women, some less attractive and less skilled than Venetia, had been just as satisfying. She had been relieved to discover that her new-found delight in the female body had not interfered with or decreased her interest in men. It had in no way diminished her desire for cock: it had only created another desire, a desire she needed to satisfy as fervently. Which she preferred was an academic question which she did not care to debate with herself, as both were equally available and accessible to her.

'I hope I will see you in London,' Venetia said.

'You will.'

Venetia picked up her negligee and slipped into it, flicking out her hair with her fingertips.

'Take care, then,' she said.

'And you.'

They kissed on both cheeks and Venetia left. Thirty minutes later Stephanie saw the speedboat racing across the calm waters of Lake Trasimeno, making a long curved wake as it disappeared into the distance. She could just see Venetia sitting on the transom and thought she saw her wave.

It was a moment of sadness for Stephanie but it passed. She poured herself a cup of coffee, kept hot by a silver Thermos jug on the tray, and allowed her thoughts to wander on to what she was planning for Andrew Harlock – now safely locked up in the castle cellars. She had promised him she would make his life a misery, and so far she was having no trouble in keeping her promise.

Chapter Two

Stephanie reached behind her back to clip the black basque in place. She attached the little metal hooks into the furthest of the three eyes that were available on the smooth elasticated back panel, enjoying the sensation of being held so tightly by the taut Lycra, satin and lace. A basque, she knew, suited her, perhaps more than any of the extensive range of lingerie she had at her disposal at the castle. With her slim waist it emphasised the curvaceousness of her hips; and at the back, where the black material finished in the small of her spine, it made the flesh of her pert, apple-shaped buttocks softer and creamier. It was equally flattering at the front, where the lacy cups of its bra pushed her firm breasts into a dramatic cleavage while the scalloped edge underneath pointed directly at the exposed black bush of her pubic triangle.

Sitting on the bed, Stephanie brushed her long black hair with a silver-backed hairbrush. Her hair was thick and very black and seemed to shimmer in the light. She brushed it in long, even, rhythmical strokes, allowing the brush to pull her head back until the tendons of her throat protested.

Discarding the hairbrush, she picked up one of the sheer, silky stockings she had already laid out on the bed. She raised her leg, pointed her toes, and inserted her foot into the pocket she made of the nylon. Then she drew the fine material up over her tanned flesh until its welt, darker than the rest of the stocking, was played out on her thigh. Taking the satin suspender of the basque, she wrapped the little rubber nub under the top of the welt then pressed it into the metal frame and trapped the nylon between the two. She adjusted the suspender so the stocking was held taut. Carefully she repeated the operation at the side. The second stocking followed, rolled out over her leg, transforming its nakedness into a sleek, sheer, almost wet-looking sheen.

Stephanie stood up and slipped her feet into very plain but very high-heeled black court shoes. She stood in front of the mirror, her legs apart, her arms akimbo. It was impossible to keep a smile from her face as she looked at herself, her breasts high and proud, her waist cinched in black satin, her long slender legs shaped by the heels and bisected by the welts of her stockings. The band of flesh, naked flesh, between stocking top and basque appeared impossibly tender and soft, as smooth and lustrous as the finest silk, its gentle bronze contrasting with the black tight satin and nylon that framed it.

She could not see the lips of her sex through the forest of pubic hair but she could feel them. They were throbbing expectantly, and her clitoris, nestling comfortably between them, was beginning to swell; her dressing, as much of a ritual as a priest putting on vestments prior to devotions, was arousing her again. Tentatively she ran one of her long slim fingers, the nail painted a deep vibrant red, between her open thighs, and gently brushed the hair, as though petting some delicate frightened little creature. The creature responded appreciatively, sending soft waves of pleasure coursing through her body. She looked in the mirror and watched her finger stroking between her legs. With her other hand she folded down the lacy cups of the basque until both her breasts were exposed, sitting comfortably on the crescent of lace this manoeuvre produced. Her red fingernails pinched her nipples playfully, and the resulting shock of pleasure raced down to her sex, generating a familiar churning sensation deep inside her. Her body responded to the increasing sexual temperature in its customary way. Almost before she realised what was happening, the finger ploughing a furrow between her legs was wet.

There was a temptation to lie on the silk sheets of her big double bed and continue what she had so casually begun; to lie back and think of what Venetia had done to her that morning, how that tongue had invaded her so tellingly. But since she had first set foot in the castle she had realised it was full of temptations, and she had learnt to pick and choose. It was better, this time, to make herself wait. Sexual pleasure, with what she had planned for the evening, would not be long delayed. She would rather have her body gently teased, pleasantly alive with anticipation, than replete at her own hand.

Slipping on a black silk robe, she tied its belt around her waist and opened the terrace door on to the balcony. A huge white moon hung in the sky, with no pollution in the air in this part of Italy to colour it, and only the smallest sliver nibbled out of one side preventing it from being entirely full. The moon lit the almost rippleless expanse of lake below in a ghostly colourless light. In the summer, when Stephanie had come to the castle in the middle of the lake for the first time, it had been warm enough to stand on the terrace nude even in the dead of night.

Now, though it was not cold, there was a chill in the air and she found herself wrapping the robe more tightly around her body.

Strangely, perhaps, though the flowers that had trailed from plants clinging all over the castle walls had long disappeared, their perfume seemed to linger in the air: a musky, heady scent that Stephanie would forever associate with lying here on the terracotta-paved terrace, soaking up the sun.

In the moonlight she could see the jetty that jutted out into the water below; and in the near-silence she could hear the slight lapping of waves against its wooden supports. It was only a month since she had been led ashore there, half-naked, her arms bound behind her, to begin life not as the mistress of the castle, but as one of its slaves. She could not suppress a shudder at the thought. For a while there had been no hope; it had seemed there would be no rescue from the rebellion Andrew had engineered. Fortunately, it had been only weeks before Stephanie and Devlin had escaped, and Andrew had been returned to the dungeons along with the other freed slaves. The chaos that he had caused was quickly righted and all that remained was to see that he – and his partner in crime, Amanda – were suitably chastened for what they had done.

She could, of course, have returned Andrew to England, and let him face trial; not for the rebellion, but for his original crimes against Devlin's company. Like many of the slaves in the cellars below, he was guilty of embezzlement and fraud. Andrew, and all the slaves he'd freed, thought he had managed to destroy all the evidence of their crimes and thus believed themselves no longer under threat. But through Venetia's cunning the files had been saved, and when presented with the choice of being returned for trial or being punished at the castle, he had begged to be allowed to stay and face rougher justice. Stephanie smiled to herself, the unpleasant memories of being Andrew's slave replaced by the delight she took in devising means by which he could be adequately punished.

The chill finally got too much for her and Stephanie walked back inside, her high-heeled shoes clacking on the terracotta tiles. She found she was still smiling as she closed the terrace doors. Before she had met Devlin, before she had come to the castle, she would never have dreamt that she would get pleasure from sexual power, from being dominant, uncontradictable, in control. Now, however, it gave her a pleasure so profound, so primal, she knew it was part of her sexual psyche. In the course of the months at the castle she had been forced, on occasion, to be submissive too: and that not had been without its satisfactions. Stephanie had climaxed profusely as she'd wrestled to obey Andrew's commands and earlier, when she had been kidnapped and imprisoned in Rome, her sexuality had been no less aroused. Just as she had begun to believe her proclivity was towards dominance, the experience of submission, of being slave rather than master, had given her new pleasures. New: but not, ultimately, equal. Being a slave, having her will forcibly denied, being bound and helpless had added a new dimension to her world. But for Stephanie, in the end she knew, it was power, power and mastery that gave her the most total satisfaction.

Like the power she felt now. Dressed for the part, her body held tight in black satin, her legs encased in sheer stockings, her high heels giving her already tall figure extra height, the excitement of anticipation, of knowing she was in command, prickled the nerves of her sex.

She glanced at her watch, a wafer-thin Patek Phillipe that Devlin had given her. It was time. She thought she'd heard steps on the spiral stone stairway that led directly from her bedroom to the cellars. They would be waiting for her to open the door.

With one final glance in the mirror, her dark brown eyes staring back at her with curiosity and amusement, her full lips painted with lipstick that matched the red of her fingernails, she gathered her hair into a single plait at the nape of her neck, and threaded it through a black velvet-covered band.

At the far side of the room, set in the silk panels that covered the walls, was a small door. There was a key in its brass mortice lock. Stephanie turned the key and swung the door open.

'Come in,' she said, walking back into the middle of the room.

Bruno, the mute servant, dressed as ever like a medieval executioner in black breeches and tunic, led Andrew Harlock forward by a chain attached to a collar around his neck. As soon as Andrew was standing in front of Stephanie, he unclipped the chain from the collar and shuffled back to the doorway. Relations between Stephanie and Bruno had not been good since Devlin had given her authority over the cellars, where previously Bruno had ruled. But he had suffered in the rebellion too, and having seen what Stephanie had devised for Andrew (and Amanda, his ally) as a result, he had somewhat changed his attitude. Now he could even manage a suggestion of a smile as he closed the little door behind him, leaving Andrew to his fate.

Stephanie smiled too. Andrew, long before the events of the last weeks, had always been a cocky and rebellious slave. He had been punished regularly for insolence and disobedience and had never accepted the system for what it was: a way of keeping him out of the clutches of the police and jail. Now all that had changed. Now he stood stock-still, his eyes cast to the floor as far as that was possible for him at the moment, his whole demeanour suggesting total submission.

In truth, he had little choice. His body was securely bound as it had been every minute of every hour of every day since his re-capture. Only his legs were allowed freedom, enough for him to walk with a shuffle; a short chain had been attached to leather cuffs strapped and padlocked around his ankles.

Stephanie had devised his bondage herself, intending it not only to prevent any attempt at escape, but to remind him graphically of his extreme servitude. It started with his head. The collar around his neck, by which Bruno had led him in, was the lowest of four wide leather straps: of the others, one ran around his chin, one around his eyes, with small ovals cut in it to allow him to see, and one around his forehead. All were joined by a strap that ran from the bridge of his nose, up over the top of his head, then vertically down the back.

Projecting from this vertical strap was a stainless steel hook. Behind his back, Andrew's arms had been secured in two leather cuffs just above the elbow. These cuffs were held together by a single metal link to which was attached a short length of chain. The chain, in turn, was fixed to the steel hook at the back of the head harness, forcing the head up and the upper arms to be held out at right angles to the body.

But that was not the full extent of his bondage. Pulled around his waist so tightly it made it difficult for him to breathe was a girdle of bright shiny stainless steel, padlocked by a hasp in the small of his back. Projecting downwards from this odd garment was a metal tail, shaped to curve down between his buttocks, its width separating them slightly. The tail was fashioned to finish in a stubby finger of steel which had been inserted into his anus. It did not penetrate very deeply, but its presence could be felt whenever he was required to move. On either side of his phallus, at its base, two thin chains ran down between his legs and up on the other side following the crease between thigh and pelvis, to clip into the metal girdle at the front of his hips.

To complete his helplessness, leather cuffs, again joined by a single metal link, circled his wrists. These were chained to a small ring set in the metal tail of the girdle at the point where it began its descent into the cleft of his buttocks.

Stephanie examined her handiwork with pride, like an engineer inspecting a new invention. She ran her long cool fingers over his bonds, over the leather on his face, around the metal at his waist, down over his buttocks to where the steel pushed between them, then up again over his tortured arms, satisfying herself that everything was in place.

'Comfortable, Andrew?' she asked, looking into his eyes. He did not return her stare.

Before, she knew, he would have gazed at her with fury and made only one reply: 'Get me out of this, you bitch.' Instead, his eyes firmly rooted to the floor as far as the position of his head would allow, he mumbled tamely, 'Yes, mistress.'

'You know it is your choice, Andrew. If you choose

not to be punished you only have to say so. You will be sent back to England immediately . . .'

He knew what that meant. It meant the police and certain prosecution.

'You know that, don't you?' Stephanie insisted.

'Yes, mistress,' he mumbled.

'So you do want to be punished, don't you?'

'Yes, mistress.' His voice contained not the slightest hint of rebellion.

'Say it, then.'

'Punish me, mistress.'

'I didn't hear "please"?' Stephanie chided.

'Please, mistress,' he said at once. 'Please punish me, please.'

'Very well. Since you ask so politely, I will.'

The exchange had thrilled Stephanie. She felt her nipples contracting against the satin of the robe as her sex throbbed.

Normally, in the castle, all the male slaves were made to wear tight, leather-covered metal pouches, chained over their genitals so inflexibly that it was impossible for them to achieve an erection. But she had ordered Andrew's to be removed tonight and replaced by a single chain, wrapped around his shaft and under his balls. It served the same purpose, but allowed her to see how his cock strained for release.

'On your knees, Andrew.' Her voice was cold and imperious. It was time to begin.

Awkwardly, his arms unable to help him balance, he thumped on to the thick carpet. Stephanie moved forward until the black satin of her robe brushed his face and he would be able to inhale the full aroma of her expensive Givenchy perfume – even, perhaps, the faint scent of sex generated by her excitement. Slowly she unknotted the belt of the robe and pulled it aside.

She slid the satin back, trapped as it was between his face and her stomach, until his cheeks were against the tight basque, his chin touching her pubic hair. Then she wrapped the robe around him, enclosing his head.

Every breath he took was scented with the musky aromas of her body. He squirmed and wriggled uncomfortably and she knew she had created the desired effect from the way his erection strained at the chain holding his cock. But this was only the beginning.

'Kiss me, Andrew.'

He had no need to ask where. Fighting the bonds that held his head so high, he tried to work his mouth down on to her belly. She let the robe drop from around his head, then pulled it off her shoulders and let it fall to the floor at her feet. Taking the leather harness at either side of his head between her fingers, she used it to force his head down until his mouth was at the junction of her thighs.

'Lick it, Andrew,' she commanded.

She felt his tongue trying to force its way past the tangle of her pubic hair and on to her labia. Bound as he was, it proved an impossible task. She felt the slightest of touches but no more.

'You're useless,' she said. Using the leather harness she wrenched his face away and stepped back. She could see his cock twitching, ballooning out against the chain that held it so implacably. It would be agony. 'Look at me.'

Stephanie set her left foot, in its black high heel, on Andrew's thigh, the toe inches from his cock. She bent forward and reached down with both hands to smooth the nylon of the sheer black stocking up her long leg, pulling it taut as if it had developed a wrinkle. Her naked breasts shifted forward, unrestrained by the basque. She saw his eyes roaming her body, watching as she refastened both suspenders, front and side, to draw the stocking tighter.

'No . . .' he moaned almost inaudibly.

She turned her back on him so he could see the big bulb of her arse. Its creamy flesh was perfectly framed by the basque at the top, the welts of the stockings at the bottom, and the thin black suspenders at the sides. With her slender legs closed there was a diamond-shaped gap at the apex of her thighs, a little mouth pleading to be filled, its upper dimensions fringed with her profuse black pubic hair. It had all belonged to Andrew, been his to command and demand, to use and abuse, to fuck and suck and play with. How he would wish it still was.

'Up,' she ordered, ready for the second part of the evening's schedule. She had to help him to his feet, the bondage being too extreme to allow him to get up unaided.

'What do you say?' she asked testily.

'Thank you, mistress.'

Despite the chain his cock had swollen. It was red and angry and looked as though it might burst.

'For what?' she insisted.

'For helping me to get up, mistress.'

'No, you idiot.'

'For letting me look at you, mistress,' he corrected quickly.

'And touch.'

'And touch, mistress.'

'Follow me.'

Stephanie turned on her heels and headed for the bedroom door. Andrew struggled to keep up, the chain at his ankle heavy and unwieldy as it was meant to be. Outside in the corridor Stephanie strode down to one of the guest bedrooms, then stood waiting for Andrew to catch up. He looked pathetic as he struggled along trying not to trip over the chain between his feet.

As soon as he stood beside her, his forehead beaded with perspiration from the effort, Stephanie knocked twice on the bedroom door.

Mrs Olivia Branchman had been waiting and opened the door quickly, knowing what to expect.

'Well . . .' she said as her eyes feasted on Andrew. 'Now that's quite a sight right enough. He's sure not going to run anyplace, is he?' Her accent was American but soft and cultured, which suited her light and very feminine voice.

'I thought you'd approve.' Stephanie indicated that Andrew should lead the way into the room, and both women watched him critically as he shuffled past. Olivia closed the door behind Stephanie.

'Stop,' Stephanie ordered as Andrew reached the middle of the room. He obeyed immediately. The room, like all the guest suites in the castle, was comfortable and luxurious, a thick, dark blue carpet toning with a lighter blue in the silk panelling of the walls. A large double bed was positioned so that it gave a view from the great windows out on to the lake.

'Well,' Olivia Branchman repeated, taking a tour around the new attraction. To put not too fine a point on it, Mrs Olivia Hortense Branchman was fat; short and fat. Everything about her was fat, with the exception of her face which was petite and small featured and topped with short blonde hair that bounced as she moved. The extraordinary thing about her bulk was that it did not wrinkle and sag and hang from her body in great spare tyres. It was firm and rounded and gave off a peculiar glow of health. In a way her body looked as though it had been attached to an air line and inflated. Her breasts were great round balloons of flesh, as were her buttocks, her belly, and her thighs: spongy cushions where it looked as though a man could drown.

It was easy to see the details of her weight as she was wearing nothing more than a thin transparent veil of white chiffon tied around her neck with a white satin ribbon. While this billowed out over her body like a tent, a pair of white stiletto heels gave her a couple of extra inches in height.

'Would you like me to stay?' Stephanie asked.

Mrs Branchman had been to the castle before. In fact, according to Devlin, access to the castle, and more particularly to its cellars, was the sole reason Mrs Branchman kept supplying Devlin's companies when she could have got a better price elsewhere. The castle was her first port of call on her annual European holiday.

'Oh yes, please do. I'm not shy. We can both enjoy ourselves.'

She stood in front of Andrew and clutched his harnessed cheeks in her two hands, squeezing them together so his mouth was forced into an odd shape. Then she ran her hands all over his body. She followed the lines of his tortured arms and ran her hand down the inside of both his thighs without touching his cock. The effort of walking from Stephanie's bedroom had made his erection shrink. Olivia's fingers caressed his buttocks right down to where the metal tail curled into his anus.

'Guess he knows who's boss,' she said. 'We're going to have to lose this.' She was indicating the chain that linked his elbows to the hook on the head harness. 'And this.' she flicked the chain under his balls.

'Of course,' Stephanie agreed, kneeling and quickly undoing the tiny hook that held the cock-chain so tight.

The effect of freedom on his cock was dramatic. It sprang up, the blood having been held back for so long, pumping wildly into the shaft. His erection was rock hard in seconds and throbbing visibly – so visibly, that, for a moment, Stephanie thought he was going to come. But he did not. Instead, a tear of fluid escaped his urethra and ran down his glans.

'Well just look at that,' Olivia said as Stephanie got to her feet and released the elbow-chain too. As soon as he was able to lower his elbows again she felt a shock of relief course through his body. He moaned out loud, unable to stop himself. He moaned again as Olivia scooped his balls into her hand and fingered them as carelessly as if they were a bunch of grapes.

'Oh, how rude of me,' she said, letting Andrew go. 'I didn't offer you a drink. I'm on bourbon rocks. Would you like something?' There was a selection of drinks on a tray, sitting on a chest of drawers beautifully crafted from solid burr walnut. Olivia had picked up her glass and filled it from a bottle of Jim Beam, taking more ice from the bucket on the tray.

'The same,' Stephanie said. She would have preferred champagne, but did not want to waste the time it would take to uncork the bottle.

Olivia handed her the crystal tumbler and touched her own glass against its lip.

'Cheers,' she said. 'You've got quite a body on you, young lady.'

'Cheers. And thank you.'

'Only true compliment you ever get, from another woman.'

'Well, you're very . . .' Stephanie could not think of a word.

'I'm very fat. It suits me that way. I like to eat. I like to overindulge all my appetites.'

She took a large swig of her drink, put the glass down on the bedside table and turned to Andrew again. Despite her weight Olivia was surprisingly strong. Taking Andrew by the wrists she pulled him backwards, twisted him round and forced him to his knees facing the foot of the bed.

'This is going to be fun,' she said with a gleeful look in her eyes. She had already stripped the blue brocade bedspread off the bed, together with all the bedding apart from the bottom sheet, which was pale blue.

'He looks too cool to me. I think we should warm him up. I like my men hot.'

Olivia sat on the foot of the bed, her feet on either side of Andrew's knees. She reached forward, grabbed the head harness and pulled him forward into her vast and pliant bosom, her cleavage so deep his head all but disappeared into it. One arm wrapped around the back of his neck held him there as firmly as a vice, while the great pillows of her breasts pushed against the sides of his face.

'Would you mind . . .' Olivia said, indicating the object that lay on the small armchair nearest the bed. It was a whip, but not one of the many available in the castle. This was Olivia's own design. It consisted of five very thin strips of white plastic, each about the width of a fingernail, fused together at the base to form a handle which had been bound in leather. Stephanie picked it up, weighing it in her hand before swishing it through the air experimentally. It made a strange, almost harmonic noise, like wind chimes. She handed it to Olivia.

'I should order one for the cellars,' she said.

'Oh yes, they're very effective.' As if to demonstrate the point Olivia brought the plastic switch cracking down on Andrew's buttocks. It hit the meaty flesh of his rump as well as the metal tail and clattered noisily. Stephanie saw Andrew's body jump, his cry of pain muffled by Olivia's tits. Immediately three very thin red welts appeared, much thinner than the welts produced by a normal whip and much more inflamed, seared into his flesh.

'Lower is better,' Olivia said almost to herself before bringing the switch down hard across the back of Andrew's thighs. Her other arm had increased the pressure on his neck to make sure he could not move away. This time not even Olivia's bosom could suppress the cry of pain. 'You see – much better.'

Olivia loved that; loved the feeling of holding a man between her breasts, of him struggling and wriggling and crying out in pain as she stroked him with her switch. Three times more she brought the switch down on Andrew's thighs, three times feeling him jerk helplessly under her arm, the hot breath of his pain expelled against her bosom. She aimed the blows well despite the awkward position she was in, each falling on new, untouched nerves, each forming welts, until the back of his thighs looked like an abstract painting: red and scarlet and crimson lines on a pink background.

It was hard for him to breathe, too, pressed against her like this. She could feel his sweat soaking into the chiffon and running down his cheeks under the harness to drip on to her stomach.

'That's more like it.' She threw the switch on the bed and leant forward to run her hands over the area she'd attacked. His body jerked against her as her fingers tortured the thin welts. 'That's got you nice and warm. Now it's time for some real loving, baby,' she cooed, like a mother talking to a child.

Olivia released her smothering grip, allowing Andrew to gulp in fresh air, and pulled the white chiffon nightdress over her head. Andrew, his vision partly blurred by sweat that had run into his eyes but which he could not wipe away, looked at the woman in front of him. Though she was fat, her bulk was far from unattractive. Her skin seemed to radiate a soft sheen, like silk. Nestling at the top of her plump thighs, almost hidden by the overhang of her belly, he could see a little tuft of blonde pubic hair.

Olivia sat back on the bed, and the mattress sagged under her weight. With the fingers of one hand, she caressed his cheeks almost lovingly, between the leather straps then round along his lips. She forced two, then three fingers into his mouth. He could taste the salt from the sweat that had collected on her hand. He sucked the fingers, hoping it was what she wanted him to do. He would have done anything to stop her using the switch again, the switch that lay so menacingly within easy reach on the pale blue sheet.

'Love me, baby,' she said, extracting her fingers and pulling his head down into her lap. She looked at Stephanie and winked broadly, then opened her thighs. She leant back on the bed and raised one foot over his shoulder until the sharp stiletto heel dug into his back just below his shoulder blade. 'Come on . . .' she urged.

The flesh all around him cut off most of the light. He groped forward with his tongue until he felt her long, rather wiry pubic hair, then followed it, like a trail, until he was on the puffy labia. Like everything else about the woman, her labia were fat, swollen and thick. He tried to get his tongue between them, to push his mouth forward, but it was impossible.

'Love me . . . Come on.' Even though her voice was muffled by the thighs pressed tightly over his ears he could hear her impatience and feared for its consequences. He tried again, tried pushing his tongue up to her clitoris, but knew he hadn't succeeded. If he could have used his hands he would have parted her thighs, but his hands were bound securely behind him. Suddenly she lifted her other leg up over his shoulder, digging a second heel painfully into his back and opening her thighs as a flower opens to reveal its stamen. In front of him the furrow of her sex blossomed and he took his opportunity, plunging forward until he felt his tongue make contact with the little lozenge of her clitoris, hot, wet, and engorged.

'Oh darling . . .' he heard her say.

He attacked his target aggressively, wanting to please her. He sucked the whole thing up between his lips, then used his tongue to find the hard central bud and manoeuvre it from side to side. He felt her body contract, little jerking spasms at each stimulus. Then, just as he was increasing the tempo of his strokes, he felt her massive thighs closing around his head. Total darkness descended. Her thigh muscles began to tighten, squeezing his head between them, cutting off his air. She was strong, very strong. He struggled, fighting for air, but he could not move his head an inch: not up nor down, nor from side to side. His lungs felt ready to burst. He bucked and squirmed to escape, tried to straighten his legs, but only succeeded in making her thighs hold him tighter and burying himself deeper. He was rubbing his face against her sex, the last of his breath panted out against her labia.

'Oh, oh . . .' Olivia cried in delight, enjoying her favourite game.

Suddenly the thighs parted. Andrew gasped in air.

Just as quickly they snapped shut again, enveloping him in flesh.

'Love me, baby,' Olivia cried.

Her sex was pulsing, he could feel it. It was wet too, copious juices running down her labia, over his mouth and harnessed face. He managed to tongue her clitoris, hoping against hope she'd realise he needed air to continue and open her thighs again. But she didn't. Instead he felt her muscles tightening, much more slowly this time, inexorably crushing his face against her sex, making it impossible for him to do anything but squirm to be free.

This was what she wanted, of course. This was her pleasure. The helpless head writhing, trapped between her thighs, its mouth open, panting and gasping for breath, making her nerves jangle: this was what she needed.

It was longer this time, much longer. He thought he was going to pass out, be drowned, drowned in pliant, spongy flesh. Desperately he tried to free his arms but he could get as little movement from them as he got from his head. He used every muscle in his body to try and thrash around, but produced practically no discernible effect. Only Olivia appreciated it, as his mouth wriggled against her sex. The effort used up even more of his air supply.

The thighs opened again. He gasped in air, but suspected his ordeal was not yet over. He was right. The fleshy walls snapped shut like the jaws of a whale, and he was trapped once more. Then a new element entered his nightmare. The heels of the shoes had slipped down his back till they rested on the top of the tail of the metal girdle. They pushed inward, between his buttocks, forcing the phallus deeper into his anus. He gasped, letting more precious air escape. But the action of her feet had loosened the pressure on his face slightly. There was a gap, a small gap admittedly, but enough for him to work his mouth forward on to her clitoris and for his nose to breathe. This was his chance. He tongued her clitoris fiercely, trying all he knew to make her feel good. If he could make her want him, if he could set her on the road to orgasm, make her need him to continue, she wouldn't torture him again.

It worked. As he licked frantically, manipulating the hard lozenge of her clitoris, tonguing it, sucking it, kissing it, he felt her body change gear. The tautness disappeared, and slackness and looseness set in as more pressing demands took over from the desire to tease. He could feel her whole sex melting under him, juices pouring from her labia. She wouldn't close her thighs on him now. In fact she was opening them, using her heels to dig the phallus into his body, deeper and deeper, spearing him; then she opened herself further so his mouth could go deeper and deeper into her sex.

'Yes,' she moaned. 'Oh yes . . .'

He was beating his tongue against her clit now, regularly, rhythmically, and feeling her response. Suddenly he felt her body contract, every muscle lock, her thighs once again clasp around his head. He felt as though he was being sucked up into her. He felt her shudder and heard her moan and then, to his enormous relief, she collapsed back on the bed, her heels sliding to the floor, her thighs releasing the gin that held his head.

'I think he enjoyed that,' Olivia said raising herself on her elbows and looking at Andrew's face; it was wet with her juices. Between his legs his cock was standing up vertically, its own fluid smeared across the glans.

'He's not supposed to enjoy anything,' Stephanie said sternly. She picked up the plastic switch and Andrew flinched involuntarily in response.

But the focus of Olivia's attention had changed. She was looking at Stephanie, her eyes examining the body so sleekly displayed in its black basque and sheer stockings.

'You're a very beautiful woman,' she said.

'So you said earlier.'

'I did, didn't I?'

Stephanie had seen that look before in other women's eyes – the look of desire – and after witnessing Olivia come so profusely, her body ached for attention too.

'Would you let me . . . I know you're not available . . .' Olivia said tentatively.

'Available?'

'One of the slaves.'

'I think I would like that,' Stephanie said, immediately feeling a thick pulse of sensation kick up from her sex. If she was honest with herself, she wasn't at all sure whether she did find Olivia attractive; but she had learnt not to make judgements on the basis of first impressions. She was certainly willing to experiment.

'Stand up, Andrew,' she ordered, his time not helping him.

He struggled to obey, the manoeuvre a little easier now the chain from his head to his elbows had been removed. His cock was rigid as Stephanie stood in front of him, letting the very tip of it graze against her pubic hair. Teasingly she rolled her hips so it glided across her thighs from one side to the other, over the black suspenders and back again, leaving a little trail of wetness.

'Wouldn't you just love to?' Stephanie asked.

'Yes mistress,' he replied at once.

'This is your punishment, Andrew. It's what you deserve, isn't it?'

'Yes, mistress.' Andrew's voice was barely a whisper.

Olivia had worked her way back into the centre of the bed. She kicked off her shoes and lay with her legs open, her big breasts pulled by gravity over to the sides of her chest. Her long blonde pubic hair was plastered to her thighs by a combination of Andrew's saliva and her own juices.

'Now, Andrew.' Stephanie tapped his cock with the switch, and saw it jerk upward. 'I want you to watch a little private show, just for you. And if I catch you looking away, this is not all you'll get.' She smacked the switch down firmly against the base of his cock. He groaned. 'Understood?'

'Yes, mistress.'

'You'd better hold this for me then, just in case.'

Stephanie planted the handle of the switch in Andrew's mouth, until he could grip it securely with his teeth. 'Don't drop it,' she added menacingly.

Having dealt with her slave, Stephanie turned her attention to Olivia. She knelt on the bed between Olivia's open legs and, with both hands, began caressing the inside of her thighs all the way up until she could feel the wetness of her pubic hair and the wetness of her labia. She could see the mouth of Olivia's sex, open like the trumpet of a flower in crimson red. She could even see her clitoris, swollen and exposed, its pinkness in sharp contrast to the deeper red below.

Stephanie replaced her hands with her mouth, beginning to lick the softly rounded flesh of Olivia's thighs. But Olivia had other ideas. She sat up, wrapped her big arms around Stephanie's back and pulled her down on to the bed on top of her, rolling over so Stephanie was underneath, swathed in the mountainous folds of her body. Her hand dived down between Stephanie's thighs and, with no fumbling or searching, found the bud of her clitoris instantly. She pressed it against the pubic bone behind, then, moving her finger from side to side, Olivia worked her way up on to her knees.

'Take this,' she said, using her other hand to feed the nipple of her huge breast into Stephanie's mouth.

Stephanie sucked it in eagerly. It felt like nothing she had felt before: the hard nipple between her lips, the surrounding flesh pressing heavily into her face, against her cheeks, even on top of her eyelids, and all the while Olivia's hand worked artfully between her legs. She knew she was going to come at almost the same moment that the first thrill made her body churn; her orgasm built so quickly, so unexpectedly that it took her by surprise. Olivia's fingers strummed her clitoris. She moved her head to one side so she could see Andrew, suddenly remembering how he had taken her, how he had fucked her relentlessly, how deep and hard that cock had gone and how she'd climaxed over it.

'Oh, oh . . .' she moaned, as Olivia's nipple slipped from her mouth. As her body locked, every muscle taut, Olivia pressed her soft breasts against Stephanie's face, then shook them from side to side. Stephanie felt the flesh ripple, its softness in such contrast to her rigidity. It was the last straw: the feeling of soft, warm, spongy tits squirming against her pushed her orgasm to new heights, and her body arched off the bed.

Gently, not wanting to disturb the aftermath she

knew would be playing through Stephanie's body, Olivia moved away, and lay down on the bed next to Stephanie, but not touching her.

Finally, after what seemed a long time, Stephanie opened her eyes. The orgasm had come as a complete surprise. She hadn't even been sure she was going to enjoy herself with Olivia but, in the end, her body had reacted hungrily.

She looked into Andrew's eyes. This was his punishment, having to watch her, her of all people, being pleasured. In a way it was worse without the restrainer on his cock. The restrainer gave him pain, but without it his cock could throb and pulse and jerk and remind him of how near it was to fulfilment – near, and yet so far. It would only have taken the lightest of touches, the finest of caresses, the tiniest of kisses to make him spunk: but he knew the touch, the caress, the kiss would never come.

All he could do was watch and obey. Though every nerve in his body was stretched taut by his need, he could only stand helplessly and watch. That was his punishment.

Stephanie smiled, knowing what must be going through Andrew's head. The sight of him, broken now, all hint of rebelliousness gone, was fuelling her lusts again. The night was young. He would have a lot more to endure before he was returned to the cellars exhausted and, of course, unfulfilled.

'Now it's your turn,' Stephanie said, turning towards Olivia. She knelt up on the bed and pointed her buttocks at Andrew, knowing he would be able to see the whole crease of her sex, the tightness of the basque cinched around her waist and the black stockings, their welts pulled into black chevrons on her thigh. She dipped her head and began to lick at Olivia's smooth, open thighs . . .

Chapter Three

'Wake up!'

She was lying in bed. She opened her eyes. It was still dark, almost pitch black in the room and all she could see was a dark shape looming over the bed.

'Get up, bitch!'

It was Andrew's voice. A hand tore the white silk sheet from her naked body.

'Get up. Didn't you hear?'

Her heart was beating ten to the dozen. She couldn't believe it, couldn't believe it had happened again. How on earth had he managed to escape? She thought they'd taken every precaution. How had he got out of his cell, out of the cellars?

A hand caught her by the wrist and pulled her to her feet. Before she knew what was happening her wrists had been locked into cold steel cuffs behind her back. Her head was pulled back by her long hair and a big rubber gag forced between her lips. It filled her mouth completely. She screamed, but not the slightest murmur got past the gag.

Now she saw other figures in the darkened room. It was not just Andrew. He must have freed the other slaves too, just as before. Hands grabbed at her body, pinching at her flesh or slapping her. She felt a hand between her legs, another on her breasts. There was laughter. She could not see any faces – it was too dark – but she knew there was at least one woman among the men.

'Bring her down,' Andrew's voice said.

They started pulling her forward. She knew they were going to take her to the cellars. She had high heels on now, precipitously high heels which made it difficult for her to walk. They opened the door in the silk panelling. She tried to tell them it was too dark to go down the winding stone steps in these heels, but the gag prevented her. It felt strange in her mouth as she tried to talk, the taste of rubber gone. She had the feeling it was moving, throbbing: as though it were alive, as though it were made of flesh.

How had he got free? She heard the question going around and around in her mind. How could it have happened? She couldn't stand it. She couldn't stand the thought of being Andrew's slave again. After everything she'd made him suffer over the last weeks she couldn't imagine what he'd do to her in return.

'Please don't, please let me go,' she said, though she wasn't sure why. Of course, not a sound was produced.

'Tie her up, tie her up tight, the bitch,' the woman's voice said, and Stephanie knew it was Amanda.

'Yes, really tight.'

'Tie her tight.'

They were in the cellars, in the punishment room where all the bondage frames were kept. She was being laid on the one that looked like a slated wooden bed. She felt her limbs being stretched out, spread-eagling her; felt herself being tied securely to each corner.

'Tighter.'

'Yes, tighter.'

She had used the device herself. The leather cuff at

each corner was attached to a pulley so that it could be tightened. She felt her limbs being pulled apart, her thighs opening, her sex exposed. She was stretched so tight she could feel her clitoris escape the protection of her labia. It was swollen and throbbing.

'Look at that,' Amanda said, and even though she could not see her face, Stephenie knew what she was talking about.

She could see the whip though: a riding crop with a leather loop at the end. Amanda flicked it against the clitoris. It was an easy target to find even though the room was dark. Each flick made Stephanie's body jerk against its bondage, and each was harder than the last.

Why didn't they put the lights on?

The gag was pulled out. A man knelt behind her head and she felt a cock being thrust into her mouth. It felt exactly the same as the gag. She sucked it hard, hoping it would spunk. She wanted to taste spunk.

Another cock was thrust into her right hand and one into her left. She closed her fingers around them and they began moving back and forth using her fists as makeshift vulvas. Their cocks were greasy, as though they had been oiled. Stephanie could feel them throbbing.

The whip stung her thighs, flicked at her breasts, stroked the side of her hips. She writhed against it, but felt no pain; only the emptiness of her sex. She badly needed it filled, filled with cock.

'Aren't you going to fuck me?' she said, but the words were only mumbled against the hard cock in her mouth.

The three men were coming, spunk pumping into their shafts, ready to spurt out. The whip went back to her clitoris. She could feel pain now, except it wasn't pain, it was a hot flush of pleasure, each stroke making it hotter. She was coming. The men were coming.

'Fuck me!' she screamed on to the cock. She struggled to get it out of her mouth so she could make them understand what she needed so desperately, but it only thrust deeper down into her throat, muffling every effort she made to speak. She arched her body off the bed, pushing her sex up at them, trying to make them see what she wanted.

The cock in her mouth began to spasm. The cocks in her hands did the same. As spunk lashed out against her throat, more hot white milk sprayed over her body, over her breasts, her navel, even over her thighs. She thought she could even feel it splashing on her clitoris. She was coming too, shaking, writhing.

The three men stood over her, their cocks in their hands, each of them hard and rigid still, each of them, she knew, just about to spunk again.

'My slave . . .' Andrew said. 'My slave again.'

They all started laughing as their hands worked up and down their cocks. The laughter bellowed through the room, echoing, booming . . . so loud it woke her up.

The Learjet circled the island, gradually losing height. It was about to make its approach to the landing strip Devlin had constructed on the mainland. It was a beautiful bright day, the winter sun low in the sky but bathing everything in its weak warmth, and making the numerous birds sing happily in the hope of an early spring.

Stephanie sat on the terrace of her bedroom watching the plane come in against the background of the cloudless sky. A silver coffee pot sat on the table in front of her together with a large bowl of fruit, some of which she had eaten for her lunch. She poured herself another coffee and contemplated what she would wear for Devlin that afternoon.

It was the first time he'd left her alone at the castle since the rebellion and he had been reluctant to go, despite her assurances that she would be all right. Indeed, most of the time she had been – apart from the graphic nightmares like the one that had woken her the previous night. They took some getting over, and twice after such dreams Stephanie had got up to check, in the cellars, that Andrew was still securely chained in his cell. But, considering her ordeal, she imagined that she had got off lightly if the only after-effect was one or two nightmares and an odd start if someone opened a door unexpectedly.

It would take roughly half an hour from the time the plane landed for Devlin to get to the castle. And Stephanie wanted to be ready for him. She had already made arrangements to entertain him tonight in the cellars, but that was different. This afternoon they would be alone.

Taking a final sip of coffee as the plane straightened up on its final approach, she went inside to prepare herself. The thought of Devlin's strange body had started a sequence of excitement in her; she felt her pulse thicken, each beat suggestive of another rhythm.

Her feelings towards Devlin were tender but she knew that was not what he would want from her; not initially at least, after a week's absence. The fact was that for all his authority and power in business, despite his control of a huge international company, Devlin wanted to be a slave, not a master. He had made Stephanie the mistress of the castle and had given himself to her totally as well. As much as any of the indentured slaves in the cellars Devlin was hers to do with as she chose. Above all else it was *that* aspect of their relationship that he would want to be reminded of.

The thought brought a smile of pure pleasure to Stephanie's lips. It was, after all, what she enjoyed most, too.

As she stood under the shower she thought of ways to please him by pleasing herself. Here, in the castle, there were so many possibilities. She could get one of the slaves from the cellars and order them to perform any number of variations on a theme. But she had already worked out a programme for this evening with Amanda – who, like Andrew, had always been a difficult slave, but was now broken and compliant – so this afternoon she decided on a more singular approach.

'Come in.'

She had waited in her bedroom for him to arrive. He had knocked twice on the door timidly. Now he opened it and advanced hesitantly into the room. He never knew what to expect, what mood she would be in.

'You're late.' Her voice was ice-cold. Her performance had begun.

'I'm sorry . . .'

'Sorry what?' she snapped like the crack of a bullwhip.

'Sorry, mistress. I had to . . .'

'I don't want your excuses. Get on your knees.'

Devlin obeyed immediately, his eyes not daring to look up at her. The position of prayer was also the symbol of submission, of subjugation.

'Come over here, then,' she said impatiently.

He shuffled forward on his knees until he knelt in front of her. She was sitting with her legs crossed on one of the big cream-coloured sofas opposite the bed. All he could see was her feet, the toenails painted bright red.

'You may kiss my feet.'

He kissed the foot that dangled in mid-air immediately, licking and sucking the bare toes.

'And the other one.' Her tone was still cold but his mouth produced a delicious feeling that made her tremble with pleasure.

His mouth dropped to the carpet where her other foot rested flat. His tongue explored the upper surface minutely.

'You interrupted me,' Stephanie lied. 'Can't you see I was getting dressed?'

'Sorry, mistress,' he said between licks.

'Oh, you will be. Get your clothes off so you can be punished. That's double punishment, being late and interrupting.'

'Yes, mistress.'

Eagerly Devlin started to pull his shirt off.

'Idiot. Not here. In the bathroom. Do you imagine I want to watch you undress?'

'No, mistress.'

He shuffled over to the bathroom on his knees and closed the door after him.

'Be quick,' she shouted, standing up.

Stephanie was naked apart from a pair of black panties made from leather so thin and soft it was like silk. It clung like silk too, following every curve of her spectacular buttocks.

She went over to the bedside table and picked up a pair of what looked like earrings, though they were not for her ears. Positioning the spring-loaded clip over her already erect nipple – the conversation with Devlin had been enough to see to that – Stephanie felt the delightful shock of pain as the clip bit into her tender, puckered flesh. The second clip soon followed. She had had them specially made in Rome to her own design. The tension in the clips was adjustable so that they could deliver just the desired amount of feeling: light, as now, or much tighter and much more painful. Stephanie had designed the front of the clip too. It was a metal hemisphere, attached to which was a silver chain about three inches long. At the end of the chain was a silver pendant in the shape of an elongated tear. Like the clips, the tears could be adjusted; the light pendants could be replaced with much heavier weights. The heavier the weight, of course, the more pressure on the clip, and the more it bit into the nipple.

Looking down at the silver ornaments, Stephanie could see the pendants swinging slightly and felt another frisson of pleasure arc through her body. She felt her sex, nestling under the thin leather, respond too, ever willing to join in. As if to comfort it, she stroked her hand over the leather that covered the flat wide plain of her sex.

The bathroom door opened and Devlin entered, naked and on his knees. His cock was standing erect.

Stephanie had drawn all the curtains and dimmed the lights.

'Over here,' she ordered, sitting on the edge of the bed.

'Yes, mistress.' The reply was unnecessary; he spoke because he loved the sound of those two words. There had been a time in his life when he could only get an erection under very special circumstances.

Stephanie had changed all that. She had discovered, almost by accident, what made him tick. Now he could feel himself harden just at the sound of her voice – his mistress's voice.

'Do you like my nipple clips, Devlin?'

He dared to look up at her breasts. 'Oh yes, mistress . . .'

His cock throbbed at the sight. Stephanie had never seen a cock like Devlin's. Not only was it huge, long and thick, it was also gnarled and misshapen, its veins standing up like string, knotted and twisted around the shaft. The sight of it had always given Stephanie a unique feeling in the pit of her stomach, a strange mixture of anticipation, memory of what it had felt like deep inside her, and sheer awe that she had managed to accommodate it at all. The idea that she had had it buried in her sex – though never all of it, that was too much for any woman – made her squirm.

Leaning forward, she swung her breasts gently from side to side. The silver tears on the end of their chains swung in unison. She positioned herself so that one struck the glans of Devlin's monstrous cock. He started, his whole body jumping. The impact stopped the swing, so Stephanie shook her breasts again to produce another blow.

'Ah . . .' he moaned, not from pain but from pleasure.

'You like that?'

'Yes mistress.'

She pulled herself back on the bed and lay flat, opening her legs and bending her knees.

'Kneel up here,' she said.

Quickly he scrambled on to the bed and knelt at her side.

'I need some attention, Devlin. You've neglected me. Use your finger . . .'

He was looking at her body. The silver tears had fallen on each side of her chest to rest on the sheets. He stared at the curve of her pubic bone smoothly covered in soft black leather, dimpled slightly over the mouth of her sex as though sucked in by it. He put out his hand and pulled the leather to one side, before wriggling his finger between her labia. Stephanie felt a surge of passion. Devlin's fingers, like his cock, were massive, each the size of a banana. Having one – no woman could take two – thrust inside her, filling her completely, as completely as any cock, was a pleasure only Devlin could give her and one she relished.

'Do it,' she said as she felt his finger poised between her nether lips. She didn't need any preparation. Just looking at him, performing for him, subjecting him to her will, was excitement enough. She was already wet.

The finger slid home on the tide of her juices, up inside her, so deep, so far she could feel it against the neck of her womb. She didn't think she would ever get used to the feeling of being so thoroughly penetrated by warm, animate, bony flesh, flesh that could bend and move and stroke right in the very depths of her.

By now he knew what she liked. He pulled the finger down until it was almost out of her, then pushed it up again, then wriggled his top knuckle in a circle against her clinging, silky sex. She moaned and he felt her whole vagina contract around him. He hesitated.

'Do it,' she cried.

And he did. In and out, opening her up, probing her, reaming her, feeling her whole body impaled on his single finger. She shook and squirmed, the nipple clips on her breasts biting tightly. It did not take long before she was out of control, her body rigid, her nerves begging for release. Then release was theirs, as the softest of cries escaped her lips and a muted, gentle orgasm trembled through her body.

Taking his wrist in her hand, she pulled his finger out of her sex. It made a distinct plop. Without a word she unclipped the silver hemispheres from her breasts, adjusted the tiny little wheels at the back of each to increase their tension, then positioned them over Devlin's nipples.

'You're useless,' she lied as the clips bit, one after the other, into the puckered flesh almost hidden in his mat of white and wiry hair.

'Yes mistress,' he said, his body shuddering with a surge of pain from the clips that immediately cranked up every sexual nerve.

'I should have you whipped.'

'Yes, mistress.' He would love to be whipped. His cock bucked, enlarging more if that were possible.

Taking the sides of the leather panties in her hands she scissored her legs together and skimmed the garment down over her thighs. She sat up and held them under Devlin's nose, making sure he could smell the odour from her sex where the leather was soaked with her juices. He did not need to be told to inhale the wonderful aroma. His body was so tense, so taut with anticipation, that it seemed to be trembling. This was everything he'd ever wanted; every sexual emotion he'd ever experienced, all wrapped up into this one beautiful, cruel woman, with her tone of utter contempt. Her voluptuous naked body was laid out before him, but forbidden to him until she allowed. She could toy with him, tease him, taunt him; his feelings were unimportant. Only what she wanted mattered.

Stephanie hooked the leather panties around Devlin's erection. She lay back on the bed, her body just as excited as she could see Devlin's was. Their need was mutual, and complimentary. They needed each other. Slowly, she opened her long slender legs.

'Watch me,' she commanded unnecessarily as she smoothed her hands down over her creamy thighs, stroking the silky flesh, teasing herself by nudging her sex with the top of her hand. But she was too wound up to take much teasing. The sight of Devlin's cock and the sensation of Devlin's massive finger buried in her body had fuelled her need, and the fire was consuming her.

With one hand she took hold of her breast, pinching the nipple already sensitised by the bite of the metal clip. Feeling a wonderful rush of pleasure, she plunged her other hand down on to her sex and pushed her finger into her labia to find her clitoris. Wildly, with no delicacy, she strummed at her clit, as though it were the string on a musical instrument, her body convulsing with the effects. She moved her fingers from one nipple to the other, provoking more sensation, the pain left by the clips mixing deliciously with the heat of her pleasure.

Her body arched off the bed. She was wild, but not out of control. This was not a performance any more, no act for Devlin's benefit; it had gone way past that. But that didn't mean she had no goal. She was angling her sex up off the bed, pointing it at him, making sure he could see her finger working on the pink bud that was the source of her feelings, while her other fingers slid into the mouth of her sex, making sure he could see it all, crimson and scarlet with passion.

'No,' he moaned, trying to hold himself back. His cock jerked involuntarily, sticky fluid dripping from his urethra. He closed his eyes and tried to block out the sight of temptation.

'Watch me,' Stephanie snapped at once.

'Please . . .' he begged, staring down at her beautiful body writhing on the bed in front of him, her thigh pushed against his knees. 'Please . . .'

The invisible strings that held Devlin back broke, as Stephanie knew they would. He physically hurled himself on to her, knocking her arched body back on to the sheet. And at last, at long last, his monstrous cock slid into her sex in one continuous, seamless movement.

Stephanie had been on the brink of her second orgasm, her own efforts combining with the expression of total desire in Devlin's eyes to almost finish her off. She'd managed to hold back until Devlin lost control, to save herself for penetration by that massive instrument; the instrument she had felt so many times before but which she knew she would never tire of, nor find the equal of with anyone else. His cock invaded her, overwhelmed her, filling her mind as much as it filled every corner, every nook, every cranny of her sex. Now, as it rocketed into her, as it took her over, she felt her body quivering, her eyes rolling back, her nipples, crushed against his chest, stinging madly. She could do nothing but feel the waves of orgasm rocking through her body, one after another, until they coalesced; until there was one continuous wave picking her up like a rag doll then throwing her down again in a heap, used, exhausted, replete.

Devlin began pumping in and out, so fast, so hard that he was completely out of control, his mind taken over by his body, ignoring the consequences of his disobedience – or rather, if the truth were known, relishing them. His hand groped for Stephanie's breast, wanting to touch her soft pliant flesh. As he felt Stephanie's wet, creamy sex clinging to his cock, as he felt his spunk rising, his eyes closed and his mind filled with images, like scenes from a film projected in the dark: images of Stephanie, whipping him, abusing him, binding him, her magnificent body encased in satin and lace, leather and Lycra, her sex always throbbing, alive, demanding. The feelings she had given him, no other woman had ever come near to arousing. Instinctively she had reached into his sexual psyche and found the key to his absolute pleasure.

His cock began to pulse, the juices of her sex bathing it in a flood of sticky lubrication. He felt his nipples aching: the clips, trapped between their bodies, bit deeper, transmitting sharp pulses of pain that seemed to reinforce his pleasure. He was coming and there was nothing he could do to stop himself.

Stephanie, her climax passed, reached over to the side of the bed. The riding crop was hidden under the pillow. Before Devlin had fully registered what she was doing she had slid it out, raised it over his back and slashed it down along the length of his buttock with all the force she could muster. Devlin's body jerked forward, ramming his cock even deeper into her body. His monstrous sword of flesh was so hot it felt like it would burn her.

'Get off me!' she screamed, bringing the whip down again, and writhing against him as though trying to get free.

His cock stabbed into her again, the two cuts from the crop like tongues of raw heat licking at his naked, unprotected arse. The searing sensation they caused raced straight to his cock. He gasped, unable to withdraw his pole again, rooted firm in the secret cavern of her sex . . . then spunked, great gobs of white hot spunk lashing against the wet silky impossibly soft walls that clung to him so tenaciously.

'God . . .' he moaned. It went on forever.

Eventually he rolled off her body, his cock only slightly deflated.

Stephanie got up off the bed, the whip still in her hand. She stood over him and slapped the whip into the palm of her hand, making Devlin flinch.

'How dare you spunk in me!' she said. 'How dare you fuck me without permission! What do you expect me to do now?'

'Punish me, mistress.'

'Exactly. Turn over and get that arse in the air.' Her voice was as cold as ice, in complete contrast to her body which was boiling, little bubbles of excitement still rising to the surface. Despite what she had in mind for tonight in the cellars, she had not finished with Devlin yet. She knew his capacity for sex as well as she knew her own. Both, in these circumstances, were extensive.

And even if they were not, she couldn't let him get away with what he had just done.

'Say please.'

'Please, mistress,' he said pathetically, his cock already thickening again at the thought of what was to come.

The chaos and damage Andrew and Amanda and the rest of the slaves had caused in the living quarters of the castle had quickly been restored. Furniture and rugs had been replaced or repaired. The huge glass dining table that had been shattered into a thousand pieces had been provided with a new glass top, the silk-lined walls re-covered where they had been splashed and the carpets cleaned or renewed.

Stephanie stood by the large Gothic fireplace where a log fire burned merrily. She wore a simple, short, strapless black dress. Her hair was pinned to her head to reveal her long sculptured neck and her legs were clad in sheer black tights – the skirt of the dress was too short for stockings. She had scented her body with a perfume by Jean Patou and stood with a crystal champagne flute in her hand, filled with her favourite champagne: Louis Roederer Cristal.

The glass dining table was set for two, with a huge display of flowers, dominated by white Arum lilies and orchids. Stephanie had ordered the food: delicate little clams from Sicily cooked in tomato with pasta, a rack of lamb in rosemary, a soufflé of pistachio nuts, and petits fours with almonds, all served with wine.

'Darling, you look beautiful,' Devlin said, coming over to her, and kissed her cheek; the game of mistress and slave had been temporarily suspended by mutual agreement. He had been working in the office at the back of the castle, catching up on the news from the rest of his empire while he'd been away in London.

'Any problems?' There was genuine affection in Stephanie's question.

'No, nothing. What about you?'

She poured him a glass of champagne, handed it to him and touched the lip of her glass against his. 'No. Andrew is suitably chastened. He had a session with Mrs Branchman . . .'

'Oh, I can imagine!'

'He begged me not to take him in to her again.'

'I bet he did. And Amanda?' Devlin had a soft spot for Amanda, Stephanie knew. At the mock trial that had been staged during the rebellion in this very room, Stephanie had been 'sentenced' to serve Andrew while Devlin had been consigned to Amanda's none too tender mercies. Naturally with his sexual proclivities, the more extreme the punishments she had devised for him – and she had a vivid imagination – the better he had liked it.

'Oh, she appears to be completely . . .' she searched for the right word, '. . . docile. In fact, I thought you might like a little demonstration after dinner.'

'A demonstration?' Stephanie could see the interest spark in Devlin's eyes: confirmation, if she needed any, that this afternoon's activities had not depleted his interest.

'You know how awkward she always was when she was in the cellars.'

'Oh yes.'

'Always arguing, never obeying orders . . .'

'The worst.'

'I think you'll find quite a difference since you last saw her.' While Devlin had been busy in the office, Stephanie had occupied herself in the cellars, completing the arrangements for tonight. Amanda was ready.

'Sounds intriguing.'

'I thought it was time for something new. You know I always like to surprise you.'

'Talking of surprises . . .'

'What?'

'Let's eat, I'll tell you over dinner.'

They finished the champagne and sat at the glass table. A linen-jacketed waiter with gold-braided epaulettes on his shoulders appeared to pour mineral water and a delicate Frascati into crystal glasses. Another arrived with bread baked in the castle's kitchens and a third with steaming bowls of *vongole*.

They ate eagerly.

'So what is the surprise?' Stephanie asked, after a few mouthfuls.

'The Baron called me.'

'Did he? And what did he have to say?'

'He sang your praises, of course. He said he found you one of the most exciting women he'd ever encountered.'

'Really?'

'You obviously gave him a good time.'

'Let's say I gave myself a good time and he watched.'

'That's what he likes to do.'

'Exactly.'

The Baron, a German from Munich, was the last guest Stephanie had entertained at the castle before Andrew had freed all the slaves. Stephanie had found him attractive: a big powerful man with a disciplined bearing that betrayed his military background. Unfortunately, from her point of view, all he had wanted to do was to watch.

'Well,' Devlin continued, 'he wants us both to go to his Schloss in Bavaria, for a holiday.'

'He did mention it . . .'

'Well, now he's invited us. After what's happened here, it would be an ideal opportunity to unwind, wouldn't it? Rest and recuperation.'

'Sounds good to me.'

'Believe me, it's a fantastic place.'

'You've been?'

'Just overnight. Business, not pleasure. I didn't have time to enjoy the facilities.'

'Facilities?'

'The Baron has a very vivid imagination.'

'And you didn't . . .'

'No, strictly business.'

'I'm sure.'

'No, I didn't indulge. That's why I'd be fascinated to go again.'

'Strictly pleasure this time?'

'Well, the Baron and I have one or two ventures we might want to put together. It certainly wouldn't hurt to accept his hospitality as well.'

'So when do we go?'

The day after tomorrow.'

'Oh dear . . .'

'What?'

'I've got nothing to wear.'

They both laughed. Since taking over at the castle, Stephanie had shopped extensively. In her old life, a life that now seemed so remote and different it seemed as though it belonged to someone else, she had had no clothes – or underclothes – appropriate to the life she now led as mistress of the castle and of Devlin. Trips to the Via Condotti in Rome, Bond Street in London and the Boulevard Haussmann in Paris had soon put that right. The Baron had already seen what she looked like in expensive and revealing lingerie. Now he would have the chance to see her in some elegant outer clothes too.

The lamb was carved in front of them by a white-coated waiter. It was pink inside and the sweet scent of rosemary filled the room. With the meat were served tiny roast potatoes in the shape of olives and *zucchini fritti*, each no bigger than a matchstick. A rich Barolo was poured into the biggest of the four crystal glasses set in front of each place. Green salad with a dressing of balsamic vinegar followed.

'So what exactly happens at the Schloss?'

'I told you I didn't go there for pleasure.'

'But you know.'

'Roughly.'

'And?'

'I think it should be a surprise.'

'A pleasant surprise, I hope.'

'Stephanie, knowing you as I am delighted to say I do, I think you'll find it a very pleasant surprise.'

'OK. I like surprises.'

They ate the soufflé and toyed with the petits fours, dipping the biscuits into the rich, syrupy Italian wine. The waiters brought tiny cups of espresso coffee.

'So are you ready for my surprise?' Stephanie asked.

'With Amanda?'

'With Amanda,' Stephanie confirmed, finishing the coffee and getting to her feet. She came round behind Devlin and dug her fingers into his shoulder muscles, massaging them to ease away any tension. 'Unless you're too tired. . . ?'

'No, no,' he said quickly. If it was something Stephanie had planned he had no intention of missing it.

'Come on then.'

She took his hand and led him out into the vestibule behind the huge oak front door. A curved marble staircase dominated the area; to the side of it hung a large modern tapestry. Behind this, in one corner, was hidden a small wooden door. Stephanie held the tapestry to one side and unlocked the door before leading the way down the spiral stone steps into the cellars.

At the bottom of the stairs the cellar was perfectly innocuous: supporting pillars of stone and structures stacked with vintage wine beside discarded furniture and other bric-a-brac. But at the far end, set in a much newer wall, was another thick wooden door. Stephanie knocked on it firmly. The noise of bolts being drawn back echoed off the stone walls. The door swung open and the large figure of Bruno – as ever dressed in a black tunic and breeches with a thick leather belt around his waist – stepped aside to let them enter. He bolted the door after them.

A long wide corridor led down to a bare, open space. Here the slaves were chained for the guests to make their choice. Along the side of the corridor were the doors to the individual cells where the slaves slept if they were not required upstairs.

There was one other door in the complex, at the far end. Here there was a suite of three rooms. Two of them were like the bedrooms upstairs: windowless of course, but otherwise luxuriously appointed with beds, silk sheets, thick carpets and *en suite* bathrooms. The third room was what Stephanie called the Punishment Room, its stone walls and floor spartan like the rest of the cellars. Here the guests could indulge their more *outré* fantasies, let their imaginations run riot, with every conceivable piece of equipment to bind and fetter and punish.

But it was in one of the bedrooms that Stephanie had arranged for Amanda to wait.

Before dinner Stephanie had dressed her personally. With the help of one of the other slaves she had squeezed and cajoled Amanda's body into a specially designed catsuit. It was made from the thinnest and finest quality black rubber, rubber that fitted so tightly it was like a second skin. It had taken nearly half an hour to cram her body into the fastener-less garment, rolling it up from the feet, easing and pulling it over her legs and belly and breasts, using talcum powder to help, until Amanda was fully encased in it. Three holes had been made in the garment: two rather small openings on her chest, from which her breasts protruded awkwardly, as the holes were too small for their bulk; and a long oval slit that ran between her legs, exposing the whole furrow of her sex from the apex of her belly to the cleft of her arse.

To complete her costume they had pulled a rubber hood, as tight as the catsuit itself, down over her head and neck. This too had three holes, for eyes and mouth this time.

The rubber was so tight, so seamless, it changed her appearance entirely. Amanda had always given the appearance of being plump, not because she was fat, but because her muscles were strong and well developed. The black rubber pulled her body into a sleek and slender shape, emphasising the feminine curves of her rump and her waist. With the orifices of her mouth and sex exposed it also made her look obscenely sexy, like a modern artist's representation of some outlandish goddess of sex. This impression was heightened by the fact that Stephanie had had her labia shaved entirely of hair, so that the pink lips of her sex were naked and exposed. The smoothness of the rubber and everything it covered was in stark contrast to the wrinkled nether lips which pouted between her legs.

They had not bound her. There was no need now, now that Amanda was broken.

'My God,' Devlin said as he eyed the slender shape. 'This is Amanda?'

She stood obediently by the foot of the bed, where she had been told to wait, not daring to move a muscle until she was given instructions.

'Amazing, isn't it?'

'Amazing. When I left she was still . . .'

'Awkward. Now, as you see . . .'

'How did you do it?'

'Drastic measures, I'm afraid, weren't they Amanda?'

'Yes mistress.' Her eyes were full of fear at the memory.

Whipping had never worked with her. She liked to be whipped, gloried in it. But Stephanie had discovered something she did fear. Having strapped her slave to a wooden frame in the Punishment Room, Stephanie had decided that after having her pubic hair shaved, the razor should move to Amanda's head. At that point her resistance had crumbled. It was the one threat she could not bear.

'Unusual, don't you think?' Stephanie said.

The room was filled with the smell of rubber and talcum powder.

'Now let's give her a little test. Bend over Amanda, hands clasping your ankles.'

Without a word Amanda obeyed. She opened her legs wide, bent over and took an ankle in each hand. The slit in the rubber suit stretched open, exposing every detail of her sex. Coming over to her, Stephanie ran her finger along the hairless furrow. She felt Amanda quiver.

'You see,' she said. 'So good.'

Devlin eyed the remarkable sight and felt his cock stir.

'Up now,' Stephanie ordered.

Amanda obeyed at once.

'Incredible,' Devlin said. As usual Stephanie had provided him with another thrilling spectacle. Her sexual imagination seemed to know exactly what would please him. How she had turned the wilful and sullen Amanda into this compliant slave he did not know or want to know. But he hoped it was not all Stephanie had planned for the evening.

'Get your clothes off.' The change in Stephanie's voice was so dramatic that Devlin almost looked around to see if someone else had come in. He started to strip off his clothes instantly. Stephanie opened the top drawer of one of the chests in the room, used to hold equipment and lingerie, and extracted two pairs of padded leather cuffs. While Devlin pulled off his trousers, his erection already getting in the way, she strapped one pair around Amanda's wrists.

Naked, Devlin stood waiting for instructions.

'Come here.'

The other pair of cuffs were soon fixed tightly around Devlin's wrists. After manoeuvring him over to stand in front of Amanda, Stephanie joined the metal link of each pair together by means of a small padlock. Hanging down from the clasp was a short chrome chain.

'Lie on the bed, hands above your head.' She had worked it all out beforehand.

A little awkwardly they managed to obey, and were soon lying on their sides facing each other. Stephanie knelt on the bed, caught hold of the chain and quickly padlocked it in turn to a metal ring set in the wall at the head of the bed.

'That's better.'

She stroked Devlin's body, then Amanda's. The black skirt of her dress crumpled up around her waist. The rubber felt warm and smooth against her hand. Taking her time, she got to her feet and unzipped the dress; then, still slowly, she began peeling it away from her body. Devlin's eyes couldn't stop watching as she revealed her body, naked but for the sheer black tights.

Once again she experienced the strong aphrodisiac of power coursing through her body. She was the mistress of the castle, mistress of all she surveyed. She could do anything, fulfil any caprice, have this hapless pair perform any number of unspeakable acts on her and for her and with her. She could make them beg and plead for mercy; she was in control of their fate.

Stephanie felt her nerves knot, a sudden spasm deep inside her sex spreading the peculiar feeling of sexual need, warm and throbbing, out from its centre. She could feel her juices begin to flow, lubricating the inner passages of her sex.

Her hand slipped into the front of her tights, tenting the sheer nylon, her fingers drawn to her clitoris like steel to a magnet. There was a wide tall mirror on the wall alongside the bed, and Stephanie looked over her shoulder to see herself in it. She felt another flush of pleasure as her eyes roamed her naked back: the perfect triangles of her scapulae standing out firmly, the straightness of her spine in contrast to the curves of her wasp-waist, the pronounced flare of her hips, her tight nylon-covered buttocks, shaped and hardened by her high heels, and her long legs, slightly parted, covered by the sheer, glistening nylon.

She looked down at her slaves on the bed. That was what they were, of course, her slaves. The words thrilled her. Her finger worked away under the tights, circling the nodule of her clitoris, fighting against the constriction of the nylon that veiled it. She could see Devlin's monstrous cock pressed against the black rubber at Amanda's belly. A trail of fluid covered the material, where the tip of his cock had leaked its sticky juices over it. She remembered how it had felt that afternoon, how it always felt; how it splayed her open, filled her, exposed all the tenderest nerves, did things to her that no one else could do. She hadn't intended this, hadn't intended to get so involved; she wanted to be the ringmaster in this circus, not a performer. But now it was too late to draw back.

She could have turned Devlin over, had him fuck her; she could have used Amanda, had her cultured, artful mouth suck her to completion. But even that would take too much time, make her break off from what she was doing. Her finger had found just the perfect place, a place so sensitive, so telling that it was propelling her speedily to orgasm. Her finger hardly moved at all – just the smallest touch, pressing down against the little button of the clitoris itself.

'Oh . . .' she gasped the word loud and long as her orgasm exploded from her sex, a shock of pleasure engulfing her body. The second before she closed her eyes she saw Devlin straining round on the bed to see her, the expression in his eyes full of lust and need and desire. The look stayed with her in the blackness as his helplessness, his total dependency on her, added the final frisson to her passion.

There was no hurry. Biding her time, letting the orgasm fade gently, Stephanie sat on the bed and peeled off her tights. The crotch and her thighs were wet. She went into the bathroom and sat on the bidet, letting warm water from its spray play gently on her labia. She moaned aloud as this produced a little aftershock of orgasm which rippled through her body. After drying herself thoroughly Stephanie repinned her hair where her exertions had loosened it and stepped back, naked, into the bedroom. She walked straight to the chest of drawers, where she found a black silk and lace teddy and pulled it up over her body; lacy panels on her hips and bosom revealed the creamy tanned flesh underneath.

They would be ready for her now.

'Well now.' She looked down at the two of them lying stretched out on the bed. The front of Amanda's belly was wet with secretions from Devlin's overexcited cock. 'I'm going to give you a treat.' It was back to the programme she'd planned; no more improvisations. 'I'm going to let you fuck.'

As she said the words she went back to the chest of drawers, and extracted a thick belt from the selection the drawer contained. The belt was made of black rubber. Kneeling on the bed Stephanie pulled the belt up under Devlin and Amanda's legs, forcing it up until it was around the top of their thighs. Quickly she cinched the belt tight, drawing their thighs together.

Back at the chest, Stephanie opened another drawer. The drawers were neatly organised. Belts, harnesses, restrainers, cuffs in one. Lingerie in satin, leather and rubber in two others. A drawer for a collection of dildos. And the drawer she delved in now, which held a variety of whips. She took out a short-tailed whip, thongs of leather with knotted ends.

'Come on Devlin, don't tell me you don't want her.' Stephanie stroked the whip across Devlin's buttocks.

Devlin immediately used his weight to roll Amanda on to her back. He tried to raise his hips to direct his cock down between her legs. The rubber belt gave but, just as he thought he had managed to gain entry, the pressure proved too much for him and the rubber snapped him back against her belly.

'Help him, Amanda,' Stephanie ordered, a stroke of the whip on her rubber-covered thigh reinforcing the message.

Amanda writhed underneath him, opening her legs

wide and trying to push her naked, hairless sex down on to his cock. But, however she tried, however close she got to achieving her goal, the rubber belt would allow so much and no more.

Together their bodies strived, squirming and wriggling against the belt, their hands bound and powerless to help. The more they moved the more desperate they became. Devlin was sweating, the perspiration making the impervious rubber slick and wet.

By now, Devlin's own need was as great as his desire to obey his mistress. Trying another tactic, he pulled Amanda over so he was underneath and she was on top. Straining back she used all her considerable strength to push her buttocks out and feed his cock between her legs. She felt it sliding down the rubber at her belly, but just as the warmth of his glans reached the top of the slit in the catsuit, the effort required to push against the constriction became too great, and her muscles collapsed. Their bodies slumped together again.

Stephanie knelt by the head of the bed. This was going to be a new experience for Devlin. She opened the drawer of the bedside table and took out the rubber hood she had placed there before dinner.

'Hold up your head, Devlin,' she said. As he obeyed she pulled the hood down over his wiry white hair and over his sweating face. There was only a tiny hole for his nose to enable him to breathe. Nothing for the mouth or eyes.

In the blackness that had descended, the smell and feel of rubber enveloped him. He could feel his whole body writhing against Amanda's rubber body; it was warm and sensuous. He felt it most of all against his cock. He inhaled the smell of rubber. It smelt like nothing else, but he associated it intimately with the sweet musky aroma of sex. He knew Stephanie had planned all this for him.

There was a bottle of body oil in the bedside table too. Stephanie took it in her hand and moved down the bed. Suddenly there was an oily wetness spreading over Devlin's cock and the rubber on Amanda's belly. It was wonderful, so slippery, so soft, his cock trapped between Amanda's navel and his own. He bucked his hips and felt his cock sliding up and down against the oily rubber, his balls pressed into the heat of Amanda's naked pubis. The rubber felt like nothing else, impossibly smooth, so frictionless, the warmth of the body underneath it making it pliant and soft. He was going to come. He thought he heard Stephanie whisper something in Amanda's ear – 'Bring him off!' – but didn't know if that was just his imagination. He was going to come. He felt Amanda moving on top of him now, wriggling her slightly rounded belly against his cock, under and down, from side to side, then using her stomach muscles to press into him. His immense tool was surrounded by rubber, wet, greasy rubber on three sides. He felt his cock pulsing on the brink of orgasm. He breathed in deeply, pulled at the leather cuffs that held his wrists because he loved the feeling of helplessness they gave him, then let every muscle in his body relax, feeling only the incredible hardness of his cock as Amanda writhed her snake-like body against him. Suddenly he felt her mouth against his face, searching for his lips under the rubber hood. When she found them she kissed him, without losing the rhythm of her belly; she forced her tongue into his mouth, forced the rubber between his lips as deep as it would go, so that not only was he engulfed in rubber, smelling it, feeling it, but he was tasting it too.

He felt his balls jerk and his cock spasm and spunk splurged out against the rubber, white strings of spunk spread across the clinging, smooth, black rubber and down over Amanda's thighs. Some even ran into the cleft of her hairless throbbing labia.

Stephanie let him enjoy the aftermath for some time, and watched as little ripples and tremors played through his body. Eventually she pulled the hood off his head and unstrapped the rubber belt. The leather cuffs followed and, a little unsteadily, Devlin got to his feet. Together they looked at Amanda lying on the bed, on her back now where Devlin had pushed her. She was still undulating, the tempo of sex still commanding her attention, her needs created but unsatisfied.

The rubber made her hot, made her sweat, its tightness a constant provocation.

'So what shall we do with her now?' Stephanie asked, trailing her finger across the white semen and watching Amanda flinch and tremble at the contact. Perhaps she would relent for once, allow Amanda to have what she clearly so desperately wanted – push a vibrator up into her open sex and watch her climax profusely. On the other hand, perhaps not . . .

Chapter Four

The cases were unloaded from the smartly polished mahogany and brass of the speedboat that had brought them across the lake. Its wake was still visible in the calm water, a vast sweeping curve gradually dissipating as the waves it had created lost their momentum and flattened out the further away they spread.

Stephanie sat in the back of the black Mercedes watching as the carefully packed luggage – Louis Vuitton leather luggage she had bought in Paris – was transferred to the boot. She was wearing a white blouse over a crisp St Laurent suit. Bright yellow, its short jacket braid was in black, and its knee-length skirt slit at the side to provide tantalising glimpses of thigh. She wore mid-brown high-heeled boots and quite opaque white stockings attached to a white satin suspender belt. Of course, with the slit in the skirt she should really have worn tights, but she was in a capricious mood and wanted Devlin to catch occasional views of a tight white suspender clasped into the white welt of the stocking.

The drive to the airstrip was no more than five minutes. The Learjet, white with the black and red logo of Devlin's main holding company painted on its tail, stood on the short taxiway, its engines running, the steps up to the cabins at the front and rear both extended.

As the car approached, Susie, the Malaysian flight attendant, appeared at the top of the front steps. As always she was dressed in a raw silk kheong sam, this one in the deepest of greens, which complemented her jade eyes.

The driver pulled the Mercedes round so Stephanie's side of the car was opposite the steps and jumped out to open the passenger door. He clearly appreciated the view as Stephanie swung her legs to the ground and her yellow skirt fell away to reveal her suspender-clad thigh.

'Good morning,' Susie said politely, touching her hands together and bowing slightly, her short shiny jet black hair bobbing forward as she did so.

'Good morning, Susie,' Stephanie said curtly, seeing the usual hint of disapproval hovering in Susie's smile and in those jade green eyes.

Devlin followed her into the luxurious interior of the plane. In the main cabin at the back was a cocktail bar, beautifully crafted in burr walnut, a comfortable leather sofa, leather armchairs and a dining table that seated four. Mounted in one corner was a television screen which picked up satellite transmissions but could also display the plane's inertial navigation system, plotting the exact position of the aircraft against a map of Europe.

Stephanie sat in one of the large leather armchairs and indicated to Devlin that he should sit opposite her. He took his jacket off first and handed it to Susie to hang up.

'Would you like a drink after take-off, madam, Mr Devlin?' Susie asked, having secured the main cabin door.

'Yes,' Stephanie said as she saw the last of the luggage loaded into the rear door and heard the crunch as that too was closed. 'The usual, and the same for Mr Devlin.'

The usual was a vodka martini made using Russian vodka, with a twist of lemon. It had become something of a tradition with her since having it the very first time she had set foot in Devlin's private jet.

When Susie disappeared into the forward cabin Stephanie looked over at Devlin. He was gazing at her, his eyes skimming over her body in much the same way as if she had been a beautiful painting.

'Do you like what you see?'

'You know I do. You're beautiful.'

'Good.'

Beauty was not a word that could ever be applied to Devlin. He was short and squat, his face dominated by a bulbous and warted nose. Hair, white and wiry, grew in profusion from his nostrils and his ears, and the hair on his head was difficult to tame in any one direction, however many times it was combed. Despite this, or maybe because of it, Stephanie was enormously attracted to him, and had been from their first meeting. It was more understandable now that she had been drilled by his monstrous cock and penetrated by those banana fingers; hardly surprising that her body spasmed and her stomach knotted whenever she looked at him.

The plane started to roll forward, the noise of the engines increasing. It swung round and Stephanie glimpsed the long runway ahead before the plane lined up along the central markings and the engine noise reached a crescendo. Like a car being revved up on the starting line but held back by its brakes, the body of the plane trembled under the strain. Suddenly it leapt forward as the brakes were released and it hurtled down the runway and into the air.

* * *

As soon as the captain announced that they could remove their seat belts, the plane levelled out and Susie appeared, ready to fix the drinks. Stephanie watched the ground below as the plane gained height and banked to fly north up the Italian coast. Apart from some odd small white clouds it was a clear day, and Stephanie could see every detail of the land and sea below. The colour of the sea varied noticeably at this height: a light blue near the shore darkening to a clover green where it was at its deepest towards the west.

Susie put two triangular cocktail glasses on a silver tray and poured the vodka martinis from the cocktail shaker. The glasses had been kept in the fridge and frosted on contact with the air. She presented the tray to Stephanie first and then to Devlin.

'*Salute*,' Stephanie said, raising her glass.

'*Salute*,' he repeated.

'Will there be anything else, Mr Devlin?'

'No, Susie, thank you,' Devlin replied.

As Susie walked back to the front of the plane Stephanie crossed her legs, the rasp of nylon on nylon drawing Devlin's attention. The slit in the skirt revealed the white suspender at the side of her thigh.

'What's your relationship with Susie precisely?' Stephanie asked, taking a sip of the ice-cold cocktail. It was a question she had been meaning to ask for some time.

'She works for me,' he replied.

' "Works for" ?'

'Yes.'

'And that's all?' She could see in Devlin's eyes that it wasn't.

'Why do you ask?'

'Because ever since I set foot on this plane she's resented me.'

'She's perfectly polite.'

'Oh yes . . . perfectly. But I can see what's going on in her mind.'

'I'm sure –'

'Devlin, the truth.'

Devlin took a large swig of his drink. 'Well I suppose we had more than a normal employer-employee relationship before you came along.'

'You fucked her?'

'Let's say she performed certain services for me. No doubt she resents the fact that you've taken over in that department.'

'I always knew there was something.'

The plane banked slightly and Stephanie looked down to see the city of Genoa disappearing under the left wing, and with it the last of the sea. Soon they would be over the Alps.

'So what exactly did she do?' Stephanie had no intention of letting it rest.

'I – well . . .' Devlin blushed, the reddening of his face exaggerated by his white hair.

'Come on, don't be shy with me.' Stephanie let her voice reflect just a hint of authority.

'She used to . . .' he hesitated again.

'Show me.'

'What?'

'You heard. Show me. I want to see what you two got up to that's so difficult to describe. Call her in here and show me.'

'I can't ask –'

'Devlin.' Stephanie snapped his name out coldly. 'Do as I say.'

Meekly Devlin pressed the call button, knowing further argument was useless. Almost instantaneously the forward cabin door opened and Susie appeared.

'Yes, Mr Devlin?'

She was looking at Devlin but he was not looking at her. His eyes were rooted to the floor, his pulse already beginning to thicken, the slave in him ever ready to be mastered.

'Mr Devlin has been telling me about you, Susie. Telling me what you used to get up to together while you were flying around.'

Susie's eyes flashed a look of hatred across the cabin but she said nothing.

'So I thought a little demonstration –'

'No way,' Susie said.

'Tell her, Devlin.' Susie had never accepted Stephanie's authority. Stephanie had only ever got her way on the plane by threatening Susie with Devlin's wrath.

'Do as she says, Susie, please.'

'But sir . . .'

'Do it,' he said powerfully.

Stephanie saw the rebellion in Susie's eyes extinguish itself immediately. Without a word she walked the length of the main cabin, unlocked the door to the aft compartment, where cargo and luggage were stored, and returned with a thick dimpled metal case, like the sort of thing used for carrying cameras.

'What happens now?'

'Mr Devlin gets on the sofa, miss,' Susie said quietly.

'Do it, Devlin,' Stephanie ordered.

Devlin put his glass down and got to his feet, his erection already tenting the front of his trousers. He lay on his back on the sofa.

Susie put the case on the small table bolted to the bulkhead and opened it. Inside Stephanie could see foam packing fitting closely around what looked like a control for an electric train and a large battery. But her eye was drawn to the third item carefully outlined in the spongy foam. It was a perfect replica of a man's cock and balls, accurate in every respect, except that where the glans should be, the top was open. The object was made from what looked like silver, and from its size there wasn't any doubt whose penis had been used as its model: this was indisputably a reproduction of Devlin's cock.

As Susie extracted it from the case, Stephanie could see a red wire hanging down from it, obviously connecting it to the battery. Susie lay the phallus on Devlin's belly and began unzipping his flies.

'No,' Stephanie said. 'Let's do it properly. Get all your clothes off, Devlin.'

Devlin showed no lack of eagerness. He sprang to his feet, putting the silver phallus to one side and pulled off his shirt, shoes and socks. He skinned down his trousers and pants together. His cock, freed from constraint, bounced up expectantly, its network of blue and crimson veins already throbbing. He lay back on the sofa.

For a second Susie hesitated.

'Get on with it,' Stephanie chided.

Susie picked up the phallus. To Stephanie's amazement she worked a little catch on one side and it opened; the object was hinged, and completely hollow. Placing the open sides around Devlin's erection Susie carefully arranged his balls in the sacs provided in the silver scrotum, then manoeuvred the shaft of Devlin's cock into the shaft of the phallus and snapped it shut. Apart from the pink knob of his glans, Devlin's cock was suddenly transmuted to shining, polished silver. The point at which the silver had been cut away to fit under the rim of the glans was padded with an edge of thick grey rubber, preventing the metal scraping against the tender flesh.

'Well,' Stephanie said, standing up to get a better look. 'No wonder you enjoy travelling by air.' She took the last swig of her drink and put the glass down. Up to this point Stephanie had felt abstracted, not involved, curious to discover the truth but nothing more. But the sight of Devlin's massive cock encased in silver like the shining totem of some primitive religion made her shiver: a shiver not of cold, but caused by a sudden sexual pulse emanating from deep in her white French knickers.

'What now?' Her voice was husky.

Susie made no reply. She turned to the case, threw a switch on the control panel, and twisted a big gnarled knob. Immediately a faint hum filled the air. Susie twisted the knob again. The humming got louder. Stephanie saw Devlin's silver encased cock begin to vibrate from the rim of his glans to the bottom of his scrotum. He moaned, his eyes looking up at her, searching her face to try to find out what she intended next.

In the days when he had had trouble getting an erection, Susie had shown him a device her sister had brought back from Kuala Lumpur as an aid to impotence. The man's cock would be clamped in a hollow wooden phallus with the glans exposed, so tight that once erect, the glans could not escape again should the cock shrink. Usually, the stretching and pleasure caused if shrinkage did occur was enough to produce another erection. Either way, Malaysian women could fuck their men with the artificial phallus in place. He had taken the idea and modernised it, adding a powerful vibrator in the metal scrotum.

Stephanie extended her finger and thumb to touch the exposed glans. She felt it throb.

'And you fuck her with this on?'

'No, she . . .'

'She what?' Stephanie turned to Susie. 'Show me,' she demanded.

The resentment flared in Susie's eyes again. She had no idea why she had agreed to go this far. She should have told Stephanie that none of it was any of her business, that it was private, private between her and Devlin. She should have, but she didn't. Instead she dropped to her knees at the side of the sofa – as she had done so many times when she and Devlin were alone on the plane – and moved the briefcase down on to the floor beside her. Turning the gnarled knob of the generator once again, she leant forward and opened her mouth, closing it tightly over Devlin's exposed glans. Her mouth was small and Devlin's size stretched it to the limit; her lips struggled to contain his breadth.

Stephanie watched her cheeks deflate as she sucked hard, the glans vibrating in her mouth.

'Is that good?' Stephanie asked, though the answer was obvious.

'Yes . . . very . . .'

'Can you come like this?'

'Yes . . .' He wasn't at all sure how Stephanie was reacting to this display, and so added, 'mistress,' as a palliative.

'Get up, Susie,' Stephanie ordered.

The cock plopped from the Malaysian's mouth as she got to her feet. There was a little trail of saliva on her chin which Stephanie wiped away with her finger.

'Unzip my skirt.' The tone of her voice brooked no argument. She turned her back and immediately felt Susie's fingers undoing the button on top of the zip, then the zip itself. The yellow skirt fell to the floor and she stepped out of it. 'Now my knickers. Take them down.' Susie's hand reached up under the jacket, found the waistband of the French knickers and pulled them down over Stephanie's long stockinged thighs until she could step out of these too. It was not the first time Susie had seen Stephanie's body.

When Stephanie turned back to face Devlin she saw his eyes feasting on her thighs and the dark forest of her pubic hair.

'Did I give you permission to look?'

'No, mistress.' His eyes left her immediately.

'Did I give you permission to look away?' she teased, keen to make life difficult for him.

'No, mistress.'

'Don't you want to look at me?'

'Yes, mistress.'

She looked down at his cock, trapped in the hollow silver phallus; she saw the way it vibrated, from his balls to the tip of his urethra, and felt a surge of need. She wanted it inside her, wanted to know how it would feel, the cold metal in contrast to the hot glans that surmounted it.

Without a word, holding his eyes with hers, she knelt on the sofa and swung one leg over Devlin's hips so that she was sitting astride him. She placed her hands on his chest; the great shaft of his cock was pointing directly up at her sex. Reaching back behind her, Stephanie grasped the base of the silver phallus firmly in one hand. Its vibrations made her hand tingle. Then she eased herself down on her haunches until she could position the glans at the mouth of her sex. The vibrations immediately seized her labia. They were powerful, snaking up to her clitoris, making her whole sex quiver.

For a moment she was content with that feeling,

letting the vibrations play over her sex, looking straight into Susie's jade green eyes. The Malaysian seemed quite unaffected by the spectacle, her face expressionless, cool, not a hint of sexual excitement in her eyes or in her body.

Strangely, perhaps, Stephanie found this coolness exciting.

'Will you do as I say?' she asked. It was not meant to be a command. She wanted to know that Susie was willing, wanted her to join in of her own free will.

She saw Susie's eyes widen slightly. Now they were gazing so deeply into the dark brown pools of Stephanie's eyes that they almost looked right through her.

'Yes,' she said after a pause, understanding this was her choice.

Stephanie moved her hand away from the phallus and, at the same time, sank down so Devlin's cock shot up into her body. She was expecting the silver to be cold, but the long contact with Devlin had warmed it through. Immediately she felt the silky walls of her sex vibrate. She squirmed down, trying to get as much of the massive cock into her as she could, wanting the vibration deep inside her, right up against the neck of her womb.

'Oh, God,' she gasped as she felt his trembling glans pushing into the centre of her body. Inside she felt the unyielding cylinder of metal like some hardy invader, its vibrations spreading out through her, touching every nerve, making her sex heave, her juices run.

Devlin started to buck his hips, moving his cock to and fro.

'Yes . . .' Stephanie moaned. The movement seemed to increase the vibrations, to transfer them from one area to another then back again. Stephanie's whole body was throbbing, sensations she had never experienced before flooding through her. She looked out of the cabin window to see snow-covered mountains. They were flying over the Alps at 35,000 feet and 600 miles an hour, and she was coming.

'Kiss me,' she said to Susie.

For once the black-haired woman did not hesitate. She leant forward, wrapped her arm around Stephanie's neck and pressed her thin small mouth against Stephanie's fleshy lips. Her tongue darted out, wet and thick, filling Stephanie's mouth. Her hand, unbidden, worked its way over the cliff of Stephanie's breasts to find her hardened nipple covered by the white blouse and lacy bra. Without breaking the kiss she nimbly unbuttoned the blouse and worked her hand under the lace of the bra. Her hand was wonderfully cool.

The longer the vibrations went on, the more they seemed to spread, reaching up to Stephanie's breasts, under Susie's hand, even to her mouth, filled by Susie's tongue. Her whole body was shaking, and now it spread into Susie. Stephanie ran her hand up the slit of the kheong sam and on to Susie's hard pubic bone. It was covered in tan-coloured tights but no knickers. With one finger Stephanie pushed down between Susie's thighs. She would have liked to strip the tights off, to make Susie pull off her dress, but there was no time. Her orgasm was too close, the waves of feeling generated by the vibrator and Devlin's cock too overwhelming for her to do anything more than grope up through the nylon. Her fingers ventured between Susie's labia to the hard knot of her clitoris, wanting to make some contact, however small. Susie was not wet. Despite Stephanie's efforts, despite their mouths being joined and the spectacle of Devlin, the Malaysian was still not excited. Even the hand on Stephanie's breast remained cool.

For some perverse reason this added to Stephanie's excitement, just as her expression of indifference had. Susie was so clean and clinical, like a nurse dealing with a patient – in complete contrast to Stephanie, who was writhing uncontrollably, impaled on the great sword of Devlin's cock and the weird contraption that surrounded it. With all her strength Stephanie pushed herself down on Devlin's cock, resisted his attempt to pull back again, and contracted all the muscles of her sex around the shuddering cylinder. Such hard contact immediately produced almost double the vibration as the motor fought the constriction, and the whole length of Stephanie's sex throbbed.

She was nearing the brink of orgasm: Susie's tongue in her mouth, her hand on her nipple, her white-stockinged thighs kneeling over Devlin's body, the juice of her lust flowing out over the silver metal scrotum. She held herself there, enjoying the exquisite feelings trembling through her nerves, taking her closer and closer to the edge, but not over it.

But her careful calculations of what she could take were suddenly upset. Deep, deep inside her body she felt Devlin's glans spasm. He was not moving, but the grip of her body and the relentless vibrations and the images in front of his eyes – the half-dressed Stephanie and the fully dressed Susie, Stephanie's hand inside the slit of Susie's dress – were too much for him to bear any longer. His cock jerked and, despite the silver cylinder that held it so tightly, managed to squeeze spunk up to his glans and out, out into the sleek wet confines of Stephanie's sex.

That was enough. As she felt his cock spasm, as she felt his hot spunk splashing out into her body, the vibrations reached their peak right in the very core of her. Her body seemed to lock, every muscle taut and hard, every nerve alert, then *snap*, like an elastic band being cut, a flood of sensation swamped her consciousness, wiping away everything but the feeling of pleasure.

From somewhere in the blanket of darkness that had been thrown over her by her orgasm, she felt Susie's mouth leave hers. The vibrations stopped. Very slowly she opened her eyes and looked out of the window of the plane. Craggy mountain tops still passed by below. She looked at Susie standing impassively by the side of the sofa.

'What do you want?' she asked quietly.

'Nothing, madam,' Susie said.

'I want to give you pleasure.'

'No, madam.'

Stephanie lifted herself carefully off Devlin's cock and stood up. The metal glistened with her juices.

'You can have anything,' she said. 'Use him. Anything.' The design of the phallus had only allowed Devlin's cock to shrink slightly; the rubber seal held his glans firm.

'No madam,' Susie repeated.

'What then?' Stephanie insisted, determined to see the woman's coolness broken.

Susie said nothing. Stephanie could see her mind working as if trying to calculate what she should do. The Malaysian flashed her jade eyes, under her very neat black eyebrows, up at Stephanie, who was suddenly aware of the height difference between them.

'There's only one thing I want,' she said calmly.

'What's that?'

'You, madam,' Susie replied, with no emotion in her voice.

Stephanie felt a shiver of pleasure at her directness. 'Sounds interesting.'

'On the sofa.' The words were hesitant. It was not up to Susie to order Devlin to move.

'Devlin.' Stephanie said at once.

Devlin got to his feet. Without a word he sat in a leather armchair opposite, his eyes never leaving the two women.

'And now?'

Susie sat down on the sofa, its leather warm from Devlin's body. She kicked off her shoes and lay flat on her back, making no attempt to take off the kheong sam. She reached up and took Stephanie's hand. Stephanie knew what she wanted. For the second time she knelt on the sofa and swung her thigh over a recumbent body, but this time facing the opposite direction, her back to Susie's face.

Immediately she felt Susie's hands slide round the top of her thighs, on to the naked flesh above the stockings, pulling her back so the furrow of her sex was above Susie's mouth. Satisfied that the position was right, the hands pulled Stephanie down until Susie's mouth touched the glistening wet labia and she extended her tongue. Gently she began licking from one end to the other, from clitoris to anus, like licking an ice cream.

She was no longer cool. Her body was alive. She could taste Stephanie's juices mixed with Devlin's spunk, a heady cocktail. Her hands left Stephanie's legs to snake down over her own sex. Quickly she worked up under the dress and down under the waistband of her tights.

Stephanie watched as Susie's hand worked between her own legs. She made no attempt to penetrate herself. She just pressed her forefinger into the very top of her labia. Her belly was sparsely covered with very black, very straight pubic hair. It hid little and Stephanie could see the tip of her finger pressing into her clitoris. She hardly seemed to move it at all, just rocking it slightly, but it was obviously enough. Underneath her she could feel Susie's body stiffening, beginning to shudder; her mouth and her tongue were getting hotter, working faster. Though the movements were tiny, the tempo with which her finger worked on her clitoris was frantic as was the rhythm of her mouth, sucking and licking at Stephanie's sex.

'I'm coming,' she mouthed, before plunging her lips back into Stephanie's wetness. Stephanie felt the whole body beneath her go rigid, saw the finger stop completely and the hips arch off the leather sofa. For a moment the tongue was rigid too, pressed hard against Stephanie's clitoris. Then the body, back, hips, and mouth slackened, and a delicious blast of hot air, an audible sigh, was expelled from the mouth, like exhaust from a car.

Stephanie eased her labia away but Susie's hands, abandoning her own sex, clamped themselves around her thighs again and pulled her back down.

'I won't come . . .' Stephanie started to say, but then she felt Susie's tongue, hot and thick and hard, shoot up into her sex. It lapped at the wetness there, then pushed further and further and further, further than a tongue had ever been, or so it seemed. It was a shock, like a jolt of electricity, deep inside her body. Stephanie reacted immediately. She had had no intention of coming again, no desire to do anything other than let Susie take her pleasure but now, suddenly, she was squirming down on Susie's tongue, pressing it deeper still, rubbing herself against the hard bone of Susie's chin. She felt her body heave and throb with pleasure. Almost before she'd realised what she was doing her body had taken over and she felt her sex convulse, a sharp, hard, almost painful contraction, followed by a slow, soft, infinite softness. Then she was melting over Susie's tongue, a flood of juices running over Susie's mouth as Stephanie's orgasm raked through her body.

Stephanie sipped her second vodka martini and looked out of the window. They were over the foothills of the mountains now, though these were still covered in snow.

After putting the glass down, Stephanie stepped into the shower and let the water cascade over her body. The shower in the plane was small but effective, and she adjusted the water so it was only slightly warm.

This was, she thought, the only way to travel. She dried herself thoroughly, dabbed her body with Joy 1000, pulled off the shower cap she had used to protect her hair and re-did her make-up before climbing back into her lacy white bra, suspender belt and French knickers. Finally, she rolled the opaque white stockings up her long legs. Her body still hummed with pleasure. As she pulled on her blouse and skirt she made a final check of her face, then unhooked the yellow jacket from the back of the door and slipped into her boots, zipping them up at the side.

The captain announced that they would be landing in Munich in fifteen minutes just as Stephanie rejoined Devlin in the main cabin. He had already showered and looked more than a little bemused – like a little boy given too many presents at Christmas.

'Are you all right?'

'Fine. Tired, that's all. I've never had such . . .' He couldn't think of the word. '. . . experiences.'

'Oh yes you have. How many times have you got Susie to use that little toy?'

'I didn't mean that. It's just something about you, Stephanie. You're so . . . direct. So sexy.'

'You didn't answer my question.'

'What question?'

'How many times, with Susie?'

'Not often. When we were alone on the plane. Never since I met you.'

'I'm not jealous, Devlin. Just curious.'

'But I never . . .'

'Never fucked?'

'No. Only you would have done that. It was fantastic.'

'I know. I was there too.'

'You always make everything so special.'

Stephanie smiled and pressed the call button on her seat. Susie appeared from the front cabin, neither her face nor her body giving any hint of what had occurred.

'Let's have another vodka martini. And a toast.'

'To what?' Devlin asked.

'To our holiday, of course. I have a feeling we're in for a very interesting time.'

'Very interesting,' Devlin repeated.

As Susie mixed the drinks, Stephanie watched her neat precise movements and felt a slight flutter inside her sex. She wouldn't forget what Susie had done to her.

Chapter Five

Susie unlatched the cabin door and the landing steps extended hydraulically from the belly of the plane. They had not landed at the main international airport at Munich, but at a small private airfield to the south.

'Well, Susie,' Stephanie said as she disembarked, 'I look forward to my next flight.'

'Yes, madam.' The resentment and disapproval that had always accompanied Susie's polite remarks up to now had disappeared. It had been replaced with what Stephanie could only describe as an overtone of longing and even of lust. 'So do I, madam. I hope you have a lovely holiday.'

'Perhaps it's time you had a holiday too, Susie,' Devlin said, as he came up to join them. 'You've never been to the castle, have you? I'm sure you'd enjoy it.'

'You've never been?' Stephanie asked with surprise.

'No, madam.'

'Oh you'd definitely enjoy it. I'd make sure of that.'

'I'd like that madam, I'd like that very much.'

Stephanie held Susie at the shoulders and kissed her on both cheeks before walking off the plane and down the metal steps. The thought of introducing her to the delights of the castle, after what she'd shown herself capable of on the plane, made her body hum.

A large white Mercedes stretch limousine was waiting at the foot of the ramp, its passenger doors open. It was distinctly colder than it had been in Italy and, as if on cue, just as Stephanie set foot on the ground, big thick flakes of snow began to fall. She hurried into the car. Its engine was running and its heater was on, and the driver closed the door as soon as they were both inside, ensuring that any chill was soon dispelled. He supervised the loading of the luggage into the boot and as soon as this was completed, climbed behind the wheel. Snow was still melting on the shoulders of his grey overcoat as the car set off.

Through the back window Stephanie saw Susie, seemingly reluctant to go inside, standing on the steps by the cabin door. She was waving one hand, and snowflakes were already peppering the dark green silk dress.

The Mercedes sped out of the gates of the airfield, and they were soon on the Autobahn heading south. The snow was falling faster now, the car's windscreen wipers working flat out to clear the glass. In the fields at the side of the road the dark ploughed earth was rapidly turning white and the branches of trees were soon fully laden.

'The first snow of winter,' the driver said in precise English with a heavy German accent.

'Is it far?' Stephanie asked.

'Thirty minutes,' the driver replied.

By the time they pulled off the three-lane Autobahn the whole country had turned white and the snow had eased up slightly. A watery sun was shining through much thinner cloud as the big car drove more slowly along the country lanes, most coated in undisturbed snow.

If Stephanie had cared to time it, she would have

found that it was exactly thirty minutes from the time the driver had spoken to the moment he pulled the car to a halt. They were at the entrance to a long winding driveway where large wrought-iron gates were set in elaborate brick pillars. The gates swung open on a signal from a transmitter in the driver's hand. Waiting on the other side was a large open sledge harnessed to four white horses. The driver of the sledge had covered the buttoned-back leather seating with a sheet to protect it from the snow. As Stephanie and Devlin climbed out of the Mercedes he quickly removed the cover and took out a delicately carved wooden block for them to use as a step, then stood waiting with the little half-door open.

Stephanie settled down into the comfortable leather beside Devlin. Any worries she had that they would be cold were soon dispelled by the driver, who extracted two huge sable rugs from a box opposite their feet. He threw these over their legs, then handed them matching hooded cloaks to wrap around their head and body. Within seconds the fur had taken off any chill they might have felt as the luggage was unloaded from the car.

As soon as the cases were on board, the driver got up on to the driving platform at the front of the sledge. He picked up the reins and a long whip and cracked it over the head of the leading horse who immediately led the others off at a walking pace.

The odd snowflake fell on their faces but under the fur they were perfectly warm. The driveway wound through open fields, then through a thick forest of conifers that seemed to go on forever. Oddly, considering they were travelling on firm-packed snow, the trees and the ground around the track had no more than a sprinkling of white. When they emerged from the woods they were greeted by an amazing spectacle. A vast lake, stretching away to the left as far the eye could see, lay before them. On the other side a mountain rose precipitously, its upper slopes coated with snow. Built snugly at its base was an enormous Schloss, a fairy-tale castle with tall spires and onion-shaped towers. Part of the lake had been diverted to form a moat, over which there was a small bridge in the same rococo Bavarian style as the castle. A drawbridge and a portcullis gave further protection.

To complete the idyllic picture, most of the gargoyles and parapets on the roofs and the equally elaborate lintels over doors and windows had been gilted with gold leaf. It looked like the castle in *Sleeping Beauty* where the Prince had come to wake the Princess with a kiss.

'Disneyworld,' Stephanie said, laughing and hugging Devlin's arm.

'It's a bit over the top,' Devlin agreed.

The sledge moved almost noiselessly, the horses' hooves making no sound as they fell in the snow, the metal runners sliding smoothly and silently apart from a crackling whisper as the blades cut ice. Only a pleasant trilling of the bells attached to the horses' harness filled the air.

The weak sun was trying to break through the clouds behind the lofty spires of the Schloss, and it had stopped snowing completely by the time the sledge nosed its way on to the bridge. At exactly the right moment, the drawbridge was lowered with a clanking of chains. There was a sharp report as it fell into place. Behind it, the heavy cross-hatched portcullis was winched up with an equal amount of groaning and protesting from the machinery.

The driver reined the horses to a halt in a large cobbled courtyard. They were now in front of the main entrance to the Schloss, formed by two massive wooden doors, braced by decorative wrought iron and fronted by a portico. The portico roof was a miniature of the spires that dominated the main building. At any minute Stephanie expected a major-domo in pink satin frock coat and satin breeches to walk through the doors.

Instead, as the driver jumped from his seat to lay out the mounting block and open the half-door, the Baron von Himmstrafer himself threw open one of the huge doors and strode out to meet them.

'Welcome, welcome,' he said, coming straight up to Stephanie, taking her hand and brushing it against his lips. He did not, as she might have expected from one of his military bearing, click his heels together at the same time. He was dressed in green plus-fours tucked into brown plaid socks and highly polished shoes, and a matching short braided jacket worn over a thick waistcoat. 'I hoped you enjoyed the sledge. It is one of my little luxuries . . . So romantic.'

'It was wonderful,' Stephanie said. She had thoroughly enjoyed the experience, the cold air on her face contrasting with the warmth under the sable rugs. 'I'd love to do it again.'

'You shall, whenever you wish.'

'I didn't think there was enough snow,' Devlin said as he shook the Baron's hand.

'There wasn't,' the Baron said. 'We have a snow-making machine. I had it out all morning. But now it looks as though we will have the real thing. Come in, come in! Everything is ready for you.'

The Baron took Stephanie's arm and led her into the house. Seeing him again had roused the same feelings she had had when they'd met at the castle. He was a big man, tall with obviously powerful muscles, and a ramrod straight back formed by years of military service. Apart from a horseshoe of almost white hair round the base of his scalp he was almost completely bald, his pate shining as though polished. His eyes were an extraordinary colour, a grey so dark it was almost slate. They were penetrating, and added to his overall aura of physical and intellectual power.

Inside the Schloss the decor was much less extravagant than the exterior, though no expense had been spared. The spacious lobby was floored with pale oak, the walls lined in the palest of cream silks. The impressive staircase was carpeted in black, its bannisters made of gleaming stainless steel – the product, Devlin had revealed, that had been responsible for von Himmstrafer's vast fortune. The Baron led them on through a pair of solid walnut doors into a large reception room where logs the size of small trees blazed in an open brick fireplace with a black slate hearth. Big, chunky modern sofas separated by a rectangular occasional table dominated the room. As well as the modern furniture there were several antiques, a Louis XVI *table à ecrire*, a sixteenth-century oak coffer and two Venetian *fauteuil de gonde* chairs. Dotted around the room on shelves set in the walls, individually lit, were various *objets d'art* in porcelain and silver, including a collection of Meissen plates.

'Please, please, make yourselves comfortable,' the Baron said, waving them towards the sofas. 'May I offer you something? A drink? I have a few bottles of Bollinger '69 left. A great wine. Lost a lot of its vigour now, but not its flavour . . .'

'That would be lovely,' Stephanie said.

‘And something to eat? I have planned a rather . . . let us say, lavish dinner this evening of course, but something light now perhaps?’

Stephanie looked at the Patek Phillipe. It was three o’clock. ‘I’d like to freshen up.’

‘Yes,’ Devlin agreed.

‘Then I’ll have something sent up to your suite. I think you should have time to settle in. Then I can show you around.’ There’s plenty of time.’

‘That would be perfect,’ Devlin said.

‘Let’s meet up here then at seven. If you’ll excuse me, I’ll get Hanna to show you up to your rooms.’

After bowing slightly again the Baron strode away and disappeared through a rather inconspicuous door on the other side of the room.

Up to that point everything had been perfectly normal: normal, that is, for an obviously extremely rich man greeting his latest house guests. Providing snow over a six-mile drive so they could be brought to the Schloss in a horse-drawn sledge equipped with sable fur rugs was certainly extravagant; but it was the appearance of Hanna a few minutes after the Baron’s departure that indicated exactly how out of the ordinary their stay was going to be.

Hanna was a tall, long-legged blonde with large blue eyes, a very straight nose and high cheek-bones. Her height was increased by the boots she wore; their heels were so high that her feet stood almost vertical. The boots were laced tightly up the front of her calves, as was a matching brown leather corset, cinched incredibly tightly around her waist. In fact the corset was no more than a wide belt, curved, boned and secured by leather thongs threaded through eyelets in the front. Above it her small but very round and proud breasts were naked. Below it the triangle of her mound, its neatly shaped blonde pubic hair and the rich curves of her pert buttocks were equally exposed. Her hands and arms were covered by leather gloves, the same colour as the rest of the outfit, which stretched right up almost to her armpits. There the gloves ended in a strap which was buckled tightly around the upper arm, preventing the leather from slipping down.

But this was not all that was bizarre about her appearance. Around her neck, again in brown leather, though much thicker than the leather of the corset, Hanna wore a broad collar. It was so broad it forced her head up, stretched her neck and made it difficult for her to look down. But the collar did not end under her chin. It was moulded to fit right over the line of her jaw, up over the mouth to just under her nose, thus enclosing the whole bottom half of her head – all the way round the back, too. At each side of the stiffened, moulded leather, just under the ear, a leather strap was fastened, which passed over the top of Hanna's head and held the collar firmly in place.

It was obvious that the leather over the mouth held in place some form of gag, as Hanna made no attempt to talk. She merely indicated with her hands that they should follow her.

Stephanie glanced at Devlin as they followed the attractive, leather-clad figure of the girl out into the hall and up the stairs. She could see him watching the way the girl's buttocks swung from side to side as she tottered on the high heels. Given their height, she walked with an ease that could only have been the result of lengthy practice. As Hanna mounted the stairs, Stephanie too stared up at her long legs, watching the planes and angles of the dark chasm between her legs change with the sensuous movements of her thighs.

At the top of the stairs, Hanna led the way along a dimly lit passageway, past numerous doors, out into a wider space where two corridors met. Hanna took the left-hand passage, then stopped at the first set of double doors.

The bedroom was huge. Big picture windows overlooked the lake, and a thick cream carpet coordinated with several other creams and off-whites, on the walls, on the upholstery of a sofa and chairs, and on the counterpane of the large bed. Their luggage had been neatly stacked on folding wooden racks. Hanna opened the doors to show them the wardrobes, the two bathrooms, and a small sitting room. She showed them how all the lights worked, and the telephones, and the two televisions. She picked up a remote control unit – one of two on either side of the bed – and used it to close and open the thick cream curtains, then to reveal a sliding panel that held a bar with every conceivable drink inside, then a fax machine, and finally a Reuters information terminal.

Her task completed, Hanna stood by the bedroom door as if to ask whether they would require her for anything else.

Stephanie very definitely did.

Coming up to her near-naked body, Stephanie looked into her light blue eyes. With her right hand she stroked her cheek, down from where the flesh was unobstructed, over the stiffened brown leather, then beyond the collar to her neck. Her hand reached Hanna's breast. She took it in her palm and weighed it, feeling the nipple as hard as a pebble against her fingers. Hanna remained impassive. She held Stephanie's eyes, staring straight at her with a sort of defiance. She was clearly making an effort not to flinch as Stephanie's hand explored the tight leather corset, down over her pouting buttocks and between her legs until her fingers brushed Hanna's pubic hair.

'Does that meet with your approval, madam?' her eyes asked without a word.

'Very pretty,' Stephanie said in answer to the unspoken question. She wanted to ask several of her own. She would have removed the gag but she could see that the strap securing the moulded leather on either side was secured by a tiny padlock. So, instead, she opened the bedroom door and indicated that Hanna was dismissed.

Devlin sat on the bed. He had watched her every move.

'Beautiful, didn't you think?' Stephanie asked, stripping off her jacket before going to look out of the window at the full panorama of the lake.

'The view or the girl?' Devlin asked.

'Both,' Stephanie said, smiling, as she unbuttoned her blouse and unzipped her skirt.

There was a delicate knock at the door.

'Come in,' Devlin shouted, necessarily since the distance from the bed to the door was so great.

The door swung open and a girl entered, wheeling a silver trolley in front of her. The girl, her hair a flaming red, was as bizarrely dressed as Hanna had been, and undoubtedly in a great deal more discomfort. Like Hanna, her neck was stretched high in a stiff moulded collar that enclosed her mouth and was strapped over the top of her head. But, at the base of the collar in the front, two long, very thin straps ran down her body, over her big meaty breasts and down over her navel. At the junction of her thighs, where her red pubic hair sprouted thinly, the straps were buckled into two corners of a rectangle of thick leather. This pad then disappeared between her legs, re-emerging halfway up her buttocks. Here, the corners were buckled to more thin straps which ran up her back to be secured into the collar again. Thus the crotchpiece was held firmly in place between her legs. There was very little give in the thick leather and it had not been cut to fit the area it was meant to cover, so it had chafed and reddened the girl's inner thighs.

Stephanie could just see, under the leather, the base of two black dildos, held firmly in place in both the passages of her body.

But as she examined the girl more closely another astonishing feature caught her eye. Both the girl's nipples has been pierced and they sported large gold rings. The leather straps running down the front of the girl's body had been passed through these rings, thereby pulling her big breasts inward and agitating the nipples every time she moved.

The redhead pushed the silver trolley between two high-backed wing chairs sited by one of the windows. She returned to the bedroom door and there, like Hanna, waited to be dismissed.

Stephanie, now stripped to her white lacy underwear and stockings, was curious to take a closer look at the nipple rings. She walked over to the girl. There was no doubt; the gold rings were not merely clipped to the redhead's big puckered teats, but ran right through them. Stephanie fingered each ring in turn, then pulled them up the long thin strap.

'Does that hurt?' she asked, feeling her own nipples hardening as if in sympathy.

The girl shook her head.

'Not even a little?'

The girl nodded.

'How interesting,' Stephanie said, signalling that the girl could go. 'I think we're going to enjoy it here, Devlin. This is my idea of fun.'

The silver trolley the redhead had brought was laden with a silver wine cooler, containing the precious Bollinger, champagne flutes of a modern design, and an array of tempting morsels all on silver platters. There was a crystal glass bowl filled with caviare, set on top of another filled with crushed ice. There were rolls of smoked salmon and a big plate of Mediterranean prawns surrounding a silver bowl of mayonnaise. On the lower level there was bread, cheese – at least three different kinds – and fruit.

Stephanie suddenly discovered she was ravenously hungry. Sexual excitement it seemed, always did this to her and, on top of the memories of what had happened on the plane, the sight of the two girls had set her pulse and her imagination racing.

Posed on the champagne bottle was a thick white card. In neat copperplate writing it read: IF THERE IS ANYTHING ELSE YOU REQUIRE, PLEASE DIAL 9.

'Yes, I think we'll enjoy it here,' Stephanie repeated, dipping her finger into the caviare to scoop it into her mouth.

The big grandfather clock in the lobby struck seven. The Baron, wearing dinner dress and a black tie, was waiting for them when they appeared on the stairs. Stephanie had taken a great deal of trouble over her appearance. She wore a full-length red dress sewn with a regular pattern of sequins that left her arms and back bare but wrapped around her neck in a little halter. This covered her bosom at the front but allowed for glimpses of breast at the sides. The skirt extended down to her ankles, tight and clinging, perfectly outlining the shape of her pert buttocks and the firm contours of her thighs. Her red court shoes, their toes decorated with a diamond of diamanté, could just be seen below the hem.

She had pinned her long black hair up into a neat chignon and had applied rather darker make-up than usual. She had emphasised her eyes with a heavy eye-liner and shadow, hollowed her cheekbones with blusher and used a much darker, redder lipstick, matching its colour on her finger- and toenails.

Devlin followed behind her, his black tie and dinner dress set off by a brightly coloured cummerbund.

The Baron's eyes sparkled his approval as she walked down the last few steps.

'Bravo!' he said. 'Simply magnificent, my dear. A triumph.' He took her hand and kissed it again. 'You are a very lucky man, Devlin.'

'I don't belong to Devlin,' Stephanie reminded him sternly.

'No, of course.' the Baron said. 'I meant to imply only that he was lucky to be able to see you so often, to live with you.'

'And I am,' Devlin added. 'Very lucky.'

They walked through into the reception room where the big fire was still consuming logs at a rapid rate. A waiter in a white tail coat, white bow tie and velvet breeches waited to pour the champagne, another bottle of the exceptional Bollinger brought up from the Baron's well-stocked cellars.

'Champagne?' the Baron asked, in case they preferred something else.

'Yes, thank you.' She saw the bottle. 'It was delicious this afternoon.'

Devlin agreed with a nod of his head.

'I thought we would have dinner, and then I'd show you the . . .' He tried to think of the right word. '. . . facilities.'

'It's a beautiful house,' Devlin said.

'Actually built by Leo von Klenze in 1826. I had the interior redesigned but my sense of history won't let me touch the exterior, however extreme it may appear.'

'It's fun,' Stephanie said as she took the champagne flute from the tray presented to her by the waiter.

'There's plenty of space, that's the main thing. Plenty of room for all the activities.'

'And what are those?' Stephanie asked.

'I think it is better that you see for yourself. *Prosit.*'

The three raised their glasses and drank the champagne, its bubbles almost gone but its colour clear and crisp like the golden tones of autumn.

'Wonderful,' Devlin said.

'Yes. Unfortunately, like all good things, it has come to an end.'

They moved through into a small intimate dining room, one of three of various sizes, the Baron explained. It was a completely circular room with no windows, its interior lavishly pleated in a dark blue material that rose over their heads like a tent. The centrepiece, above their heads, was a rose ruched in a different material but in the same blue. Hanging from this central rose was a small chandelier; illumination from this spilt down on to a circular table underneath, set with white linen, silver cutlery and sparkling gold rimmed crystal glasses. Three high-backed sculptured chairs that might have been Charles Rennie Mackintosh originals surrounded the table.

The Baron explained that he had asked his kitchen to prepare German specialities and serve German wines. They ate white asparagus and wild boar with *Spatzel* and apple cake. The sweet *Eiswein* served with the cake Stephanie thought particularly good and said so.

'Yes, it is gathered at midnight after the first frost, hence "ice-wine".'

The waiters brought coffee and tiny petits fours in chocolate, each one bearing the Baron's coat of arms.

'And so. We are soon ready for the evening's entertainment I think. I have an establishment like yours, but with some essential differences.'

Stephanie had been eager to ask about the two girls.

'Those girls this afternoon – they are slaves?'

'No. Not in the sense you mean.'

'What then?' Devlin asked.

'My friends, my acquaintances. They come here as my guests. It is entirely voluntary. But once they are here, they must spend two-thirds of their time as slaves and one-third as masters. That is the strict rule. If they cannot agree to that then they do not come. If they find they cannot obey as a slave, then they must leave the Schloss immediately and without question; and, naturally, they would never be allowed to return. As an incentive to good behaviour that seems to be quite adequate. Many of my guests wish to return regularly.'

'Do many disobey?'

'No. Usually they find that any inconveniences they may suffer are outweighed by the many delights. Of course, if you are of a submissive nature in the first place, we do not insist that you become a master. Fortunately, it seems, there are always more people of that persuasion.'

'Oh definitely,' Stephanie said, looking at Devlin.

'So, would you now like the tour?'

'Absolutely.'

Stephanie felt a pulse of anticipation as the Baron came up behind her. He swung the dining chair back as she stood up.

He took her hand and looked deep into her eyes.

'I can see your excitement,' he said, stressing the word 'see'. At her castle, despite the endless opportunities offered in the cellars, Stephanie had been unable to tempt the Baron to do more than watch. To cater for his predilection she had organised a series of spectacles for him, and on his last night had herself been the main exhibit in a sexual tableau. When he looked at her now, was he remembering how she had looked, her body clothed in black lingerie, her sex open for his inspection? Or how she'd responded to being fucked by one of her slaves, or sucked by one of the women, her legs spread open, her sex angled at him through a two-way mirror?

'You've seen more than that,' she reminded him.

'And I hope I will again.'

Devlin watched the exchange with no jealousy. His relationship with Stephanie allowed him to feel no emotion other than the physical needs she provoked in his body. She aroused him totally, and as long as she continued to do so he really didn't care about anything else. He was, after all, fundamentally and above all else, her slave; it was not for him to question her. Their relationship was unequal, one-sided. He owed her total obedience; she owed him nothing.

The Baron led them through the house. Not wanting to destroy the facade of the building, he had built four pavilions into what had once been the stable block, applying the same rococo style von Klenze had used on the original. These pavilions were connected to the original Schloss and to each other by means of Perspex tunnels running from the back of the house on the first floor.

At the door to the passageway, after they had walked the length of the house and up a narrow staircase, the Baron paused.

'There are four pavilions,' he explained. 'Each have a different theme. Each guest is shown all four themes by means of a viewing gallery, and then may choose which they prefer. Are you ready?'

Stephanie felt her pulse surge again as the Baron punched a combination of four numbers into the computer lock on the heavy metal door. It swung open with a hiss of hydraulics, and he ushered them through. The Perspex tubing which formed the passage was dotted with snow on the outside, and ice crystals had formed in lacy patterns. Stephanie could see the lake and the mountains, and, under her feet, a piece of formal garden.

The passage veered to the right and they were confronted with another metal door. As they approached, the door swung open, activated by a photo-electric cell set in the Perspex.

The Baron led the way through the second door on to a metal gantry above a large rectangular hall. Immediately below the gantry was a sheet of what looked like glass.

'This,' the Baron said, indicating the glass, 'can only be seen through from above. From below it looks like a normal ceiling.'

Stephanie looked down through the 'glass'. Below, perfect in every detail as far as she could tell, was a Roman villa of the first century A.D., spacious and meticulously built, complete with a patio leading out to a swimming pool. As she walked further along the gantry she saw a large living room and three bedrooms, all furnished with Roman artifacts and drapes corresponding exactly to the period.

But it was not the authenticity of the surroundings that most attracted Stephanie's attention; far more interesting was what was going on inside them. All the rooms were deserted apart from the largest, where all the inhabitants of the pavilion were gathered. There were perhaps twenty people in total, with slightly more women in evidence than men. A rostrum supporting a Roman throne had been erected at one end of the room, on which was seated a rather portly man. His hair was combed forward in the Roman fashion, his body clothed in a white toga, and his feet in leather sandals. Seated at his feet on either side of the throne were two almost identical blondes wearing very short togas, their long blonde hair brushed neatly over their shoulders.

In front of the throne was a stone slab about three feet off the ground, roughly the size of a single bed. All the other participants stood around this slab. Stephanie could see the portly man's lips move, but could not hear what was being said.

'Can we hear?' she asked the Baron.

The Baron nodded. He took from his pocket a small unit resembling a remote control for a television, and pressed one of its dozen or so buttons. Immediately sound filtered into the gantry: not natural sound, but relayed from some speaker system.

'What do you have to say for yourself?' Stephanie heard the man on the throne saying.

'Nothing, master.' The words came from a petite auburn-haired girl who was being held by two burly men at each arm.

'Then you will have to be punished.'

'No, master, please don't punish me. I did nothing –'

'You have to be punished until you learn to obey. Slaves must obey.'

The master nodded to the two men. With a minimum of effort they stooped and grasped her ankles, then lifted her bodily on to the stone slab. Four metal rings were set in each corner of the stone. With leather thongs the men quickly bound the girl's wrists and ankles to the rings, spreading her across the slab. The assembled crowd looked on eagerly, examining the girl's naked body.

'The candle . . .' the master said.

While one of the men busied himself with stretching the woman's body out more tightly, retying each leather thong in turn, the other picked up what looked like a small but heavy stone basin and placed it squarely on the bound woman's navel. Sitting in the middle of the basin was a large thick white candle, which the man lit. He then blew on the flame until it burnt brightly. As the captive woman breathed in and out, the round bottom of the basin rocked and the candle moved from side to side. Once there was enough hot wax, this movement spilt the liquid over the woman's body, making her writhe in pain, which in turn increased the oscillation of the bowl and sprayed more wax over her.

'The quieter you are, the less you will feel,' the master explained, getting up from his throne to stand by his captive's head. 'Try to breathe deeply, try not to move,' he counselled, stroking her cheek then dropping his hand to her naked breast. He squeezed it hard, making her try to buck him off, but this only caused the bowl to gyrate more wildly, causing hot wax to fly all over her thighs. 'See,' he tutted.

With a click of fingers directed at the two blondes, he strode back up on to the rostrum. One of the blondes immediately loosened the leather belt that held the toga at his waist while the other came up behind him to part the loose white material and slip it off his body. Under his considerable paunch his cock was beginning to swell.

One of the blondes fell to her knees in front of the master and gobbled the growing erection into her mouth. The other stood behind him with her hand snaking down between his buttocks to find his anus.

The master's action seemed to be a sign for the rest of the room to dissolve into sexual activity. The group divided up into couples, threesomes, foursomes. Men and women began to kiss and fondle each other, lying down on the floor or across the Roman-style benches that littered the room.

The woman on the stone slab had managed to bring her breathing under control and the candle remained more or less vertical. But one of the men had decided that, of all the available women in the room, the auburn haired captive was his target, and so he began running his hand up her thigh. Desperate not to have more hot wax splash her body, the woman tried to remain passive as the man's hand reached her belly. His fingers artfully descended into the folds of her labia, sparsely covered with wispy auburn hair. As his finger circled her clitoris, he grinned down at her, knowing perfectly well what he was doing. The feelings he was generating in her sex made her pulse rise, her breath shorten and her navel flutter. Instantly the bowl swung, the candle gyrated and a shower of hot wax, more than before as it had pooled for longer, stung her naked flesh.

Her tormentor laughed, withdrew his hand, and went to join a threesome of two women sitting astride a man, one on his cock and the other on his face. The newcomer hauled the woman on the man's mouth over to one side and replaced the tongue that had licked inside her with his rampant and throbbing cock.

On the rostrum, the master's cock was thrusting into the blonde's mouth at an ever increasing rate. The other blonde had also sunk to her knees and had replaced her finger in his anus with her tongue. Unfortunately for her, that was not all the master could feel.

'Stop!' he shouted. 'You bitch, you bit me!'

'No, master,' the blonde said, cowering away as the man turned on her.

'How dare you contradict me!'

'I didn't, master.'

'I know what you did.'

'Please, master . . .' The blonde sounded genuinely frightened.

'Brutus, Agrippa,' the master shouted. Two naked men immediately disentangled themselves from intimate liaisons with other slaves.

'Please, master,' the girl whimpered.

The two men stepped up on to the rostrum, their cocks erect and glistening. They grabbed the blonde and pulled her to her feet.

'Over there. You're going to regret biting me.'

At the back of the rostrum on the wall was a large lion's head, its mouth holding a golden ring rather like a latter-day door knocker. A white rope hung from the ring. In a matter of seconds the two men had pulled the girl's toga off her body and lashed her hands together with the rope, and she was tied to the ring, her arms stretched up above her head until she was on tiptoe. They turned her round so she faced out into the room.

'Please . . .'

The master stared into her face. 'To prove how

kind and considerate I am, I'm going to let you choose your punishment.'

'Please . . .'

'You can have the pins or the cream.'

'Please, master . . .'

'Which is it to be, the pins or the cream?'

Clearly the girl knew precisely what these alternatives meant, having seen them used before. 'Please, master, it was an accident. I didn't mean –'

'You don't have much time to choose. In ten seconds Brutus is going to gag you. If you don't choose by then, I'll use them both.

'Both?'

'Both. So which is it to be?'

Brutus advanced with a braided leather strap, into which had been woven a wooden oval block.

'Seven, eight, nine . . .' the master counted.

'The cream!' the blonde blurted out, just before the wooden oval was forced into her mouth and tied fast behind her head, trapping her long blonde hair.

'Good. Octavia, bring the cream.'

The other blonde had already gone to a small cupboard at the side of the rostrum. From it she took a small earthenware pot, decorated with Roman figures and highly glazed, and carried it over to the master. She then took a wooden bowl and filled it from a large stone water butt at the far end of the room, before bringing it back up to the rostrum with a small towel. As soon as this was accomplished the master dabbed a finger into the jar. It emerged with a gob of green cream, which he immediately smeared on the unfortunate blonde's very erect nipples. A second gob was plastered between her labia. Satisfied, he washed his hand in the wooden bowl and dried it on the towel.

'Now,' he said, turning back to the others. 'Continue.' He clapped his hands and the orgy began again, the men and women resuming the encounters they had interrupted to watch the girl's bondage. Mouths, hands, cocks, penetrating, sucking, caressing, kissing: every conceivable sexual act was openly performed.

The blonde put the bowl down and sank to her knees again. While she slipped the master's cock between her lips, another slave came up from the floor to replace the errant blonde behind him, and pushed her tongue between his buttocks to penetrate the mouth of his anus and make him moan. But this time he didn't face out into the room. He stood facing the captive blonde. The others, too, whatever their activities, arranged themselves to watch the girl.

The cream did not take long to work. The blonde began to moan, a long continuous moan, shaking her head from side to side, as if trying to get rid of the gag. At the same time she was raising one foot off the ground, bringing her knee right up to see if she could rub it against her breast. Her nipples and labia were prickling with a hot, itching sensation, like being stung by a nettle over and over again, except the feeling was totally rooted in sex. Within minutes the sensation had completely engulfed her. She had never wanted to touch herself more. She would have given anything, done anything to be able to pinch and caress her nipples, to scratch and knead her clitoris, to use her hands to bring herself off. The cream was creating her need, making her body heave, filling her with a desperate desire: to scratch the enormous, throbbing, pounding itch that had grown in the tender flesh of her erogenous zones. All she could do was move her legs, try to force her knees against her breasts, try to rub her thighs together against her labia. But it wasn't enough. She needed more. Much more.

The desire increased, swelled, mounted in her, got so great she thought she would faint. It was worsened by the fact that, in every corner of the room, she could see women getting what she needed so desperately, cocks and tongues and fingers working labia and nipples. She knew she would come the instant she felt the slightest touch; she could come from a fingertip poised against her nipple. But she knew that touch would never come. All around her men and women came, watching her, watching her body writhing against the white rope, watching her helpless frustration.

'Yes . . .' the master said, pulling the other blonde's head back just as his spunk jetted from his cock. He aimed it all at the helplessly bound girl, and the hot white semen splashed her thighs, adding to her maddening desire to feel the release he had just felt.

The woman on the stone slab had remained quiet, glad that, temporarily at least, attention had turned from her. But now the master picked up the little jar of green cream and advanced on her.

'Did you think we'd forgotten about you? Poor thing. So neglected . . .' He started to smear the cream on the prostrate woman's nipples. 'This should warm you up.' His finger applied it to the lips of her sex. Almost instantly the candle on her belly began to oscillate as the stinging sensation ate its way into her body.

'Shall we move on?' the Baron said.

'Oh, yes . . .' Stephanie had been so fascinated by the spectacle that the Baron's voice came as something of a shock.

'Interesting, don't you think?'

'I, ah . . .' Stephanie found it hard to say anything. She was watching the hot wax spray on to the woman's body, and the way she reacted. She made herself tear her eyes away and look at Devlin. He appeared cool and unmoved by what they had seen.

'Not your scene,' she said and stroked his arm.

'Not tonight, anyway,' he said.

'This way.'

The Baron led the way across the gantry to another metal door. He punched the same combination of numbers into its computer lock and it swung open with a hiss.

'I take it you wish to proceed?' the Baron asked solicitously.

'Oh yes.'

'Then, please . . .' he said, indicating that they should go first.

Chapter Six

The Perspex corridor leading into the next pavilion was no more than a few strides long and the door at its end was already swinging open as the one behind them closed. Again Stephanie could see the lake through the transparent panels, and at that moment the moon emerged from behind a cloud, lighting the water in a ghostly silver.

Once again they found themselves on a metal gantry running the whole length of the building, screened off from the view of those underneath by the same one-way ceiling. But whereas the Roman pavilion had been bright, with a feeling of openness, the interior of this space was dark and enclosed. As Stephanie's eyes adjusted to the light she saw they were in a reproduction of a cavernous, vaulted cellar. The meagre illumination came from big candles mounted on black iron candelabras and from a central chandelier, also in black iron. This took the shape of a huge wheel of iron spikes, into which candles had been stuck. In one corner, under a black canopy of metal, a forge burnt with red-hot coals, bars of metal sticking out from its depths, occasionally shooting sparks into the air.

Hanging on the stone walls were pairs of metal rings from which several men and women were chained, their wrists stretched apart above their heads. All were dressed in various medieval costumes, the women in tight bodices and full skirts, the men in tights and tunics. Some were fully dressed while others had had their clothing torn away to reveal a breast, a buttock, a cock or a tuft of pubic hair.

The ringmaster of this particular circus appeared to be a large, muscular man dressed in black tights, a massive black codpiece around his loins and a leather top. This amounted to no more than a broad band of black leather on his chest, held by two wide straps over his shoulders. His navel and arms were naked and glistened with sweat.

'Confess,' Stephanie heard him shout as the Baron adjusted the volume on the speaker system.

The reason for his perspiration was obvious. He stood in front of an accurate copy of a medieval rack and his big muscular arms were turning the spokes of its rope drum at the top of the frame. Tied into the rack was a strikingly beautiful brunette, her face finely featured, her eyes a brandy brown. The tight bodice of her dress had been pulled off her breasts, which were big and meaty, and the skirt ripped away so that her legs and belly were bare. Several men and women stood around the rack watching eagerly.

'No,' the woman gasped.

'Confess!' the Inquisitor yelled again, turning the spokes of the drum a further notch.

'Never,' the woman cried defiantly.

'You are a witch,' the Inquisitor said and bent over her until his face was inches from hers, his sweat dripping down on to her cheeks. 'Confess.'

'No.'

The woman struggled, her wrists and ankles tied into leather cuffs. These were in turn attached to the rope that wound around the drum at the top of the machinery. There was a definite excitement blazing in her eyes.

'Very well,' the Inquisitor said, reversing the spokes on the drum. The woman's body relaxed and she gasped. 'We have tried the rack. Now we will introduce you to the iron maiden. Get her up.'

Four of the spectators, two men and two women, untied the woman's wrists and ankles and hauled her to her feet.

'Bring her over here,' the Inquisitor ordered. As he walked the length of the cellar he took a short leather whip from a selection of many hanging from the walls. Each of the slaves tethered to the metal rings he stroked hard with the whip as he passed: one man across his thigh, almost catching his cock; a woman across her breast; another, whose face had been turned to the wall, and whose skirt was tucked up around her waist, twice on the buttocks, which he then stopped to fondle briefly. She moaned with pleasure.

The brunette was frogmarched over to the side of the room next to the forge, struggling and fighting every inch of the way.

Standing against the wall was what looked like a coffin, made from sheet metal and hinged at the front. A small barred window in the shape of a diamond was set in the door at head height. The Inquisitor strode over to it, and with a creaking of hinges pulled the door open.

'May I introduce you to my friend the Iron Maiden,' he said, smiling broadly. 'You will remember, no doubt, that it used to be equipped with rather unpleasant iron spikes. We have made some changes, but the principle remains the same . . .'

The woman stared into the narrow and cramped

interior, empty except for some odd black padding, cut out in a human shape.

'Strip her, quickly.' The assembled crowd, who had all moved to this end of the cellar, obliged readily, pulling away the woman's already torn skirt and blouse.

A female stepped forward holding a carefully shaped leather mask, designed to fit over the contours of the eyes and nose to exclude even the faintest hint of light. While the others held the brunette tightly the woman pressed the mask over her eyes and strapped it tightly at the back of her head.

'Bind her hands.'

The woman's hands were dragged behind her back and bound with a single leather thong.

'Do you confess to being a witch?'

'I am not a witch,' the woman said firmly.

'Put her in then. And may God have mercy on your soul.'

Not struggling now, the brunette was pushed into the metal casket, facing outward, her figure encased in the padded shape. Slowly the Inquisitor closed the door. There was a simple but strong hasp which he locked by means of a metal pinion.

He stood back and took a thin, narrow candle from a small rack on the wall, spiked it on an empty candle holder and lit it with a taper from the forge. The candle burnt rapidly.

'No woman has ever lasted longer than half a candle,' he said to the crowd.

The Inquisitor peered through the diamond shaped window and could see the woman's eyes blazing in the dark interior. He picked up a bulbous wooden rod, curved like a scimitar, and inserted it in a hole that had been made dead in the centre of the casket door. There was no doubt from its shape and breadth that it was intended to be a crude dildo. From his movement it was clear that the Inquisitor was making no effort to penetrate the woman with this device; he was merely inserting it until it rested at the apex of her thighs, so that she was fully aware of its presence.

Inside the casket the brunette was hot. The heat from the forge had warmed the metal, but it was not unbearable. Like the interior, the door was padded, lined with a strange, fleecy, spongy material that pressed into the front of her naked body. The blindfold was effective. She couldn't see the slightest hint of light. She heard and felt the wooden rod being inserted and thought for a moment this was the beginning of her torture, but it merely nudged between her thighs.

The padding moulded every curve of her body. Apart from the inside of her thighs, which were tightly pressed together, and the underside of her arms, bound against her back, there was not a single part of her body that was not touched by it. Even the undersides of her breasts and the sides of her face and neck pressed against it.

It was the soles of her feet that she noticed first, perhaps because they were pushed into the padding the hardest. They began to prickle as though the fleecy lining was made of a thousand tiny pins. She lifted one foot off the floor as far as she could – which wasn't very far in the confines of the casket – but this only made the feeling in the other foot worse. The fibres seemed to be working their way under her skin.

Almost before she had had time to register the discomfort, her breasts began to experience the same sensation, like tiny needles sticking into her tender flesh, making her squirm. If her hands hadn't been tied behind her back she would have scratched the incredible itch the material created, but she couldn't; that made it worse. Squirming against the padding only increased the feeling, driving the needles of the fabric deeper.

She gasped. The feelings from her breasts intensified, and were joined now by a prickling on her rump, on her outer thighs, on the cheeks of her face, on her waist and belly. Soon every bit of her body touched by the fleecy padding was alive, every inch of her flesh crawling. She could not help but squirm and writhe. If she managed temporary relief for one small part of her body, it was only at the cost of increasing the irritation in most of the rest of her.

'Oh no, no . . .' she said aloud. The fibres on her belly seemed to have worked down into her pubic hair and on to her labia. That was the worst of all. She felt the wooden shaft in front of her and used it to scratch at her sex, but as she pushed against it, the wood slipped away.

The Inquisitor saw the wood move. He'd heard the gasps. He looked at the candle. It was a quarter burnt down. At halfway he would put the question again.

Suddenly the sensation in the woman's body changed. The feeling of being pricked by a thousand pins and needles turned to a slow, sensuous heat. The fibres of the padding seemed now not to be sharp at all, but soft, incredibly soft. They seemed to be caressing her, caressing every part of her with a touch so delicate it made her swoon. Waves of pleasure flooded over her, not just from her nipples and breasts and labia, but from every part of her body. Her arms, her thighs, her feet, the back of her neck, her waist and her buttocks seemed to be just as sensitive as her sex. Her whole body was heaving. It was as though the fibre had created a thousand clits, centres of sensitivity spread right across her body, all equally capable of delivering exquisite sensation, all throbbing with pleasure.

'Please, please,' she moaned, not really knowing what she was saying.

As quickly as it had come that phase ended and a new feeling began. The fibres seemed to be drumming against her now, in exact time to her own thick, racing pulse, stroking her body up and down. It was impossible, she knew; nothing had changed. But in the blackness behind the blindfold it felt like the fibre was moving, swaying, like seaweed in the swell of a wave, to and fro against her body.

That feeling created another need. Suddenly, instead of being spread out everywhere, the sensation became concentrated. It homed in on the thrumming centre of her sex, the lozenge of her clitoris squeezed between her labia. Almost unconsciously she pushed her belly forward against the wooden shaft but, once again, it was unsecured, and slid away. She was desperate for contact, desperate to feel something hard against her sex, something she could push into her labia, against her clit, that would free it, open it, fulfil it.

'Please . . .'

The Inquisitor heard her plea and saw the wooden shaft move out again. He looked at the candle and smiled. It was exactly half burnt down.

'Do you confess to being a witch?'

'No!' she screamed, half hoping that noise, a lot of noise, would distract her from her torment. It didn't. Her whole body was screaming instead, screaming with sensation that built and built, that fuelled her need and increased her frustration. The wooden shaft was there, right in front of her, in exactly the right place for her to use it. If only she could squirm against it, push it right up into her soaking wet sex. She knew she was wet. She could feel her juices running over her labia and down her thighs. All she wanted was the hardness of the shaft. It would only take a second – not a second even. Was that too much to ask?

'Please . . .' she begged, her whole body quivering. As the fibre continued to tease her, her breasts and nipples, her buttocks, her thighs, all joined together, pumping more and more need into her pounding sex.

'Do you confess?'

'No . . .'

'You want the shaft?'

'Yes . . .'

'Confess.'

'No.'

The Inquisitor held the shaft and eased it forward until he could feel the resistance of her body.

'Oh, yes . . .' the brunette groaned.

Immediately the Inquisitor pulled the shaft back.

'Oh no, no, please . . .'

He pushed the shaft in again.

'Thank you, thank –' Her gratitude turned instantly to alarm as the shaft was pulled away. 'No, no!' Her whole body was sweating, her mind, in the enforced darkness behind the mask, able to see nothing but a picture of a dildo slipping effortlessly between the lips of her sex. She could see it in every detail, a beautifully shaped imitation of a penis, the acorn of the glans carved in wood, the little slit of the urethra, everything perfect as it plunged up into her. She could even hear it, hear the noise it would make as it parted her labia, the silky whisper her juices would sing as it penetrated her. She had to have it, she had to.

'Please . . .'

'Do you confess?'

'Anything, anything.'

'Confess.'

'Yes, yes, damn you, I'm a witch. Please give it to me, please . . .'

The Inquisitor looked at the candle. More than half its length had disappeared. She had been stubborn. More stubborn than most. He looked into the casket through the little window and watched the brunette writhe hopelessly. He started to count out loud.

'One, two, three . . .'

'Please.' Ever more desperate.

'Four, five, six . . .'

She angled herself towards the shaft, knowing it was coming, her body heaving with total frustration, desperate for release.

'Seven, eight, nine . . .' He smiled again, delaying the last count. 'Ten.'

His hand seized the wooden shaft and pushed it forward. Even though he could not see it, he could feel it forcing its way effortlessly into her body.

'My God, my God . . .' she moaned continuously.

The woman was impaled on the shaft. It lunged up into her, stretching her clitoris, opening her. Almost before it had come to rest the brunette started to come, her whole body centred on the head of the dildo. At last, the teasing, the frustration were released. She came like she couldn't remember ever coming before, every nerve stretched to breaking point, the muscles in her body convulsing against the strange padded fibre, sensing once again its potency.

'I'm a witch,' she said softly, when finally her body came to rest.

'Yes, my dear, you are.' The Inquisitor took the pinion out of the hasp and swung the door of the casket open. Without support the woman almost fell to the floor.

'Shall we move on?' the Baron said as the woman was helped over to a wooden bench to rest.

Again Stephanie felt momentarily disorientated, so involved had she become in the woman's plight – even though she had had no idea of exactly what was going on in the confinement of the iron maiden. The sound of the brunette's voice in extremity had been enough to make her imagination run riot. Her final moan had seemed to vibrate through the room forever, her vocal cords, like every other part of her body, stretched and throbbing with pleasure.

'Shall we move on?' the Baron repeated, gently touching Stephanie's elbow to snap her out of her reverie.

'Oh yes, sorry.'

'Or would you like to stay?'

'No, no, let's go on.'

Under the tight long dress, Stephanie's body felt suddenly hot. She could feel her nipples pressing hard against its silk lining. Between her legs her sex had responded too, sending little messages to tell her it had been awakened from its temporary slumber. A slick of moisture had begun to dampen the gusset of the sheer tights she was wearing; the dress was much too tight to allow her to wear panties.

The Baron had already opened the door at the end of the gantry by the time Devlin took Stephanie's arm. He led her over to it, recognising only too well the tell-tale signs of her excitement, though he had been only mildly interested in the spectacle.

To Stephanie's surprise, the exit door from this pavilion led not to another length of tubular Perspex but to a short flight of stairs which took them down to what she judged to be ground level. Another metal door opened automatically at the bottom of the stairs.

They found themselves this time not on an overhead gantry but in a passage along the side of the building. This time the same one-way glass, or whatever the material was that allowed them to see without being seen, had been used to form the wall of what looked like a Victorian prison. It was easy to see why a gantry would not have been appropriate to view the interior of this 'theme'; most of the space was divided into small cells, with the exception of the far end which formed a large recreational area.

Unlike the other two pavilions, this one, it was immediately apparent, was occupied only by women. Each of the six or seven cells were occupied by two women. Their basic uniform was a dirty grey jacket and fatigue pants, but there was no such regulation in their underwear, and as Stephanie walked to and fro looking into each cubicle, she saw a variety of lingerie. Everything from plain cotton to luxurious silk and satin was in view as the inmates stripped off their uniforms to prepare for bed.

In one of the cells a couple of women were already naked and engaged in oral sex, their mouths buried between each other's thighs, licking and sucking and panting their pleasure.

'This is the only non-guest,' the Baron whispered as he adjusted the sound system. 'Brunehilda I hired especially.'

As he said this, a woman in a black uniform and shiny black boots and gloves unlocked the door into the recreation room. She then relocked it behind her. She was a strawberry blonde, her hair wrapped into two plaits like a young child's, which was completely at odds with the rest of her appearance. Everything else about her suggested a female shot-putter. She looked incredibly strong, with her squat, heavy legs under her short black skirt, her barrel chest, her thick wrists and her bulging biceps.

Around the uniform jacket she wore a belt, attached to which was a chatelaine of keys. Tucked under her arm was a swagger stick. Walking down the corridor of cells she gazed through the peep-holes set in each metal door to inspect the inmates in her charge.

The moment she saw the naked couple engrossed in their mutual cunnilingus, she unlocked the door of the cell and threw it open with a crash.

'What do you think you are doing?'

The women's heads came up and they tore away from each other. They cowered into the corner and wiped their mouths dry as the Warden advanced.

'Nothing, mistress,' one of the women managed to gasp.

'Nothing!' The Warden pulled the swagger stick out from under her arm and slashed it across the woman's naked chest. At its tip it had a fine network of thin lashes that caught the woman's large breast at its meatiest part. 'Do you think I'm stupid? You know the rules. If you want to go down on each other, you first go down on me.' Her accent was very guttural and Germanic.

'Yes, mistress. We thought . . .' The other woman, much smaller and thinner than her companion, stammered.

'You do not think. You did not think at all.'

Another blow from the swagger stick caught the second woman across her thigh. 'Well, you're going to get your punishment right away. Come here.' She indicated the floor in front of her. 'Hands behind your back. At once!' Hooked into the belt around the Warden's waist was a little leather case. She opened it and extracted two pairs of traditional metal handcuffs. She quickly snapped one pair around the smaller woman, then manoeuvred the other so her wrists were cuffed with the central span linked across the first pair. They were effectively bound together back to back.

'I've got a little present for my girls,' she smiled. 'You, unfortunately will not be joining in, though I'm sure you will hear everything . . .'

'No mistress, please. Punish us tomorrow,' the smaller woman begged, knowing full well what the present was.

'Oh, don't leave us in here,' the other one added pathetically, knowing it was useless to argue.

'The rules are here to be obeyed, no?'

The Warden gave both women a parting stroke across their thighs with the swagger stick, then marched out, locking the door behind her. Then, one by one, she unlocked all the other cells, opened their doors and barked out at the occupants, 'Recreation room at once. Schnell, schnell . . .'

Excited, the women gathered, all in various states of undress, none stopping to put clothes back on. A steady parade of slim thighs, tight buttocks and every possible shape and size of breast assembled in the large room at the end of the hall. The only thing that all the women had in common was that they wore what appeared to be regulation issue black high-heeled stiletto shoes.

It was clear that this was something of a routine; all the women seemed to know perfectly well what to expect. They whispered to each other and giggled. On the Warden's instructions, two of the women carried a heavy wooden trestle into the middle of the room, its upper surface padded and covered in suede, a leather strap secured at the base of each of its legs.

'Inspection, schnell,' the Warden snapped.

Without further instruction, the women hurried to obey and lined up smartly in two ranks like soldiers on parade. They stood with their heads up and their arms straight down at their sides, the variety of lingerie they wore as great as the variety of shapes and sizes in their figures. Some of the women were tall and slim, others small and plump; the rest covered the whole spectrum in between. Hair colour and length varied too, from jet back and long to tightly cut and the lightest of blondes.

The Warden strode down the two ranks of prisoners, her black boots clanking against the stone.

'Very nice.'

Her second inspection was much slower. She stopped in front of every prisoner to examine her minutely, using the swagger stick to touch their bodies. She prodded one prisoner's brassiered breasts, inserted it in the waistband of another's panties, then pulled the elastic out and let it snap back painfully. She used her gloved hand to squeeze the cheeks of the tallest woman, moulding her mouth into a puckered O. On a rather plump woman, in a black suspender belt and stockings but otherwise naked, she used the tip of the stick to lift each breast in turn. Then she ran her gloved hand down into the woman's thick mousy pubic hair, examining her labia and making the woman flinch.

'Very sensitive, Fraulein,' she said, moving her leather-covered finger deeper between the woman's legs.

'Yes, Warden.'

'You're on report.'

'No, Warden.' The woman looked genuinely shocked.

'Don't contradict me.'

'I haven't done anything, Warden.'

'You are being insolent.'

'No, Warden . . .'

'How dare you argue with me! Be quiet.'

The woman was about to argue further but decided against it.

The Warden moved on to the second rank. Again her swagger stick and gloved hands made free with the prisoner's semi-naked bodies. A distinctive and quite tall redhead, her long legs encased in black opaque stockings, her sex barely covered by a tiny black lace G-string, was given the same treatment as the plump woman, but did not react in any way. This seemed to displease the Warden too.

'Get on your knees,' she ordered.

Without a word the redhead sunk to her knees.

'You know what is required.'

Again without demur, the redhead began to lick the shiny black leather on the Warden's boots, from the toe to the top of the calf. She started on one boot then moved to the other, pressing her head between the Warden's legs to get at the back of each boot.

'Such a good Fraulein,' the Warden said, watching the girl work, and using the lashes on the swagger stick to caress her naked, curved back. 'I choose you.'

'Thank you, mistress,' the redhead said, pausing halfway up the second boot. Apparently, she knew full well what this meant.

As soon as she had finished the redhead stopped, her head still bowed, waiting for instructions.

'Up,' came the order and the redhead scrambled to her feet and stood back in line.

Satisfied that all was in order, the Warden went over to the door of the recreation room. She found the appropriate key on the bunch at her belt, unlocked the big mortice lock again and strode out of the room, leaving the door open. But almost as soon as she had disappeared she reappeared, this time leading a naked man by a chain around his waist. She shepherded him in and relocked the door. Coming from behind him she shoved him in the back so hard and unexpectedly that he went sprawling on the floor.

'Well, ladies, I present to you the entertainment for tonight. Shall we make him comfortable?'

The women broke ranks at once and crowded round the naked man, pulling him up to his feet, putting hands all over his body. The hands nipped and pinched at him, feeling his muscles, his buttocks, his nipples, his cock and balls: hard, spiteful fingers with long nails raking over his flesh. His cock, flaccid when he had been led in, stiffened rapidly and hands wrapped around it, squeezed it – not at all gently – while others cupped his balls.

The man was comparatively young but he was not very healthy-looking or athletic. His body was soft and sallow and though he was not fat he was beginning to develop a paunch. He had brown curly hair and a jowly round face.

The women, knowing the procedure, dragged him over to the wooden trestle.

'Over,' the Warden ordered – unnecessarily, as several hands were already forcing the man's head down and pulling his arms out in front of him. Nimble fingers made short work of folding the leather straps at the base of the legs around his wrists and ankles. Once they were buckled, he was pinioned to the frame.

'Back,' the Warden commanded and the women, with obvious reluctance, retreated to form a circle around the bound victim. 'This thing,' the Warden continued, 'this animal, this abomination, was caught this evening trying to break into this prison. To break in here. Can you imagine anything so foolish, *Liebchen*? What was he trying to do, rescue an inmate, or just get in among you with his *Pimmel*?' To emphasise this point, the swagger stick nudged against the man's cock. 'So, we have to teach him a lesson, no?'

'Yes!' the women roared together.

The Warden caressed the man's backside almost lovingly. In this position it was spread open, the puckered mouth of his anus clearly visible, his heavy balls hanging down between his thighs. Her hand slipped down between his legs, caressing his thighs, then cupping his balls in her gloved palm.

'A stocking, if you please,' she said.

The redhead who had licked her boots rolled down one of her very black hold-ups and handed it to the Warden, who, in turn, handed the redhead the swagger stick to hold. She flexed the stocking in both hands, stretched it out tight until it was no more than a thin ribbon, and felt under the man's thighs. There, the Warden threaded the nylon under the shaft of his penis and around his balls before tying it tight.

From one of the pockets in her uniform jacket the Warden extracted a single rubber glove. She removed the black leather from her right hand and fitted the thin surgical rubber in its place. Casually she penetrated the man's anus right up to the knuckle of her forefinger. He moaned.

'Begin,' the Warden said.

The redhead raised the swagger stick and stroked its lashes down on to the man's thighs. The man jerked against his bonds but did not cry out. The redhead passed the whip to the next woman in the circle who used it on the man's back, before immediately passing it to the next woman, who beat his other thigh . . . and so on right the way round the circle until the last blow fell on his thigh again, all with the Warden's finger firmly planted inside the man's rear.

The man had began to moan, then gasp and even scream at the harder strokes, and she felt his body contracting around her finger. It excited her, made her pulse race. She withdrew her finger, stripped off the glove, pulled on the leather one and took back the swagger stick. The man's body was reddened all over, except his buttocks which had not been touched for fear of accidentally hitting the Warden's arm. That was not to last long. Moving to one side the Warden raised the whip, then slashed it down on the virgin territory.

'No!' the man screamed.

Five strokes followed, hard, well-aimed blows delivered with the Warden's considerable power. Each fell on a new area of flesh, creating an instant network of fine red welts. Each burnt a shock of pain into the man's body that served only to fuel his excitement, and his cock swelled, hardening against the confinement of the nylon tied so unyieldingly around it.

The Warden's gloved hand, cool to the touch, smoothed over the rump it had tortured, making him squirm with a combination of pain and pleasure. Then her own desires, the heavy, relentless throb she had aroused in herself, began to demand her attention.

She turned to the redhead. 'Come on. It is time.' She unlocked the recreation room door, ushered the redhead through and closed it behind them with a resounding clang. The mechanism of the lock clicked loudly as the key was turned on the other side.

For a long moment none of the women moved, waiting to see if the Warden was going to return. She didn't.

Then, as if by some secret signal, pandemonium broke out. The women were literally falling over themselves to get at the hapless man. The tall, long-haired brunette got down on the floor under the trestle and managed to get his cock in her mouth. The plump woman slapped his buttocks with the palm of her hand. Another big-breasted woman rubbed her tits all over his whip-reddened back; still another, also on her knees, forced his head up by holding his hair and kissed him full on the mouth.

The rest of the company began unbuckling his limbs. Soon, though he was pulled this way and that like a rope in a tug of war, he was pressed down on to the hard stone floor.

Immediately the plump woman crouched over his face, forcing her nether mouth on to his lips.

'Make it good,' she cried, and wriggled her hips until she felt his tongue delving between her labia.

'Make it good,' another woman echoed, having won the battle to see who would mount his hips and use his rampant cock. She lowered herself on to his bone-hard shaft and almost orgasmed instantly. Groping hands covered her body, rubbing and pinching her thighs and buttocks and breasts, exploring her clitoris, picking her up off his shaft and slamming her down again, wanting to make her come quickly so they could have their turn. Hands encompassed the plump woman too for the same reason, pinching her nipples and stroking her breasts. They soon got their reward. Both women raced to orgasm, unable to contain their excitement.

Woman after woman replaced them, squatting over his face or astride his hips. His cock was soon sore, his tongue aching, but any flagging was punished by a rain of slaps. He knew coming would be no escape either. They would suck him back to erection and use him again. That was what he was here for. To be used.

His first orgasm came just as the long-haired blonde was climbing on to his cock. Unable to control himself long enough to allow penetration, his rod jerked and shot spunk over the thick thatch of her pubic hair.

'Seen enough?' the Baron asked.

Stephanie looked around to see Devlin still staring at the spectacle. The blonde was licking the man's spunk from his cock. When she had finished she slipped the shrinking member into her mouth, just as another woman shuddered to a climax on the man's face. A massive erection tented Devlin's trousers.

'Devlin finds this much more interesting, I see,' Stephanie said.

'Yes, yes.' Devlin tore his eyes away.

Stephanie knew what he was thinking, of course. He was imagining himself as that man, surrounded by eager, hungry women, overpowered and helpless, his body beaten and singing with delicious pain; his cock bound and sore, his mouth tasting their juices. This was definitely more to Devlin's liking.

'Do you want to stay?' the Baron asked.

'No, no, let's move on,' Devlin said, rearranging his erection by putting his hands in his pockets.

'I think you'll find the last pavilion just as interesting as a matter of fact.'

The Baron led the way to the next door, punched in the computer code and watched as the door opened automatically. On the other side the Perspex tubing extended no more than a few feet to the next building, still at ground level. The entrance door was already ajar.

'How is the man selected?' Devlin asked, his mind still obviously on the previous spectacle.

'With difficulty,' the Baron replied. 'Obviously there can only be one man at a time, and many of the male guests want to participate. We put them on a waiting list then draw a name at random. No one is allowed a second visit. At least, not so far . . .'

'And Brunehilda? You said she is not a guest?'

'No. I felt it needed someone with particular qualities and expertise. All the other woman are guests though. It is very popular among the women.'

'Yes, I imagine it is,' Devlin said quietly.

Chapter Seven

The Baron ushered them through the last door. Again, rather than offer a view from overhead, the room allowed them to watch through a false wall on the side, for very much the same reason as in the prison. Here, too, the pavilion was divided into individual rooms in this case, four of them – rather than being one large space.

They were now looking into a perfect reproduction of a *fin-de-siècle* Parisian brothel. The first room was a reception area, where clients chose their partners from among the women lounging on a circular love-seat or red *chaises longues*. From there, the women would be taken to one of three bedrooms, each differently equipped, but all dominated by a large double bed with an elaborate brass bedstead. Red seemed to be the predominant colour throughout all the rooms: heavy red drapes, walls lined in red silk, a deep rich red carpet. The period detail was so complete that the rooms were even lit with hissing gas lamps in brass and translucent white glass.

In the first room there were eight girls and six men. Clients of the brothel were of both sexes and would choose who they wished to be entertained by. The men were stripped to the waist and wore identical black velvet breeches. At the front of these was a flap of material, buttoned on either side of their hips, which could be removed easily in order that a female client might examine the man more closely before making a choice.

The women were more colourfully dressed. Most wore red or white corsets laced at the back and tightly boned, over which their breasts spilled unadorned. Some wore only the corsets and the 'drawers' of the period, two white lacy legs joined at the waist but with no crotch. Others were dressed in long frilly skirts and petticoats. All without exception wore white silk stockings held by garters just above the knee, and buckled red shoes.

The door of the brothel – an art nouveau creation of stained glass – opened, and a stout, bald man entered.

'Good evening, Monsieur André.'

The woman who spoke was older than the girls and wore a tight-fitting black satin dress under which was obviously an even tighter corset. The corset pushed her big bust into a spectacular cleavage under the V-neck of the dress, pinched her waist into hourglass proportions, and emphasised the flare and curvaceousness of her big hips. She wore little fingerless black lace mittens.

'Good evening, Madam Lilly.'

The man kissed her on both cheeks and immediately began to inspect the girls. His eyes ran critically over each one, Lilly following at his side.

'If I may suggest, Monsieur. A new addition. Claudine.' The Madam crooked her finger at one of the girls.

A slender auburn-haired girl got up from the love-seat and stepped forward. Her red corset was set off by a white skirt supported by rows of frilly petticoats.

'Monsieur,' she said crisply, curtsying.

'Oh, very nice,' he commented.

'Claudine, please,' the Madam said with a trace of annoyance in her voice. It embarrassed her that the girl had to be told what to do.

Claudine spread her legs apart, bent right over and grasped her ankles in her hands. The nearest girl to her stood up and flipped the skirt and petticoats up over her hips so they hung down over her head. Now her buttocks and the deep chasm that ran between them were perfectly exposed.

'Yes, very nice,' the man said, his eyes roving the furry labia being presented to him.

'Mmm . . .' Claudine said, wiggling her bum from side to side.

'She is a virgin?'

'Monsieur André, have I ever let you down? Straight from the Auvergne. A very strict father. She has run away from home.'

Claudine stood up, the skirt falling back over her legs. She stroked the bald man's face and ran her hand down the frilly shirt under his frock coat.

'You would have to be gentle with me, Monsieur. I know nothing of the ways of men.'

'Of course, my child,' he said, letting himself be led away to one of the bedrooms. At that moment, another man entered through the stained-glass door.

'Good evening, Monsieur,' the Madam said politely. 'And what can we do for you?'

The man said nothing. He was dressed in tight-fitting red velvet trousers, a patterned silk waistcoat, a frilled red silk shirt and a black frock coat. He walked up to the love-seat and circled it, looking at each girl in turn.

'These are not to my taste,' he said, having surveyed the girls on the *chaises longues* too.

'What is your taste, Monsieur?'

'Something more . . . esoteric.'

'I see. Then perhaps you'd care to follow me.'

As the Madam led the man through the pavilion, the Baron and his guests followed, unseen. They passed the bedroom where Claudine had undressed Monsieur André and was now letting him take her clothes off, and another where two corseted women were engaged with two fit-looking naked men on the same bed, and finally arrived at the last bedroom. Like the other two this room was decorated with deep red drapes and carpet and had the same gas lights and brass bedstead. Unlike them, however, one whole wall was adorned with sexual implements of every kind. Some hung from brass hooks, other lay on shelves. There were whips, ferules, paddles and tawses. There were dildos and leather harnesses, cuffs, straps, hoods, masks, and a wig block with wigs of hair in three or four colours.

Two women sat on the *chaise longue* beside the bed. Stephanie recognised them immediately: it was Hanna and the redhead who had brought them lunch. Both were still dressed as they had been earlier: Hanna in the tight leather corset and gloves, and the redhead in the long thin straps that ran the length of her body. But now, though their necks were stretched in the high collars, the pieces of their costumes that had held their jaws and mouths had been removed. Like all the other women in this pavilion, both now wore white stockings gartered above the knee and buckled red shoes.

'Hanna and Mischa,' the Madam announced to her client as both women stood up. 'Is this more to your taste?'

'Very much to my taste,' the man responded.

'Good. Then I will leave you to it.'

'I would like you to stay,' the man said.

'No, Monsieur, I'm afraid I have other duties.'

'Another time?'

'If you wish, I could make some arrangement for another time.'

The Madam smiled and closed the bedroom door after her.

'So what is it to be, Monsieur?' Hanna asked, unbuttoning the man's frock coat. 'The Chair, the Prayer Stool or the Spindle?'

'The Spindle,' the man replied at once. He knew precisely what he wanted.

'The Spindle it is,' Mischa said. She was standing in front of the man rolling the gold rings in her nipples between her fingers. Then she pulled the leather straps that were threaded through them outwards, drawing her nipples with them and elongating her big breasts. 'You like this?' she asked.

'Very unusual,' the man said.

'Very sexy,' Mischa added.

The man stood passively while the two girls stripped off his clothes. His body, though not fat, was soft and very pale. His hair was the darkest of blacks and his chest was matted with it, as were his arms and legs. The area around his cock was so thick with black curls it was impossible to see the flesh underneath. His uncircumcised penis hung down flaccid, the tube of his foreskin completely covering his glans despite the two beautiful, lewdly dressed women peeling away his clothes.

As soon as he was naked Hanna went to a long narrow cupboard door set flush with the wall. She opened it and folded the door right back against the wall, then pulled a metal frame down from inside the cupboard where it had been stacked vertically. The frame extended across the deep red carpet. It was like the axle of a coach, a long thick metal pole with both ends attached to the hubs of wheels. But the wheels did not touch the ground. The pole was mounted on two triangular structures near each end which allowed the wheels to turn and the long pole to rotate freely. One end of the pole disappeared back beyond the wheel into the cupboard and through a circular hole in the wall. Welded across the pole were three short metal rods, one near each wheel and one in the middle. Hanging down from these crosspieces were leather straps, smaller ones on the outermost crosspieces and a single wide strap from the one in the middle.

Almost as soon as the Spindle had appeared the hairy man had got an erection. He had been on it before.

Mischa took him by the hand and led him over to the frame, the leather straps running down her body flexing, pulling on the nipple rings as she moved.

The man knew what to do. He lay down on the thick red carpet, his spine parallel with the long metal pole. Mischa immediately took one hand and Hanna the other, and they pulled his arms up, buckling them by the wrist into the leather straps on the first crosspiece. Satisfied they were secure, the girls pulled him up on to his knees so they could get the thick wide strap from the middle bar around his waist. Tugging it tighter and tighter, they drew him up until his back was hard against the Spindle, and secured him there. Then his ankles were drawn into the remaining straps on the third crosspiece. He was trussed to the metal pole like a chicken on a spit, his cock pointing down almost vertically.

The two girls went over to the shelving where the equipment was stored. Each brought back three wide leather belts. Hanna strapped hers around the Spindle and the man's upper arms, shoulders and lower chest, while Mischa tied her three around his calves, thighs and navel. They buckled them all tight, so tight his flesh bulged on either side of the unyielding leather.

The man's cock was throbbing now. His foreskin only half covered his glans and his hairy balls had risen slightly.

Hanna had taken a gag from a hook on the wall, a big ball of rubber secured by a leather strap. Without ceremony she stuffed it into the man's mouth, making his cheeks bulge, and strapped it around the back of the pole so it held his head firm too.

Above the point at which the Spindle disappeared into the wall, through a metal-lined hole, there was a small wheel, its circumference no greater than that of a cup. Mischa went to the wheel and turned it. There was a hum of an electric motor, and the Spindle began to rotate, turning the man exactly as if he were on the spit of a barbecue. She allowed the device to make two and a half rotations and then stopped it with the man on top, his penis sticking up like the lever on some strange machine.

'Well,' Hanna said, standing by the man's face. 'You're in quite a state, aren't you?'

The man looked up into her eyes. Hanna's hand grabbed his cock and squeezed it hard. She took his foreskin and pulled it back to reveal the pinkness underneath. He moaned. Bending over, she sank her mouth down over it and pushed its length as far down as it would go, until the hard sword of flesh was almost in her throat. She felt it pulse and withdrew immediately.

Mischa turned the wheel again, causing the Spindle to revolve at a very slow pace. She then slid down on to the carpet, positioning her mouth under the man's erection. As soon as the cock reached her she clamped her lips over it, sucked it hard, then clung to it, limpet-like. The movement of the slowly turning Spindle pushed her head down then pulled it up, up until the cock was forced from her mouth as it rotated out to the side and away from her. That was where Hanna began. As soon as the erection was within range she plunged her own mouth over it, licking and sucking it for all she was worth until it was pulled over and away from her by the rotation. Over and away and down to Mischa.

It was a fantastic sensation. Two hungry mouths sucking at his cock, the feeling of helplessness, not being able to prevent himself from falling out of their hot sucking mouths. And then there was the effect of gravity, forcing his body against his bonds, then against the Spindle. His balls, like his body, pulled one way then the other. It was too much. He knew he wasn't far from coming. As he rotated he saw their bodies, their breasts, Mischa's nipple rings, Hanna's tight leather corset. Once again, her mouth closed over his cock, sucked it until it was yanked out with a wet snapping sound. Mischa angled her head up, captured the wayward member, clung to it as it pushed her down then pulled her up, until it was finally dragged away.

He was coming. The mouths were making him come. He had to time his spunking but he didn't think he could. He was out of control. His cock ached, throbbed, pulsed, spunk pumping from his heavy balls. There was an interval of no more than seconds, but which seemed like hours, between contact with one mouth and the other. If he spunked then, if the last touch of the sucking clinging mouth brought him off, he would spend in mid-air, a terrible, painful waste.

Mischa's mouth was the hardest to resist because as he rotated, as she clamped her lips over his cock, her weight pulled on it, making it feel harder, making it throb, and the movement made his balls slap against her face. One more, one more turn and he would surely come.

Hanna's mouth sucked him in deep. He felt his cock torn away, descending. Now, he told himself, he had to come now. He opened his eyes, wanting to see more. He felt his arm brush Hanna's leather glove. He watched as Mischa's body came into view, her nipple rings rubbing against the straps, the crotch-piece of leather held so tightly between her legs. She raised her head to meet him. Now, he screamed at himself, come now! As the wetness of her mouth engulfed him he tried his hardest to spunk. He felt his cock slipping deeper as he rotated downward, right back into her throat, her tongue pressed against his throbbing shaft. But he did not come. Inexorably, his cock began its upward journey. Her mouth clung to it but it slipped away slowly, dragged away until his cock was at her lips and out . . . And at that moment, as his cock plopped free, he came, strings of hot white spunk spraying from his body, before Hanna could close her mouth over his spasming glans.

'So,' the Baron said. 'Now you have seen it all.'

Stephanie looked at Devlin. He was watching intently as Mischa got to her feet. Spunk had lashed down on to her body and she was wiping it away with her finger, then licking the finger clean. They left the

Spindle rotating, the man's cock, deflated, flapping from side to side; they knew his movement would soon produce another erection.

If Devlin had imagined himself as the helpless victim in a prison of sex-starved women, Stephanie knew he empathised even more with the man on the Spindle. She could see his massive erection forming a bulge in the front of his trousers. It was, after all, just the sort of thing he loved.

Very gently Stephanie ran her hand down the front of his trousers, found the tip of his cock, and squeezed it.

He looked at her and smiled mischievously.

'Very imaginative,' she said.

'Very,' he agreed.

'I think we'd better get the design, don't you?'

'Definitely.'

'I'd be delighted,' the Baron said. 'We have one or two other items, too.'

'The Chair, and the . . .' Devlin tried to remember.

'The Prayer Stool. Yes. Equally . . . affecting, I think you'd find. And now, if you'd like to follow me, I suggest we try an excellent Napoleon brandy I've had decanted for the occasion.'

'A brandy would be a great idea,' Stephanie said. She really needed a drink. Devlin had not been the only person affected by the spectacle they had just seen; Stephanie had felt her own body respond too. As had been the case that afternoon, her nipples had puckered the moment she had seen Mischa's pierced flesh. She began to wonder what it would feel like to have cold loops of metal permanently embedded in such tender flesh. At first the idea had shocked her but now, as with so many things in her life, the initial shock had changed into curiosity, and curiosity into the first stirrings of desire.

She shuddered involuntarily. The Baron was watching her. He had watched her closely in all the pavilions, seen her responses, read her body language. He had hardly taken his eyes off her: but then, she was an exceptionally beautiful woman.

The logs crackled and hissed in the grate. Blue and orange and yellow flames leapt from one to the other, consuming the wood and throwing heat out into the room.

'Well. *Prosit*,' the Baron said, raising his glass.

He had handed them crystal brandy balloons into which he had carefully poured a viscous amber liquor. He had swilled the clear, sparkling liquid around in each glass three times, watching as it coated the sloping interior.

Stephanie took a large swig and felt the brandy warm her body. It slipped down her throat without the slightest hint of fieriness.

'Delicious.' Devlin had sipped more judiciously.

'Well, I hope you enjoyed my little pavilions.'

'Beautifully done,' Stephanie said. Though the principle was the same as that of the castle, everything at the Schloss was done on a much bigger scale. The Baron, she thought, must be a very rich man. 'I bet people are queueing up.'

'Yes, I suppose so. Well, now you've seen all four, if you would like to choose one to end your evening . . . I'm sure you both need some relief. Of course, we will be waiving the rules in your case. You may enter as either master or slave.'

Stephanie sat down in one of the wing chairs by the fire. She knew Devlin would expect her to speak first.

'Devlin is my slave,' she said pointedly, looking straight into the Baron's slate-grey eyes.

The Baron looked from her to Devlin, who did not meet his gaze.

'I see,' he said with no emotion.

'Yes.'

'I am not surprised. You are beautiful enough to enslave any man.'

'Thank you. And you should know after all, shouldn't you?'

'Yes, yes indeed.' He appeared lost in thought for a moment. 'So it will be you who does the choosing, naturally.

'Naturally.'

'And?'

Stephanie thought for a moment. Of course she could please herself; but tonight she also wanted to please Devlin. 'I suggest I become the Madam of the brothel, and that Devlin becomes a very submissive client.'

The Baron laughed. 'Oh, I think that would be most appropriate.'

Stephanie stood up and smoothed the tight red sequinned dress down her body. 'And you, Baron?' she asked.

'Me?' He looked startled.

'What are you going to do?' Stephanie had been too engrossed in the various spectacles in the pavilions to pay much attention to the Baron. But that was not to say he didn't fascinate her.

'What will you be watching?'

'You think I would miss the opportunity to watch you? If that is permissible, of course.'

'I think it is a pity.'

'A pity?'

'That watching is all you want to do.'

'Perhaps . . .'

'Perhaps what?'

'We will talk of it again.'

'I would like that.'

'It is a promise. Meantime, you will not object if I watch.'

'I would be offended if you didn't.' Stephanie turned to Devlin. 'Up,' she ordered, in a tone of voice that indicated their most profound relationship had been resumed.

She did something she had wanted to do since she'd first seen Mischa. She pulled her into her arms and kissed her. She kissed her full on the mouth, sucking her tongue between her lips, and felt her breasts: more particularly, the gold nipple rings being crushed against her as they hugged tightly.

Stephanie had been laced into a white satin corset, so tight it restricted her breathing. The corset had no bra and her firm round breasts hung naked above it. She wore no knickers, so, at the bottom of its front, the corset ended just at the point her pubic triangle began. At the back it extended only as far as the base of her spine, exposing her generous apple-shaped rump and the deep cleft between her buttocks, fringed at the bottom with pubic curls.

As she kissed Mischa, she gripped the leather straps that ran down the girl's back and pulled them up, tugging the leather crotchpiece up between her legs, pushing the two dildos it held in deeper, making her moan against Stephanie's mouth. Stephanie was high with excitement, her body already singing, her nerves on edge, tingling and sharp. All day long she had been stoked up by the activities the Baron had shown her, and now her mind was sorting through all the images, flashing them up like snapshots one after the other.

Stephanie broke the kiss and turned back to Devlin. She walked right up to him until the buckled leather shoes were against his feet and the white gartered stockings on her legs were touching his knees. He could breathe the musky aroma that seeped unmasked from her excited sex. Her hand ran along the side of his face up into his thick wiry hair and round to the back. She pulled his face up to look at her.

'So what's it to be, Devlin?'

The Madam had shown her all three devices, explained how they worked and what they could be made to do, while Devlin waited outside.

'What do you want? The Chair, the Praying Stool, or the Spindle?'

Devlin had seen the Spindle, of course, and was tempted. But he hoped that by the end of their stay at the Schloss he would be able to return to this pavilion and try all three.

'The Chair,' he said firmly.

'Very well,' Stephanie said, releasing his hair only to press his face into the white satin of her corset. She wondered whether to make him fuck her first, to take him on the big bed and let Hanna and Mischa watch while he lanced her with that monstrous cock. She could feel it throbbing against her white silk stocking. Opening her legs slightly she trapped it between her calves, then squeezed them together. She heard Mischa giggle at the sight. She felt her body swell – ready, willing, able – but she controlled herself. There would be plenty of time for her pleasure when Devlin was in the Chair.

'Get your head down,' she ordered, walking away. Obediently, like the true slave he was, Devlin obeyed. His forehead touched the carpet, while his backside necessarily protruded into the air.

Stephanie picked up a leather strap from the selection on the wall. It was no more than a long thick strip of leather shaped into a handle at one end.

'Warm him up for me,' Stephanie said to Hanna, handing her the strap. 'Three to start, I think.'

Hanna had been standing waiting for instructions. Her soft pliant body contrasted with the unyielding leather that encased her waist; the corset was laced on so tight, reducing the size of her waist so dramatically, it looked as though she might snap in half. She took the strap from Stephanie, flexed it once in the air and brought it down hard against the palm of her gloved hand. Then she marched over to Devlin and without hesitation lashed the strap down on his exposed rump three times in quick succession.

Devlin moaned at each stroke. His erection was pressed, by his position, into his navel. Three hot fingers were now branded across his buttocks, each separate and distinct. They burnt into him, reaching deep inside him like surgical probes, rousing his sexual psyche, touching his secret depths. It felt as though the fingers of pain were inside his cock, inside his nipples and inside his mind, provoking him, caressing him, making his body seethe.

'Another,' Stephanie ordered.

Thwack. Hanna's aim was perfect, her arm strong. Devlin moaned again as a new welt stung his rump, renewing his agitation.

While Hanna was busy Mischa had pulled the Chair from its cupboard. She dragged it out into the middle of the room.

'Stand,' Stephanie commanded.

Devlin obeyed, resisting the temptation to touch the heat of his arse with his cold hands – much as he would have loved to. He looked at the strange object that stood before him.

The Chair bore no resemblance to any chair he had ever seen. In fact it looked a bit like a spider, except that its eight identically curved limbs were divided top and bottom: four running up to the 'body' from the floor, and four sticking grotesquely in the air. The limbs were shaped like guttering, made from stainless steel tubing, while the 'body' was no more than two small concave metal dishes, bolted to a solid square frame from which the eight limbs protruded. The limbs could obviously be adjusted to point at several angles. The upper limbs and the frame were festooned with leather straps and buckles.

As Devlin's imagination worked overtime trying to imagine how the Chair operated, Mischa was busy clamping more pieces to the basic structure. Two curved steel plates fitted on the inside of two of the protruding limbs, and what looked like a surgical instrument screwed into the base of the frame just under the dishlike seat.

'Well, Devlin, this is your choice.' Stephanie could see the fear in his eyes as well as the excitement. 'Let's get you comfortable.' She patted the two concave dishes to indicate where he should sit.

Awkwardly Devlin shuffled between the stainless steel limbs and sat on the seat. Cold metal greeted his buttocks, sending a shiver through his body as it soothed the heat in the red welts left by the strap. The pleasure soon died. The seat was uncomfortable, the two dishes pulling his buttocks apart.

'Hanna,' Stephanie said. Hanna was ready. She came up behind Devlin and slipped the padded leather blindfold over his eyes, plunging him into total darkness. From now on he would only be able to feel; he would not be able to anticipate what they were going to do to him, nor where the next assault on his naked body would come from.

Immediately Hanna and Mischa took his arms, pulling him back. He thought he was going to fall until he felt his arms being pressed back into the curve of the top two limbs. These veered away from his shoulders at a peculiar and painful angle. He felt leather straps securing his arms into the tubing, at his wrist, above and below his elbow, and right at the top of his arm. There was no support for his head or back until Hanna pulled an extension from under the frame, a curved neck-rest. She adjusted it until it fitted exactly under Devlin's neck, thereby supporting his head. It only made the Chair marginally more comfortable.

In the darkness Devlin felt his legs being lifted up into the tubing at the opposite end of the frame. Again straps bound them in place inside the curving cavity. The steel plates he had seen Mischa fit to this part of the structure he could now feel, cold and hard against his inner thighs.

Stephanie completed his bondage. She stepped between his open legs and pulled a strap attached under one buttock up around the top of his pubic bone and across his pelvis. There, it buckled into a strap from the main frame just under his other hip, pressing his body down into the metal seat. She repeated the process on the other side, so that his navel was crossed with leather straps and his buttocks could not move an inch in any direction.

He flinched as her hand brushed his massive cock. She stroked it almost tenderly, rubbing the little tear of fluid that had developed at its tip into the pink flesh of his glans.

She stood back and let the two girls make the final adjustments. Under the seat, the two hinges that allowed the tubular limbs to be spread further apart were geared to the two dishes containing Devlin's buttocks. Each girl took an ankle, and they pulled his legs apart, stretching them out, and, by means of the gearing, stretching his buttocks apart too.

They had done this before. They knew what it felt like. They liked to do it slowly, teasingly. They made only the slightest movement at first, then let the realisation of what was happening, how one movement was effecting another, sink in. This way, the victims imagined the contraption was designed to split them apart.

'No,' Devlin screamed as he felt his body being spread, his legs opening, his buttocks separating. Slowly, relentlessly they pulled. 'Oh God, no . . .'

'That's enough,' Stephanie said. At once Hanna knelt and locked the legs in position. 'Well, Devlin.' She stepped between his legs and took his cock in both hands. 'Quite an experience, isn't it?'

Now that the movement had stopped, Devlin felt the most incredible rush of pleasure mixed with relief. He had never, in all the countless trials Stephanie had put him through, felt so helpless, so completely bound, so vulnerable and exposed. His cock was so hard it felt like steel. His anus, with his buttocks forced apart, was actually open, wide open. It felt like it was alive, a mouth groping in the darkness. The thought occurred to him, as no doubt it was meant to, that it was sensitised enough to feel like the sex of a woman. He wanted it played with and penetrated.

Stephanie kneaded the flesh of his cock. Even with two hands making fists around it, one on top of the other, his glans still poked out from the top of her fingers. She bent over and licked the trail of fluid that had escaped his urethra. His cock pulsed in her hands.

The Chair was a wonderful device, she decided. She was definitely going to get one for the castle. She might even have herself tied into it when she was in the right mood. The thought made her shiver.

She released his cock and stepped back. For maximum effect, the Madam had told her, the victim must be left awhile, so that the helplessness, the vulnerability, could work its way into him. With the ability to move and the ability to see taken away, all the feelings and senses were narrowed down, concentrated on the way the body had been tied and spread. The cock and the anus, in the blackness, became the centre of his world, the only thing that mattered. It was impossible to think about anything but how he was going to be used and abused.

Stephanie walked over to the bed. 'Come over here, both of you,' she said, wanting Devlin to hear. 'Bring a dildo.'

Hanna, nearest to the shelving, selected a large black dildo with a flared base, as Stephanie lay on the bed. The sight of Devlin bound and spread so tautly had affected her profoundly, and her body was now coursing with excitement. But she knew that the root cause of her stimulation was not the odd contraption in the middle of the room; it was her power. She had chosen this scenario. She knew it was what Devlin wanted, but it was also what she wanted. She could have gone to any of the other pavilions. She could have countless slaves obeying her commands, doing whatever she desired them to do. That was what turned her on, that was what she'd discovered about herself and what she loved.

'Lick my nipples,' she commanded Mischa. She could have asked her to do anything and she would have done it without question.

Mischa knelt on the bed to obey, the leather straps on her body pulling at the nipple rings. She sucked one of Stephanie's nipples hard, then licked it while her hand fingered the other.

'Use the dildo, stick it up my cunt.' Stephanie was deliberately crude for Devlin's benefit; she wanted him to know exactly what was happening to her.

Hanna knelt on the other side of her body. She placed the head of the dildo at the mouth of Stephanie's sex as Stephanie parted her legs, and pressed. There was no resistance; the dildo slid home on a flood of her juices.

'Turn it on,' Stephanie ordered, thrilling to the feel of the big phallus inside her. She wasn't in the mood for subtlety.

Hanna obeyed and a muted humming filled the room. Stephanie squirmed, feeling the head of the dildo deep inside. The vibrations were deep and powerful, affecting her whole sex.

'Harder,' she demanded.

Hanna pushed the dildo up further, until the flared base was right up against the labia and would go no further.

'Frig my clit.' Stephanie's voice was husky with passion.

Hanna's gloved fingers responded immediately, like a machine, an automaton programmed to obey. Stephanie gasped as she felt leather pushing the lozenge of her clit from side to side.

'Oh yes,' she moaned. 'Yes, yes, faster . . .'

Mischa's mouth transferred from one nipple to the other. She took it in her teeth and bit into the corrugated flesh.

'Yes . . .' Stephanie felt her excitement building. There were so many sensations, so many images in her mind. The power she had, the absolute power; the helpless Devlin; the girls working on her body, and the knowledge of what they would do with the Chair: it all made her blood race. She looked down at Mischa's pierced nipples, and the strange feeling that sight gave her added itself to the cocktail of excitements.

'I want to suck your nipples. Feed them to me,' she ordered, making sure Devlin could hear.

Mischa moved up the bed, knelt over her face and used her hand to guide her pierced nipple into Stephanie's mouth, complete with nipple ring and leather strap. Stephanie used her teeth, catching the strap between them, then pulling it back. She drew the nipple ring gently out, stretching the big breast, watching the way the metal distended the tender flesh. She thought she knew how it felt, tangling the sexual nerves. She saw Mischa shudder.

'The other one.' She was so close to orgasm – the vibrator unrelenting in her sex, Hanna's finger equally remorseless – that she wasn't sure if the words made sense, but Mischa moved her body until her other breast was over Stephanie's mouth. Stephanie bit into the leather again and felt Mischa's body contract as the nipple ring stretched her flesh. Suddenly she felt herself melting, her body slackening around the dildo; her eyes rolled back and an infinity of feeling exploded inside her, making her scream out and arch her buttocks off the bed. Endless seconds passed; she was suspended in ecstasy.

How long it was before she collapsed back on to the bed she did not know. She felt the dildo being expelled from her body as though in slow motion, its final exit making her shudder again. She looked at the two bizarrely dressed girls who knelt beside her, awaiting instructions. She looked over at Devlin strapped into the Chair. Now it was his turn.

'Did you enjoy that, Devlin, hearing your mistress come?'

'Yes, mistress,' he said.

Stephanie got up and walked over to his bound body. She ran her fingers along his lips then forced them into his mouth.

'So now we begin.' She saw his cock twitch as she said the words. She nodded to Hanna who had taken up position between his legs.

Hanna dropped to her knees. In front of her was the instrument Mischa had fitted into the base of the frame. The device was scissor-shaped: the handles were like those of normal scissors, but the blades in the closed position resembled a hollow tube. Quickly Hanna coated the tube with a colourless oily cream, then pushed the instrument forward on its pivot.

Devlin started in the darkness behind the blindfold as he felt the cold steel nose against his anus.

'Do it,' Stephanie ordered as Hanna looked up to receive the final command.

'God.' Devlin's voice was thin and reedy as the metal slid into him. He shook with pleasure. His anus felt so sensitive he thought he was going to come. It was like being a woman; he couldn't get that thought out of his mind. The Chair had opened him, exposed him, sensitised him. As he'd listened to Stephanie's pleasure, his anus had throbbed. Now it was being fucked.

The cannula slid deep into his body, the lubricating cream making the journey effortless. Hanna, satisfied it was all the way home, locked it in place by tightening a bolt on the pivot.

Mischa, meanwhile, was fitting two wide, padded, U-shaped sections into brackets that protruded either side of the central frame. They looked like armrests, but were much wider. As soon as they were securely in place Hanna fetched a little red velvet stool to enable Stephanie to get up on to the rests. She climbed on and swung one thigh over Devlin's prostrate body so she was kneeling precisely over his cock.

Devlin heard the movement and suddenly felt the familiar heat of his mistress's sex only a fraction of an inch away. If he could have pushed his hips up he would have touched her labia, but the straps over his navel prevented even this degree of movement. It did not stop him trying.

Hanna resumed her position kneeling between Devlin's legs. Mischa was at her side with a long thin probe, a plastic shaft tipped with a ball of cotton wool, in her hand. As Hanna reached forward and gripped the handles of the instrument inserted in Devlin's body, Stephanie eased herself down so that the tip of his cock nestled in her soaking wet sex.

'Ah . . .' Devlin moaned. Any contact with his cock, however light, was incredibly welcome after so long without it.

Hanna began to open the handles of the instrument, pushing the hollow blades apart at the same time.

'No!' Devlin screamed immediately.

She opened them wider, feeling the resistance of his body.

'No, no, please . . .' He was being eased open, this time from inside.

Stephanie pressed herself down on to his cock a little more until she could feel it at the mouth of her sex.

'No, no, no,' Devlin was shouting as Hanna opened the handles wider. 'I can't take it.'

But he could. The fear, the pain were translated instantly into such hot burning sensual pleasure that he felt spunk pumping into his cock. They were prising him apart. He strained against every strap, pulled and twisted and writhed, and did not manage to move one inch. He pressed his thighs together, trying to close himself, but the steel they had fitted to the inside of the metal limbs did not yield at all.

Wider and wider the two blades spread. In fact the movement was minuscule but the feeling was enormous.

'I beg you.'

Hanna stopped. Devlin breathed again. Mischa handed Hanna the probe and they waited for Stephanie to give the order.

Stephanie pushed herself down on the throbbing cock. She had never felt it so hot. It was as though it were on fire. Her clitoris was throbbing too. This was so exciting she was coming again.

'Do it,' she managed to gasp.

Hanna inserted the probe into the channel in the instrument designed for this purpose. Devlin was so open he felt nothing until the cotton tip reached the very top of the cavern opened by the cannula. As the tip nudged forward it felt as though it were touching the absolute centre of his sexual being, as though every layer of protection, every shield had been peeled back to expose the throbbing, defenceless central core. It felt as though he had been laid up and dissected so that the most sensitive part of his anatomy could be reached, and now he was being licked by a tongue of fire. Time ceased to exist. Everything ceased to exist except the tongue inside his body and his cock, spurting his spunk up towards Stephanie's labia, towards the mouth of her sex which was pursed as though ready to kiss it. His cock jerked so violently it escaped the kiss and instead sprayed spunk upward, on to her clitoris, over her black pubic hair and down over her thighs.

His orgasm went on and on and on. He pressed himself down on the probe and felt his body leap again as though charged with a jolt of electricity.

Stephanie grabbed his cock and guided it to the mouth of her sex, this time pushing down on it until it was inside her. That was all she needed. She had felt everything Devlin had felt, the empathy between them so total. She knew how he had been touched, excited, spread open. Knew her orgasm was going to be almost as powerful as his.

Just before she lost control, before her eyes rolled back and her body convulsed around Devlin's massive pulsing cock, she looked at the blank wall in front of her. She knew the Baron was there, watching her: her body, her breasts, her sex. She could see his expression, his hunger. That was the final thrill.

Chapter Eight

It was the sun streaming through the gaps in the heavy curtains that woke Stephanie. She slipped out of bed quietly so as not to disturb Devlin and drew back the curtains a little to enable her to look out. If she had ever seen a more beautiful view in her life, she couldn't remember it. The lake stretched out into the distance, surrounded by a dark green forest of conifers sprinkled with snow which gave on to the steep craggy mountains on the horizon. A flock of ducks near the bridge leading to the Schloss decided as one that they wanted to take to the air; they kicked and skimmed the water until their big wings developed the lift to hoist them into flight.

Though the sun was still low in the sky its heat was thawing the snow on the tops of some of the trees. Now and then there were sudden flurries as the melted snow crashed to the ground bringing most of the rest of the snow with it.

Stephanie felt pangs of hunger. After showering quickly and brushing out her long hair she slipped into a lacy, white silk teddy and matching negligee. When she had tucked her feet into white high-heeled satin slippers, she went in search of food.

Downstairs she found the Baron sitting in a small breakfast room with panoramic views over the lake. It opened on to a terrace where in summer, no doubt, meals were served.

'Good morning,' he said, jumping to his feet. 'You look enchanting, if I may say so.'

'Thank you.'

'Did you sleep well?'

'Very well. And it's such a beautiful morning.'

'I thought a boat trip on the lake. The sun is so warming at this time of the year . . .'

'How lovely.'

He pulled back a chair at the table and Stephanie sat down. A waiter appeared with a silver coffee pot and poured steaming black liquid into the white porcelain cup already set on the table.

'What would you like for breakfast? We Germans eat meat and cheese as well as sweetbreads. But you may prefer something more English or French?'

'Yes, croissants please.'

The waiter left at once. The Baron's plate was laid with two slices of salami and an odd rubbery looking cheese speckled with little seeds.

'Devlin is still asleep?' he asked.

'Yes. He was quite exhausted by your . . . ingenuity. I hope you will give me the designs for those devices.'

'Certainly. I'll have them shipped out to you. I thought you'd find them interesting. And what of the other pavilions?'

'All very imaginative.'

'But not exciting?'

'Oh yes, yes . . .' Stephanie was trying to think of how to describe her feelings.

'Go on.'

'Actually, to tell you the truth I'm not sure how I feel. I think it was all too much to assimilate in one go. My mind's still working on it. I need time. Ask me later. My subconscious will have sorted it out by then.' That was exactly how she felt. Last night, in the *fin-de-siècle* bordello, she had certainly orgasmed explosively; but the other pavilions had their attractions too, and she wasn't at all sure which affected her most. She knew her mind would sort through the options in its own time.

The waiter returned with a basket of croissants, brioches and rolls wrapped in a white linen serviette. He set them on the table with a selection of jams in circular white pots and a silver butter dish.

Stephanie ate hungrily, consuming a croissant and a brioche. Not once did she take her eyes off the Baron, who sat coolly sipping his coffee.

'And you?' she asked eventually.

'Me?'

'Did you enjoy last night's festivities?'

'Very much.'

'You watched?'

'Oh yes. My dear, you are an exceptionally beautiful creature. I wouldn't let the opportunity of watching you take your pleasure so wholeheartedly go to waste.'

'And what about your pleasure?'

'My pleasure?'

'Is that all you do, Baron? Watch?'

The Baron turned to look her squarely in the eyes. 'You asked me that before.'

'Yes. I said it was a pity. And it is. You are a very attractive man. I thought that when you came to the castle. I still think it. You promised me last night we'd talk about it again.'

'Yes I did.'

'It's not just idle curiosity, you see.'

'What is it then?'

'I told you, I find you very attractive. In my life

recently I've tended to get what I want. I would like to think I could have you.'

The Baron smiled indulgently and touched Stephanie's hand as it rested on the table.

'I find that very flattering.'

'But?'

'There are no buts.'

'But you only want to watch?'

'Yes. No . . .' The Baron hesitated. Stephanie could see him deciding what he was going to say next. 'I am a businessman, my dear. I will make a deal with you. Tonight, if you will let me watch you in one of the other pavilions – whichever you care to choose – I will tell you what you want to know. I will tell you what would give me the ultimate in sexual pleasure. Is that a deal?'

'Certainly.'

'Good.' The Baron got to his feet. 'Meantime, I have another surprise for you.' He looked at his watch. 'Can you be ready by twelve?'

'For our boat trip?'

'Exactly. I think you'll find it interesting.'

'I find *you* interesting.'

'If you'll excuse me.'

Stephanie took in the Baron's stiff upright stance as he walked across the room. The exchange had left her body tingling and she found herself hoping that the deal they had made would satisfy more than his voyeurism.

Though in the sun it was warm, any area of shadow would be cold so Stephanie wore a thick pair of tights, leather trousers and a cashmere sweater under her fur coat. Devlin, who had had his breakfast sent up to their room, had to deal with some urgent business that had come up when he'd called his London office, and so decided to beg off the trip. Now he sat by the window as a servant arranged a desk for him and brought over the fax machine from the panelled recess.

'I'll watch your progress,' he said, indicating the lake outside, as she kissed his cheek and set off downstairs.

The Baron was waiting for her in the lobby. He wore a long sheepskin coat and fur-lined boots.

'Charming,' he said. 'You look charming.'

Taking her arm he led her through a labyrinth of corridors, all beautifully decorated in coordinated shades of pastel peach with individually lit paintings on every wall. Some Stephanie recognised as being the work of Beckmann, Ernst and Marc; the others were equally modern and all by German artists.

They eventually arrived at a solid oak door.

'Here we are. Are you ready for your surprise?'

'Definitely.'

The Baron pushed the door open and stood aside for Stephanie to enter. She found herself in an enormous boathouse with a U-shaped concrete jetty which projected into the lake. At the far end two doors had been opened and Stephanie could see the vast expanse of the lake beyond.

Sitting in the water was not, as she'd expected, a fast sleek powerboat, but a perfect reproduction of a Roman slave galley. There was a square forecastle at the prow and an open pit divided by a gangway down the rest of its length. Sitting in the pit on each side of the gangway were six male slaves, their oars held vertically aloft. At the moment the slaves were shrouded with red blankets against the chill of the boathouse caused by the water.

The Baron ushered Stephanie up a small gangplank which led inside the forecastle. Here the period detail gave way to modern convenience. A large window allowed them to see down the length of the boat, and another overlooking the bow gave a view in the other direction. The interior was warm and comfortable; a Roman-style couch covered with silk cushions and an occasional table made up the only furniture.

As soon as they were seated Stephanie saw a modern powerboat nose into the boathouse. The driver took a line from the bow of the galley and began towing them out into the lake. He then cast the line off and the powerboat sped away; the forward momentum carried the galley further out into open water. An enormous black man wearing a leopard's skin across his incredibly muscular body then appeared, and walked down the central gangway, plucking the blankets off the slaves. They in turn pushed their oars through the large circular rowlocks in the side of the wooden hull. Apart from a leather harness, which was no more than two thick shoulder straps joined to straps across the chest and navel, the slaves were naked. Their wrists were chained to the oars, their ankles to the deck.

'Row,' the black man roared, his voice ringing out across the silence of the lake.

The twelve oars dipped into the water in unison and were pulled back hard. The galley picked up speed.

'In . . .' the slave-driver urged, '. . . out.'

It was obvious that the slaves were practised rowers. Their movements were precise and the boat moved quickly. Soon Stephanie could look back and see the whole of the fairy-tale castle, its towers rising against the background of the mountain beyond.

'Come out and have a closer look,' the Baron suggested.

He led the way through a small door out on to the gangway. The sun, now much higher in the sky, shone down fiercely, and some of the slaves were sweating from the considerable effort of pulling the large oars.

The slave-driver carried a long whip in his hand, its lash thinning at the tip. Stephanie saw its imprint on several of the slaves' backs and shoulders.

The fresh air against her face was exhilarating, and the warmth of the sun increased her sense of well-being. She stood at the aft of the boat, and watched the slaves toiling on the oars. The Baron certainly had a vivid imagination. But there was more to it than that, she thought. He had seen her penchant for authority and this was its ultimate expression: standing here on a boat driven on by sweating, naked men. They were all hers, all under her control, all doing this for her. It was as if the Baron had organised a graphic demonstration of exactly what it meant to be in her position, to be mistress of all she surveyed. She felt her body respond. It was thrilling.

They appeared to be heading for a small chalet on the far side of the lake. Back inside the cabin of the forecastle Stephanie sipped brandy from the Baron's silver flask and tried to make out the details of the building they were approaching. A plume of smoke rose from its chimney.

'Does this amuse you?' the Baron asked.

'It excites me. You knew it would, didn't you?'

'I thought it might, from what I saw of you at your castle, and last night. You are happiest, I think, when you are dominant.'

'So it appears.'

'Appears?'

'It wasn't always like that. I hadn't really found out about myself – sexually, that is. Then I met a man who, shall we say, took me on a journey through my own feelings.'

'Devlin?'

'No. Not Devlin. Devlin was later. If I'd met Devlin first I'd have been too frightened. But by the time I came to the castle with him I was ready. The first man created the raw material; Devlin refined it. Then I took control.'

'And kept it.'

'Yes. Though I hope I am still open to new experiences.'

'I hope so too,' the Baron said cryptically.

After a few more minutes' hard rowing the galley was steered up to a wooden jetty. The path from the jetty ran up to a chalet build in the traditional way with whole tree trunks. It looked as if it had been designed by the brothers Grimm, as did the castle, now far away on the other side of the water.

'Are you hungry?' the Baron asked as the gangplank from the forecastle was laid out. 'Lunch has been arranged.'

'Not yet,' Stephanie said, resisting his attempt to lead her ashore.

'There's a lovely ride along the shore from here. The horses and sledge –'

'No,' Stephanie interrupted. She had something else in mind. She brushed passed the Baron and walked down the central gangway looking at each of the sweating slaves in turn. A slave with curly blond hair caught her eye, and a short but muscular man whose brown hair had almost been shaved away.

'These two,' Stephanie said to the black overseer. 'Unchain them.'

The slave-driver looked at the Baron, who had followed Stephanie, to see if he were to obey.

'Do as she says. Bring them inside.'

Stephanie smiled broadly at the Baron. 'You don't mind a change of plans?'

He smiled back. 'Of course not.'

'Your plan worked.'

'What plan?'

'To excite me. And I'm not good at containing my excitement. Not with all these naked men around.'

'My dear, you must do whatever you want to do.'

'Thank you. Let's go inside.'

They walked down the gangplank and up a path to the chalet.

'I can see why Devlin enjoys being your slave,' the Baron said as they walked. 'You are very . . .'

'Demanding?' she suggested.

'Powerful.'

The front room of the chalet was warm and comfortable; a huge log fire blazed in the grate. A large mirror hung on one wall, and a big soft sofa stood in front of the fire, covered in a white fur rug.

The black overseer had shepherded the two slaves in behind them. They stood passively, side by side, stripped of their leather tops.

'I will leave you, my dear,' the Baron said. He turned to the slaves as Stephanie took off her coat and warmed herself by the fire. 'Obey everything without question or you will be put in the pit for a very long time.'

'What's the pit?' Stephanie asked.

'They know.' Smiling slightly he turned and left, taking the overseer with him.

Stephanie looked into the mirror. It occurred to her that it might well be two-way, and that the Baron was going to take up position behind it to watch the proceedings. By now, at least, he would know what to expect.

'What's the pit?'

'The worst punishment,' one of the slaves said gloomily.

'Then you'd better do everything I tell you, or I'll come along and watch.'

'Yes, mistress,' they said in unison.

The familiar throb of absolute power was coursing through Stephanie's veins, like a strong electric current. With a finger she indicated a spot in front of her and the two men walked up to it. The man whose hair was close-cropped was nearly a foot shorter than the curly-haired blond, but his body was bigger in every respect, including his still-flaccid cock. Apart from his pubic hair his body was entirely hairless. The blond, on the other hand, was covered with thin blond hair. Both their cocks were circumcised.

Stephanie pulled her sweater over her head and saw their eyes fall on to the black bra she wore. It was three quarter cup and pushed her breasts together, creating a tunnel of cleavage.

'You, what's your name?' she was looking at the blond.

'Alex, mistress.'

'Undo my trousers, Alex. The zip's at the side.'

Alex, his fingers trembling slightly, did as he was told. The trousers slid off her hips and caught up around her knees.

'And your name?' she said to the other one.

'Terry.'

'Both English, too. How convenient. No language problems.'

Stephanie opened her legs and allowed the leather trousers to fall to the floor. She stepped out of them and threw them aside.

The men's eyes roamed her body, the thick black tights shaping her long contoured legs. She reached behind her back and unclipped her bra, letting the shoulder straps slip off her shoulders then leaning forward slightly so her breasts spilled out of the black cups. Her nipples were already erect.

She knew what she wanted, exactly what she wanted. The last two days had been an orgy of complicated, ritualistic sex, full of harnesses and dildos, bondage and restraint. What she wanted now was cock, simple, straightforward cock. Choosing two men was greedy, of course, but she was greedy, and over the last six months her body had become used to getting exactly what it wanted. Looking now at their cocks she saw she had already provoked a stirring.

'I want you to fuck me,' she said simply.

She looked from one to the other, wanting to see whose cock was bigger. Both were circumcised, but neither was fully erect. She reached out and grasped both firmly in her hands; they began to swell.

'Come on, don't you find me attractive?' she chided, pulling both cocks towards her and making the men moan.

She took her hands away. Terry had the biggest cock. It was much wider, though only slightly longer.

Stephanie felt her body pulse. She sat on the sofa and pulled the tights off her legs. She should have had the men do it really, but she was in no mood to tease them, to flaunt her body in front of them as she did with her slaves at the castle. Her need, a need that was increasing by the minute, making her pulse race and her breathing shallow, was too great.

She had worn no panties. Lying back on the white fur she opened her legs and bent her knees. She opened her legs wide, feeling the way her labia parted. For a moment she did nothing, just lay there suspended in a cocoon of anticipation. She felt her body churn, ached for the inevitable assault, waited to hear the words that would thrill it inexorably, the words of command she would utter.

She turned her face to the side, looked at the two men and then beyond them, into the roaring fire. The flames all seemed to be licking out in phallic shapes. Just the thought of the power she possessed made her quiver, like a plane on a runway, its engines whining but held back by its brakes.

She let the brakes out. 'Alex, come here,' she commanded.

He walked over to the sofa, his cock bobbing in front of him.

'Fuck me,' she said, the words making her nerves knot as she knew they would.

Alex could hardly believe what he was hearing. He'd imagined this was all a tease, a torment devised by the Baron. It wasn't possible he was actually going to be allowed to have this woman. His cock jerked at the thought.

'I gave you an order,' Stephanie snarled, not brooking any delay. Her body arched up towards him.

Full of trepidation, expecting her to change her mind at any minute, Alex knelt between her legs, looking down at her magnificent tanned body. He lingered over her labia fringed by thick black hair and the open mouth of her sex, glistening with her juices.

'Yes . . .' he whispered to himself, not caring any more what the game was, knowing it was too late now; now he would make it whatever happened. He threw himself down on to her, his rock hard cock shooting up between her legs and instantly finding the way into the tunnel of her sex.

Stephanie gasped. His cock was hot and ardent. She knew he would not be able to hold out for long but, for once, she didn't want that. He was pounding into her like a man possessed, ramming his cock right up into her, his balls banging against her anus, his pubic bone grinding against her clitoris. She could feel her juices coating his shaft, feel them flowing out of her body.

She looked across to the fire. Terry stood watching, his stout body tense, his cock still erect.

'Here,' she ordered.

He obeyed slowly, as though in a trance. She watched his cock and balls jiggle up and down as his thighs moved. As soon as he was in range she reached out her hand and took hold of his cock, as if it were a handle with which she could support herself. He had big hairy balls, in contrast to the odd hairlessness of the rest of his body.

Having a cock in her hand and in her sex made her body tense; it was readying itself for what was to come. An automatic reflex told her Alex was passing the point of no return. She squeezed the cock in her hand tighter and felt it respond.

Alex was pounding into her so hard she couldn't distinguish the individual strokes. They combined in a blur of motion, which suddenly stopped. He arched his back, raised himself up on his arms, made his body a bow to push his cock as deep as it would go, deep into her wet, clinging tunnel, up until he thought he could feel his cock at her womb. He pictured it in his mind's eye, his throbbing glans being kissed by the flesh deep inside her, then boiled over, his spunk, held back for so long in the pavilions, sputtering out in the place he had found for it.

Stephanie felt it but strangely did not respond in kind. She had got exactly what she wanted, exactly what she'd imagined she wanted, but her mood had changed suddenly and unpredictably. She wanted more. Now it was her turn to be wild.

She pushed Alex off her and rolled on to her knees on the floor where she sucked Terry's cock into her mouth, sucking it so hard it made him wince. She was gobbling it, eating it, wanting to feel it twitch and jerk in her mouth. She had her back to the big mirror and wondered if the Baron was following this. She opened her legs as wide as she could, pushing her buttocks further up in the air, so that he could see her if he was watching. He'd already seen every detail of her sex: last night, and at her castle, he'd seen her sucked and fucked and spunked on.

The tempo of her body changed as her needs began to assert themselves. She had no idea what she wanted but her body seemed to have overcome its strange laxity.

'Fuck me,' she said, crawling up to the sofa. She laid the top half of her body on the white fur, leaving her knees on the floor. The fur tickled her nipples. 'Like this,' she added, wiggling her rump at Terry in case he was in any doubt.

Terry fell to his knees behind her, his hands on his hips. The beautiful curve of her arse nudged his navel as his cock ploughed into the furrow of her labia. Stephanie pushed back on it, opening herself, wanting it inside her. The mouth of her sex was open and gobbled his cock up greedily just as her lips had done earlier.

Immediately she felt him inside her, immediately she felt his hardness against the boiling lake inside her, she felt herself begin to come, as though a switch had been thrown in her body. She had never felt so wet, so hot, so needing.

'Fuck me,' she cried, wanting to feel him stroking into her but she was already accelerating to orgasm. 'Oh, oh . . .'

His cock slammed into her. Its width stretched her labia apart, exposing her clitoris. He sent his hand down between her legs to finger it.

Stephanie looked across at Alex who was watching, playing with his cock; it was already beginning to rise again. Then the rhythms of her body took over and she could do nothing but feel. She closed her eyes and concentrated on the bone of flesh that stabbed effortlessly into her and the finger that played so expertly with her clit. Sensation came in waves. Her mind was full of images: images of last night, of Devlin, of the women's prison. But just as the waves began to join each other, the troughs and crests coming so close together there was only one continuous sensation, her mind lighted on one particular image. It was the black leather torso of the medieval Inquisitor as his hand inserted the wooden shaft into the sealed casket and the victim screamed her confession. That was it, the last spark that made Stephanie explode in flames. Her body convulsed, trembling, out of control, as Terry's cock plunged into the tight channel where only minutes before Alex had already come.

Stephanie did not want it to end. Her body was still high and she didn't want to come down. She knew her body well enough to know it wasn't finished yet.

'Come here,' she ordered, looking at Alex. Terry's cock was still pumping into her.

Alex could see what she wanted. He knelt on the sofa in front of her face. She pulled his hand away from his cock. It was only slightly hardened. Leaning forward she closed her lips over it, all of it, balls and all. Using her tongue on the rim of the glans, she felt it swell dramatically. It tasted of her.

'Mmm . . .' she murmured. She could no longer hold the balls in her mouth and they slipped from her lips one by one. She pulled her mouth back and dipped her head to suck his balls individually as they hung under his now rigid shaft. Alex moaned. She felt his cock throbbing against her face.

She turned her head to Terry. 'Bugger me.'

That was what she wanted now.

Terry did not hesitate. His cock was soaking wet. He moved it higher, found the little bud of her anus and pushed forward, sinking in halfway at least at the first stroke.

'Oh . . .' Stephanie gasped. A wave of pain that was so close to pleasure as to be almost the same thing raked through her nerves, taking her up higher, beginning the next cycle of completion.

She pushed back on him, pushed until he was right inside her filling her. The sensation had forced her eyes closed but she groped forward with her mouth until it found Alex's cock. She sucked it in, wanting to feel two cocks in her body.

Terry was powering to and fro, using her arse just as he had used her sex, pushing higher and deeper. She felt his finger on her clitoris, still pushing it against her pubic bone, moving it from side to side. It was making her gasp, but the sound was muffled by cock.

She wanted to tell Terry what to do but he knew. As she drove Alex's cock into her mouth, deep into her throat, she felt Terry's fingers opening the mouth of her sex, then probing inside: two fingers, then three. Deep, deep inside they pushed, until she felt them up against his own cock, separated only by the thin membranes of her body.

He pushed his fingers until he could feel his cock, stroking its glans, pressing it, as it slid in and out of her anus.

Stephanie was out of control. She was going wild with passion, wild with pleasure, wild with the feeling of being penetrated and used. She was so close to coming it was almost unbearable. In the darkness behind her closed eyelids, she saw the Inquisitor approaching her, his mouth forming the word 'confess' and then, as Terry's cock bucked and spasmed in the tight confines of her rear, as Alex's cock forced its way down her throat, she came. It was longer than before, more intense, her body locking itself around the invaders. She came over Terry's fingers and over his cock, the feelings of his and her orgasm fusing together like bolts of blue lightning.

Just as she regained her ability to feel, as she came down from her high, the cock in her mouth started to jerk. Her mouth had used it as a gag, sucking on it, forming words over it, expelling superheated air from the endless orgasm over it, using it to quell her feelings. But it was not a gag. It was alive and starved of sex. Even though he had only just come, Stephanie's treatment – and the incredible spectacle in front of his eyes – was too much for Alex, and spunk jetted out again into her willing mouth.

Stephanie sucked his cock forcefully, ran her tongue on to the slit of the urethra and felt the force of the spunk that shot out. Without warning her body convulsed again, pushed back on the cock and fingers still hard inside her, and she came again. All at once she tasted spunk and felt it trickling down her throat and her sex and her arse.

'Did you watch?'

They were sitting comfortably in the cabin of the galley, sipping champagne and watching the scenery go by as the boat was manoeuvred along the lake. They had taken the sledge ride then returned to the chalet to lunch on smoked salmon and quails' eggs, and then Stephanie had suggested they take the galley for a little excursion too.

'No,' the Baron replied.

'Oh, why not?' Stephanie felt disappointed.

'I thought you were entitled to a little privacy.'

'I can assure you, Baron, if I wanted privacy I would ask for it.'

'Well, to put it another way, let's say I prefer to reserve my pleasure until the evening.'

'This evening? In the pavilions?'

'Yes.'

'Um . . . I was thinking about that.'

'Really?'

'Yes. While I was engaged with those ardent young men.'

'I hope they were satisfactory.'

'Oh, perfectly.'

'No need to put them in the pit?'

'Well . . .' Stephanie was tempted to discover what the pit was. 'No, I suppose not.'

'And what were you thinking?'

'Oh, about the pavilions? The mind's a funny thing, isn't it? How it works. Consciously, I was most attracted to the bordello.'

'And unconsciously?'

'It appears the Inquisition has been playing on my mind.'

'That would be interesting. A female Inquisitor.'

'Oh, no,' Stephanie corrected quickly. 'I don't want to be an Inquisitor. I want to be his victim.'

The Baron laughed. 'Now that I did not expect.'

'Yes. Very definitely.'

She could see a sparkle of excitement in his eyes as he imagined the scene. 'That is easily arranged.'

'Good. And this time you will watch?'

'My dear, I wouldn't miss this for all the world.'

'Don't forget our deal,' Stephanie reminded him.

'I haven't.'

Stephanie stood up. It was warm in the cabin and she had discarded her fur coat. She slipped it back on her shoulders.

'And now . . .'

'Now?'

'I would like to see how fast this galley can go. I like speed.'

The Baron followed her out on to the central gangway. He issued orders to the muscular black overseer who immediately smiled broadly, displaying his large white teeth. His eyes admired Stephanie who, he was sure, had been the source of this idea.

The overseer strode out into the middle of the boat raising his whip aloft as Stephanie climbed up on to the top of the forecastle.

'In . . . out. In . . . out. In . . . out.'

The rowing got faster in time with the commands, and soon the boat was gliding through the water at some speed.

Stephanie heard the whip crack out but did not look down into the pit where the slaves toiled. She turned her face into the wind the movement was creating, letting it flow through her long black hair. She knew they were all watching her, hating her for making them work so hard, for the pain from the lash of the whip. But they all wanted her too. She knew that.

'Faster,' she cried, hearing their groans and listening to the relentless lash of the whip as it urged them to greater and greater effort, greater effort for *her*. She felt her body thrill with sheer unadulterated pleasure, the pleasure of power.

'Faster,' she repeated.

'Had a good day?'

Devlin was still sitting at the table by the window, papers strewn about him.

'I saw the galley. Very impressive. I bet you enjoyed that. You looked wonderful, standing there, like a figurehead on a pirate ship.'

'Have you forgotten everything I taught you?' she snapped, the experience on the galley still shaping her mood.

Devlin looked up. There was no mistaking her tone of voice.

'No, mistress,' he said quietly.

'Come over here.'

He got up and started to walk towards her.

'How dare you. Get on your knees.'

He fell to the floor and crawled over to her, the master of a multi-million-pound empire reduced, instantly, to an abject slave.

'I should have you whipped. Get your head down on the carpet and don't move.'

Stephanie took off her fur coat, dropped it on the bed and went into the bathroom. Despite her exertions with the two men, or perhaps because of them, and certainly because of the feelings she had experienced on the galley, her body was tingling. In the bathroom she stripped off her clothes and stood under the shower, adjusting the water until it was as hot as she could take it.

The powerful needles of water cascaded over her body. She closed her eyes and raised her face into the stream, feeling the water running in little rivulets down over her breasts, channelled by her pelvis into her thick pubic hair. She rubbed soap against herself, around and over her breasts, down over the slender contours of her thighs and up between her legs until her black pubic hair was white with lather. Her body seemed to be vibrating, humming like a tuning fork after it had been struck. As she rubbed the soap into her labia she could feel how swollen they still were, pumped up, engorged. Her breasts, too, largely neglected by the two male slaves, felt incredibly tender, her nipples flashing with pleasure as she brushed over them.

But it was not only her body that buzzed with sexual tension; her mind raced too. As though in a film she saw herself on the galley. Her imagination ran riot. She could imagine herself naked, whip in hand, walking up and down the gangway, scourging the slaves to greater effort. Her body would provoke their erections, all eyes would be on her . . . The thought made her shiver with excitement.

And then there was the pavilion. What lay ahead of her tonight was the opposite side of the coin. Standing on the galley, in the prow, the absolute mistress of twelve naked men was a perfect example of what she found most exciting. But that was not to say the thought of what she would experience tonight didn't excite her too.

Perhaps, she thought, it was only possible to get

such extreme pleasure from her mastery, because she knew exactly what it was like to be a slave. Over the last months she had experienced both. She had used and been used, subjected her slaves to her whims and been subjected, in turn, to the caprice of others. She knew what it was like to be in someone else's power, what it felt like to be controlled, to lose the ability to decide even the smallest things, and most of all to be dependent, totally dependent for satisfaction on the arbitrary desires of a master.

She rubbed herself dry with a towel, feeling again how the sensitised nerves in her breasts and labia reacted to her touch. She knew exactly what she needed now, and, like everything else in her life over the last months, her need was going to be easily satisfied. It was overindulgence of course, considering what had happened this morning and what was going to happen tonight, but frankly she didn't care.

Devlin was waiting for her in the same position she had left him, his forehead pressed into the thick carpet.

'Get your clothes off and hurry,' she said, framed by the bathroom door, her legs open, her arms akimbo, naked apart from high-heeled black slip-ons.

As Devlin pulled his shirt off anxiously, Stephanie lay on the bed next to her fur coat.

'Hang my coat up,' she ordered, picking up the telephone and dialling 9. 'Come in, please,' she said into the phone. Devlin hung the fur in the wardrobe then stripped off the rest of his clothes. His monstrous erection was at full stretch.

There was a knock on the bedroom door almost immediately.

'Come.'

Mischa entered the room. Her outfit was different

today. Gone were the long leather straps passed through her nipple rings; her big breasts were unencumbered, as was the rest of her body apart from her legs. These were clad in what were, in effect, stockings, but made from black leather and not nylon. They stretched over her flesh right up to her crotch, where they were secured in place by a strap sewn into the top edge. The strap was buckled tightly and bit into the soft flesh, its upper edge almost brushing her labia on the inner thigh. A pair of ultra-high heels were Mischa's only other clothing.

'Come over here.' Stephanie indicated the bed.

Mischa obeyed at once and tottered forward on the heels. The hair on her belly was as bright a red as that on her head, but it was sparse, and her labia were clearly visible.

Seeing the nipple rings again had given Stephanie an instant jolt of desire, her own nipples puckering in sympathy. She'd forgotten how fascinated she'd been by them yesterday.

'Devlin, bring me the riding crop.' Stephanie had brought the whip from the castle. It was her favourite; the right weight and the right pliancy. Devlin extracted it from the drawer where it had been left and brought it over to the bed. 'Give it to Mischa.'

Devlin obeyed. As usual, he had no idea what Stephanie had in mind. She was quite capable of making him watch as she used the girl, quite capable of denying him pleasure except the pleasure he took in his obedience.

But that was not what she had in mind. She wanted no preliminaries, no complications. She was still in the same mood as she had been that morning.

'Fuck me, Devlin,' she said simply, lying back and opening her legs. Her mind could never adequately prepare her for the physical impact his size made on her body.

Devlin wasted no time. He knelt between her legs and positioned himself, pushing forward until his cock was nudging her labia.

'Yes,' she said.

He drove his cock right up into her. It was not difficult. She was wet. His shaft stretched every membrane in her sex; his glans was hard against the mouth of her womb, but his balls were still in mid-air. No woman could take all of Devlin. He was just too big. Stephanie ran her hand down over his buttocks to grasp his balls. She heard him moan as her hand squeezed them tightly.

'Fuck me, Devlin.'

He bucked his hips. His cock slid back then up again, back and forth, filling her each time. There was no experience in the world like this. Because his cock was so big he could not grind against her clitoris, but there was no need. The breadth of him stretched her labia so far apart, so tight that the clitoris was pulled up against its own hood. The combination of the massive throbbing cock and the tiny butterfly movements against the little bud of nerves was perfect.

'Whip him,' Stephanie managed to say. She had what she wanted, Devlin's cock buried inside her, but she wanted more. She wanted his pleasure as well as her own.

Mischa did not hesitate. She raised her arm and brought the whip swinging down on Devlin's buttocks just as he was completing his outward stroke. The whip sent his cock surging back up again, a new welt of feeling burning into him. His manhood was throbbing now, the pain transformed to pleasure so quickly it was impossible to distinguish between the two.

'Again,' Stephanie gasped, sapped by Devlin's assault on her. Her body was heaving, her sex contracting around his great rod of flesh, but her eyes were riveted to the gold nipple rings on Mischa's breasts as they quivered with the effort of using the whip.

'My nipples,' she whispered into Devlin's ear. His hands groped between their bodies until his fingers found the corrugated buttons of flesh. 'Pinch them, pinch hard . . .'

She was coming and knew Devlin was coming too. She had to close her eyes. She wanted only to feel. She felt his cock, boiling hot, throbbing, pulsing. Spunk was seething up into it from his balls, still held firmly in her hand. It filled her completely. She thrust her body down, wanting the impossible, wanting to take more.

Thwack. She got her wish. The whip propelled Devlin's cock into her. Suddenly his body went rigid, his cock spasmed and he spunked, his balls jerking in her hand. The whole length of his shaft throbbed, as spunk jetted out, out against the silky wet walls of Stephanie's sex.

'God, God, God . . .' she screamed, her body taking over, as she convulsed around his cock, and she was reduced to nothing but delicious, unfathomable sensation. With one final effort she forced herself down on the huge rod of flesh, then exploded in ecstasy as she felt his spunk already running down the sides of his cock and out of her body.

'Oh, Devlin,' she said as the tension in her body seeped away and she could open her eyes again. She looked at Mischa, standing beside the bed, whip in hand. Her bizarre costume showed off her beautiful, sweating body, and her pierced nipples were as hard as stone. Stephanie felt another *frisson* of pleasure.

Chapter Nine

'This way,'

Stephanie had not seen the woman before. She had been led from the bedroom, down a long dark corridor and a flight of stone steps, and now her guide was holding open the door to a small, dimly lit room.

The woman was dressed from head to toe in black, an amorphous black dress which gave little idea of her shape, though she was probably slim. She wore a black scarf tied over her hair and her face was thin and sallow. She carried a black nylon holdall.

Stephanie walked through the door. The woman followed and closed it after them.

The room was bare and windowless. At its centre was a steel pillar running from floor to ceiling and bolted to both by a steel plate. A single weak bulb hanging down from the ceiling was the only source of light.

The woman dropped the holdall on the floor.

'Clothes off,' she said, the first words she had spoken. Her accent was strongly Germanic.

Stephanie was wearing only a white towelling robe from the bathroom, its breast pocket emblazoned with the Baron's coat of arms. She shrugged it off her shoulders. As there was nowhere to hang it she let it fall to the floor.

'Grasp this tightly,' the woman ordered, indicating the pillar.

Stephanie obeyed. The woman was treating her like a slave, like someone whose opinions, likes and dislikes were irrelevant. The thought made Stephanie's body tingle: it was, after all, what she expected.

Behind her back the woman unzipped the holdall. Stephanie could have turned to see, but did not. A slave would not have moved, and she wanted to be the perfect slave. She had cast herself in this role and was determined to play the part. No one knew better how a slave should perform.

The woman came up behind her and threaded a coarse thick garment around her waist and under her breasts. It was a corset, heavily boned to fit tightly around the waist. Its bottom edge sat uncomfortably on the top of the hips, while its upper nestled under the breasts.

The woman was threading laces through the eyelets in the back. Satisfied they were in place she began to pull the laces together, yanking Stephanie back away from the pillar until she was hanging on to it for fear of being pulled over. The corset bit into her, tighter and tighter, making her fight for breath, the bones down its length like hard fingers trapping her ribs.

Eventually, after endless tightening and minor adjustments, the woman established that the laces would go no tighter and tied them off.

'These on now,' she ordered, holding up a dirty white cotton blouse and a rough, very full skirt which was equally grubby. With difficulty – any movement made the corset bite deeper into her body – Stephanie obeyed. Bending over was the worst, she discovered, as she stepped into the skirt; the corset dug sharply into her navel and made her gasp.

As soon as the cotton blouse was tucked into the skirt, covering Stephanie's breasts, the woman in black picked up the holdall, stuffed the white towelling robe into it and walked out of the room. She slammed the door shut and Stephanie heard a key grinding in the lock.

Stephanie looked down at herself in the rough peasant clothes. The blouse had no fastenings of any sort, split at the front right down to the waist, and held in place by the skirt. Her breasts, sitting awkwardly on top of the corset, were clearly visible on either side of the neckline. The material of the blouse and skirt felt coarse against her skin, so used to the finest silks and satin and lace. The corset would have felt coarse too, no doubt, but it held her so tightly that the area it encased was numb. She had thought the corset she had worn in the bordello was tight, but it was nothing compared to the iron grip of this model.

There was nowhere to sit down except on the bare wooden floor, and the room was not heated. Since she was expecting to be collected again at any moment, and she could imagine the pain the corset would inflict on her if she did try to sit on the bare boards, Stephanie waited on her feet. She had been told to leave everything in the bedroom, so her Patek Phillipe was there and she had no idea of the time.

After a while she leant against the wall. A little later she eased herself to the floor, but the corset dug into her so much she had to lie flat to escape its worst effects.

Time passed. Despite the shallow breathing the corset necessitated Stephanie felt drowsy. She closed her eyes. She might have dozed off. She certainly did not hear the key turning in the lock.

'Well, you're a lovely one.'

She opened her eyes to see a big burly man standing

over her. He was dressed exactly like a medieval peasant, baggy shapeless breeches and a tunic over a formless, collarless shirt, his feet in primitive leather sandals. He was dirty and smelt foul.

'What do you want?' This was not what she'd expected.

The man dropped to his knees. His hands, ingrained with dirt, started pawing her breasts, as she struggled with the corset to sit up. She tried to slap his hands away but this only provoked them into attacking her legs, scrabbling up under her skirt.

'A beauty,' he said again, undeterred by her protests as she tried to stop his hands reaching her thighs. 'We'll have some fun . . .'

'No, get off me.'

'We'll have some fun.' His fingers poked at her belly, trying to get down between her legs where her thighs were tightly clamped together.

'No!'

'Come on.'

'Get off me!'

His fingers had pried between her legs; she could feel them up against her labia. Whatever was going to happen to her, she didn't want this man doing any of it, let alone touching her sex.

He leant forward to kiss her using one arm to pin her back on to the floor. He was strong. She tried to wriggle away but he held her firm. As his mouth approached she could see his rotten teeth and smell his sickly odour. She shook her head from side to side but he blocked this with one hand then slid his mouth over her cheek on to her lips. Having found his lip, Stephanie grabbed it with her teeth and bit hard.

'Ah!' he screamed, jumping to his feet immediately. 'I knew it. You're a bloody witch. A witch.' He shouted it at the top of his voice. 'The bitch is a witch!'

Before Stephanie knew what was happening the room was full of people, all shouting, all scrambling to get their hands on her. She was pulled to her feet.

'The bitch is a witch,' they all screamed, men and women, all clad in medieval peasant clothing. 'The bitch is a witch.'

The man she had bitten led the procession. Out of the little room, down a long dim vaulted corridor made from old stone and lit only by flaming flambeaux every ten or so yards. In the corridor they hauled her off her feet and she was carried horizontally at shoulder height, her arms and legs held firm in endless pairs of hands.

She saw the vaulted corridor give way to a much larger space. They were in the medieval dungeon now. She felt her heart skip a beat.

'Witch, witch, witch . . .' the crowd chanted as they manhandled Stephanie to her knees on the floor in front of the Inquisitor. 'Witch, witch, witch.'

'Silence,' he ordered.

He was dressed as he had been before, black tights and codpiece and the wide leather straps that revealed his barrel chest and muscular arms.

'The woman must be allowed to speak,' he said solemnly. 'This is a very serious accusation.'

'Witch, she's a witch,' the man Stephanie had bitten shouted.

'Let her speak. Well my dear, such a pretty thing, you stand accused of hideous offences. What have you to say for yourself?'

'He was going to rape me,' Stephanie blurted out before she'd really thought about what to say. But it was true.

'That's a very serious charge, too,' the Inquisitor said.

'She put a spell on me. She enticed me. She's a witch.'

'Are you a witch?' The Inquisitor took Stephanie's chain in his thumb and forefinger and used it to raise her head to look right into his eyes. Stephanie shuddered. His eyes were so dark it was impossible to tell which colour they were.

'He tried to put his hand –'

'Are you a witch?' he repeated emphatically.

'No. He tried –'

'Be quiet. You are not a witch, you say. Did you not entice this man with your spells?'

'No, he tried to put his hand –'

'Silence.' The word rang out across the dungeon. As well as the crowd gathered round her, the slaves chained to the walls, in various stages of undress, were watching intently too. 'You will have to be put to the test. It is known a witch can feel no pain. You will be tortured. If you feel no pain you will never confess and we will know you are a witch.'

'But what if I do?'

The Inquisitor smiled broadly, glad she had asked the question.

'Then you will confess, to stop the torture.'

'Confess to what?'

'Confess to being a witch. Which would mean you were a witch, since no one would confess to such a terrible thing unless it was true.'

'The bitch is a witch,' the crowd bayed again.

'First the rack. Put her on the rack.'

Hands dragged Stephanie to her feet. Whereas before the hands had concentrated on carrying her, now they fondled and nipped at her body, pinching her breasts and thighs and prodding up between her legs.

As they approached the rectangular rack, Stephanie glimpsed the roaring forge at the far end of the room. Then she was plucked off her feet and hoisted up on to the wooden frame. In seconds she felt her ankles and wrists being strapped to the top and bottom of the frame and heard the ratchet of the drum that tightened the mechanism being turned to take up the slack.

The crowd gathered round to peer down at her, all talking at once, still prodding and touching her body.

'Silence,' the Inquisitor demanded as he took up position at the spoked wheel that turned the drum. The chattering stopped immediately and the hands disappeared from Stephanie's body. 'You are to be put to the test.'

He turned the spokes of the wheel by one notch on the ratchet. Stephanie felt her arms and legs being stretched.

'Confess,' he said, lowering his face until it was inches from hers.

'No,' she said defiantly, staring back into his black eyes.

'Very well.'

She felt his big hand descending to the waistband of the skirt, ripping it away and pulling the material out from under her legs. The crowd roared approval as her naked belly came into view, and applauded again when he tore away her blouse. The Inquisitor's hand rested on her belly.

'One last chance,' he whispered menacingly.

Stephanie said nothing.

She saw his hands going to the spokes and heard the ratchet turn. She braced herself for the worst, but though her body was stretched out slightly, that was not the main effect of turning the wheel several notches at a time. Instead, Stephanie felt a smooth metal object pushing between her legs. It grew until it was poking out from her pubis. The Inquisitor stopped turning the wheel.

Stephanie lifted her head to look down at it. The object was shaped like a dildo, curved up over her belly, and made of some shiny bright metal. It looked as though Stephanie had sprouted a cock. It was not uncomfortable.

The Inquisitor did not put the question again. As the crowd watched intently – most of them, Stephanie noticed, stripping off their clothes to reveal breasts and cocks and labia – the Inquisitor's hand altered a small mechanism in the gearing of the wheel, then began to turn the spokes again.

This time Stephanie definitely felt her body being stretched, but all the force was coming from her ankles, pulling her down, pulling her labia on to the metal phallus which jutted up between her legs. At the same time the phallus began to move. It was not a vibration, but a steady sawing movement, up and down. As Stephanie was hauled down on to it she felt her labia open and the inner curve of the phallus push right against her clitoris, its motion immediately rubbing the tiny button of nerves.

'Oh . . .' she gasped involuntarily. It was a wonderful feeling. On the inner surface of the metal it felt as though there were a series of tiny bumps, each nudging against her tender flesh as the phallus moved up and down.

'Confess.'

'No.' Stephanie moaned as she saw the spokes turn again. Her body was already throbbing. She felt her ankles being pulled, her wrists being stretched out against their bonds, as her whole body was pulled down and the phallus embedded itself even deeper between her nether lips and up against her clit. The tighter she was stretched, the more her legs and arms were pulled at her shoulders and hips, the more she seemed to feel the phallus sawing between her legs. Every tiny bump on its surface assumed mammoth proportions in her mind as they rubbed against her.

The Inquisitor was bending over her again, satisfied she was stretched to the maximum. The nerves in her joints were aching with tension but it was a delicious pain, a pain that seemed to magnify what was going on between her legs. The Inquisitor's hands were on her breasts, kneading them aggressively, pinching at her nipples.

Stephanie gazed around her. The crowd were still watching but some were less concerned with her fate than their own. A man stood with two women vying for position with their mouths on his cock. Another woman was bent over one of the wooden benches that were dotted around the dungeon with a man taking her from the rear, while a second waited his turn. Others used their hands, penetrating the sexes of the women, circling the cocks of the men, while they watched Stephanie's torment.

The phallus was relentless. Her clitoris was held against it so hard, her legs stretched down by her bondage so tightly that it was impossible for her to move at all, even to wriggle or squirm against it. Instead she could only feel, feel what the tiny bumps were doing to her, feel how it squeezed her clitoris hard against itself and her pubic bone. She had never felt a sensation like it. The pressure seemed to exaggerate the movement of the phallus, making the sawing motion ripple through her body in giant waves of feeling.

She was coming. The Inquisitor could see it.

'Confess,' he said, his face inches from hers. 'Confess or I turn it off.'

'No . . . don't . . .' Stephanie couldn't bear that. She didn't want it to stop, ever. She saw his hand move to the spokes of the wheel. 'No!'

'Confess.'

'Please, please, please,' she begged.

'Confess.'

'Yes, yes,' she shouted at the top of her voice as the phallus rubbed against her clitoris. She was going to come, come over the grating phallus as the Inquisitor's hands found her breasts again. He pinched her nipples and drew her breasts up away from her body, filling her with yet more sensation.

Stephanie's eyes rolled back in their sockets. She would have liked to keep them open, to watch what was happening all around her, but it was impossible. What was happening in her body was too demanding. Being stretched as she was seemed to have sensitised all her nerves, putting them under pressure as her clitoris was, but she was unable to bring them the slightest relief.

She felt her body tremble as the relentless phallus ground into her.

'Oh, oh, oh . . .'

'Witch,' the Inquisitor said, pulling on her nipples, stretching her breasts as every other part of her body was stretched.

That was the final straw. Her orgasm burst over her, raking through her nerves, exploding in her mind. But, unlike any other time, her body could not respond by bucking and twisting and writhing; her limbs were stretched beyond that. This fact seemed to double the sensation, like sound echoing in a confined space. Her orgasm echoed through her body, bouncing from one set of nerves to another until she thought it would never end.

'If you're a witch, you have to be punished,' the Inquisitor was saying, finally releasing her breasts. The words seemed so far away it was almost as if they came from a different dimension.

He was unwinding the wheel, the phallus was retreating, and Stephanie's limbs at last were able to relax. A naked woman, one of the few not involved in the various couplings that were going on all round the frame, unstrapped the leather bindings on Stephanie's ankles and wrists, touching her lasciviously on the journey between the two. 'There is only one punishment for witches, only one pain they feel. The pain of the fire.'

With his strong arms the Inquisitor dragged Stephanie to her feet and pulled her over to the forge. Hanging down from the wooden beams in the ceiling in front of the hot fire was what looked like the bar of a trapeze. The two strong chains that held it were joined by a metal ring, which was supported in turn by a single chain looped through a pulley. This allowed the bar to be raised or lowered.

The naked woman who had untied her had followed them over to the forge. She was plump with mousy coloured hair and disproportionately large breasts. She went to a dog-legged handle on the wall and wound the bar down to head height. Stephanie saw two metal cuffs at either end of the bar, into which the Inquisitor quickly fixed her wrists. The woman wound the bar up again and Stephanie's arms were raised until she was almost on tiptoe. The pain the rack had caused in her shoulders was suddenly renewed.

The pain in her arms, though, was the least of her worries. What concerned her most was the proximity of the coal-fired forge, exactly like the sort of thing she'd seen in old-fashioned blacksmith's shops: a bed of coals topped by a metal cowl which ducted the fumes away. The fire was hot and Stephanie could feel sweat beading on her forehead.

'Witches hate fire,' the Inquisitor intoned, coming up behind her and running his hands over her breasts. They continued down over the corset to her belly, her sweat making his fingers wet.

He came round in front of her and went to the furnace, stoking it with coal and using a pair of leather bellows to make it glow red again, hotter than before.

Whether it was the heat, or the tightness of the corset, or the niggling fear – which she knew was ridiculous – that the irons resting amid the coals were brands intended for her, Stephanie didn't know, but she was finding it increasingly difficult to breathe, each breath coming in a shallower pant.

But for all her discomfort, her body had not stopped throbbing. As they knew it would, of course, the experience on the rack had not extinguished her need, but made it worse. Though she had climaxed she had done so without being penetrated and that had left her wanting more, wanting above everything the feeling of a cock filling her sex, wanting to hold it, squeeze it, cling to it.

The Inquisitor stripped off his gloves, then pulled off his codpiece, boots and breeches. His cock was already erect, big and heavily veined, its circumcised glans much broader than the rest of his shaft, like a long, thin mushroom. He took it in his hand and stroked it up and down in his fist before disappearing behind Stephanie's back. With her arms in this position, it was too painful to strain her neck round to try and see what he was doing, especially as it was taking all her energy and concentration just to breathe.

But she knew instinctively what he was going to do. Without warning came the whistle of a long thin whip and a stripe of pain seared across her buttocks. The pain coursed through her in waves, routed by her body to the seat of her sexual nerves where it became an almost unbelievable injection of sheer pleasure.

'Yes,' she screamed, wanting more.

'Witches love pain.' The whip whistled through the air again and another seething blow produced another rush of pleasure so pure it would have taken her breath away had she had any breath to spare.

Sweat was running down her body in rivulets. The corset was soaking. The sweat ran out from under it, down her navel, over her thighs, and down between her legs. Her pubic hair ws so wet it clung to her flesh, matted and, for once, allowing her labia underneath to be seen.

'Ah . . .' she gasped as the whip struck again.

She loved it, gloried in it. She shook her whole body, wanting to feel her bondage, the welts on her arse, the ache in her clitoris, the pull in her shoulders; she wanted to feel it all at once.

The Inquisitor came up behind her and pushed her forward so she was closer to the heat, his cock pressed into the cleft of her buttocks. The heat seeped into her body. The Inquisitor's calloused hard hands snaked around her waist, caressing her breasts and her belly. She struggled against them but her struggling made no difference.

She could feel his cock sliding against her sweating flesh.

'I'd mark you,' he whispered in her ear, not wanting anyone else to hear. 'I'd mark you with fire.'

Her body shuddered. She couldn't escape the image; she saw in her mind those irons being drawn from the fire to brand her a witch. She was a witch. She'd confessed it, hadn't she? She was starting to believe it. The heat was cooking her brain. Everything around her was so real, it was difficult to remember any other world.

'No . . .' she said.

'Yes,' he whispered.

She struggled again, this time feeling his cock slip down between her legs. It was liquid there, not with sweat but with the sap from her body. Almost before she knew it his cock was inside her and he was using his hands to pull her back on to him, driving himself deeper.

Some of the rest of the company had come over to watch, some still coupled, others naked but, for the moment at least, replete. The plump woman came to the forge and worked the bellows again, sending a shower of sparks flying up the cowl. She put on a single heavy suede glove and picked an iron out of the burning fire, its tip white hot.

Stephanie's eyes were rooted to it. The Inquisitor was driving his cock into her liquid depths, driving harder and faster, his own need suddenly urgent. His strangely shaped cock slipped effortlessly in her juices and their bodies slid against each other in a sea of sweat.

The iron came nearer. Stephanie could see it was a brand: a complex design on a round plate, a coat of arms – the Baron's coat of arms, no doubt.

They were going to do it. They were going to brand her breast. This was it. This was what it was like. This was an Inquisitor's dungeon, the world as it used to be, a helpless innocent branded as a witch and consigned to torment for the pleasure of others.

The Inquisitor plunged forward once more, held Stephanie by the hips so tightly she couldn't move, then stopped, waiting for his cock to spasm. Stephanie felt it jerk inside her and hot spunk spat out into her. Then he moved, wriggling his body against her, as if to extract every last drop of spunk from his cock. And that was what took Stephanie over the edge too, sent her plummeting down, reeling and falling. Her mind was full of images, of torture and mayhem, as her body succumbed to the ultimate pleasure, coming over the hard cock impaling her.

It was too much. She didn't have the breath for it, she was too hot and too exhausted. As her muscles took the last of her energy, convulsing to the dictates of her orgasm, fighting the constrictions that held her, the world went dark and, like a rag doll, Stephanie's body collapsed. She hung from the bar, limp and overwhelmed.

Stephanie woke with a start, her heart pumping violently as though she had woken from a nightmare. It took her a few minutes to get her bearings before she realised she was back in the luxurious bedroom, alone in the big bed.

As her heart rate returned to normal she tried to focus on the events of last night. At the time they seemed so real – too real, even. It had become harder as the evening progressed to remember that she wasn't really being tormented by some diabolical Inquisitor in a medieval dungeon. As time went by she had been drawn into the fantasy, becoming more and more convinced that it was a real Inquisition and she a real victim of it. Now it was the very clarity of this memory that gave the whole experience a dreamlike quality. She knew she had been taken to the bare room and laced into the tight corset. She remembered lowering herself gingerly to the floor. Perhaps the rest had been a dream?

She threw aside the cream silk sheet and looked down at her naked body and realised it had not. There was a distinct mark in her tanned flesh where the corset had dug into her, though she was relieved to see no scar from a brand on her breast. As she got out of bed she felt a sting of pain and glanced over her shoulder into the mirror that hung on one wall. There were three distinct, very red welts across her buttocks.

The strangest thing, she thought as she ran her bath and applied a soothing cream to the welts, was that, despite the fact she had seen the dungeon before, seen its false ceiling and known how it was used to view the proceedings, she had not thought about it at all. From the moment she had been carried into the Inquisitor's presence she had been able to think of nothing but the injustice of what was happening to her – being falsely accused of being a witch merely because she refused to have sex. She hadn't for a second imagined the Baron standing in the gantry looking down at her, watching her being used and abused, watching her, like the woman in the casket, being made to confess.

But, of course, she knew the Baron had been there, and that he had watched, just as he'd watched her at the castle a month before. She knew his eyes had seen her stretched on the rack, the phallus thrust between her thighs; had seen her strung up in front of the forge to be fucked by the Inquisitor; and, presumably, seen her unconscious body released.

What else he had done she did not know. She did not know whether he masturbated while he watched, or had one of the girls fellate him or bring him off in some other way. The Baron, with those icy slate-grey eyes, remained an enigma in that department. Not for long, however. Stephanie had her deal with him and she was determined to collect her end of the bargain; she had certainly fulfilled her obligations as agreed.

Chapter Ten

For dinner Stephanie wanted to look her best. The Baron had been away for three days, leaving them the run of the Schloss. They had played tennis in the indoor court, swum in the almost Olympic-sized pool in a conservatory kept at almost tropical temperature, and rested. They had watched movies in the small private cinema and taken the limousine into Munich to have dinner in its best restaurant.

Though they had been encouraged by the Baron, neither Stephanie nor Devlin had wanted to go to the pavilions. Devlin's sexual psyche was well satisfied by Stephanie, who, on the second night of the Baron's absence, had been particularly demanding and had used him mercilessly, commanding absolute obedience as she'd relieved her own sexual needs.

Tonight the Baron had sent word he would return, and hoped they would both join him for dinner.

Stephanie had chosen a gold lamé catsuit, its shimmering surface clinging to every inch of her spectacular body, even delineating the cleft of her buttocks. Its neckline was a deep V that ran from her throat to the gold belt she wore at her waist, giving glimpses on both sides of the firm pillows of her breasts. She wore her hair down, brushed out over her bare shoulders. Her gold Patek Phillipe watch was her only jewellery and matched her gold high-heeled slingback shoes.

'You look wonderful, my dear, if I may be pemitted to say so,' the Baron said, once again waiting at the bottom of the staircase at the appointed time.

'Thank you, Baron,' she said, giving him her hand to be kissed.

'Good trip?' Devlin asked as they were led through into the sitting room where the big log fire burnt merrily in the grate.

'I think so. And I hope you have enjoyed the Schloss.'

'We did. It's been a lovely holiday for us, Baron,' Stephanie said.

'Our life had become a bit of a trial,' Devlin said, only realising what he had said when Stephanie laughed. When Andrew had taken charge at the castle, there had been a very real trial.

'Sorry, private joke,' Stephanie explained.

'I'm glad you have had a good time. That was my intention. I certainly had an exceptional visit to your establishment.'

A waiter poured champagne, the Baron explaining the last bottle of Bollinger had not survived and he had been forced to serve them Krug instead.

'Well, here's to us all,' the Baron toasted. They raised their glasses and sipped the chilled wine.

Stephanie saw the Baron's eyes roaming her body, the tight-fitting material emphasising her slender curves, particularly her hourglass waist and the generous flare of her hips. Her buttocks, too, shaped by the high heels into pert, taut packages, were alluringly displayed.

'I suggest we go straight in,' the Baron said as they stood by the fireplace. 'I'm famished.'

They went through into the little tented dining room with Stephanie leading the way, the two men following her. Neither set of eyes was able to leave the undulation of her gilted hips.

The main aim of the conversation as far as Stephanie was concerned was to remind the Baron of their deal, her part of which was complete, but she decided she would leave that topic until after the meal.

'My chief is determined to show off his French repertoire tonight,' the Baron informed them as a *feuillette de fruits de mer* arrived, a cask of puff pastry overflowing with lobster, oysters, prawns and mussels in *beurre blanc*, and the wine waiter brought chilled Montrachet.

They talked and ate the beautifully cooked food, elaborately presented on huge round plates that the Baron declared proudly to be German. *Tournedos aux morilles* followed the seafood, and a soufflé of passion fruit finished the meal served with another glass of the syrupy *Eiswein*.

'So, Baron,' Stephanie said as she finished the melting dessert and took a sip of the wine, 'now it's your turn, isn't it?'

'My turn?'

'We made a deal, didn't we? You didn't think I'd forget?'

The Baron smiled.

'What deal?' Devlin asked.

Devlin had joined in all the conversation over dinner but Stephanie decided that she did not want him to share in this exchange.

'Be quiet, Devlin,' she snapped.

Devlin looked embarrassed – an embarrassment Stephanie knew he would find exciting – but kept quiet.

'Ah yes, our deal.' The Baron looked into

Stephanie's dark brown eyes, suddenly remembering how she had looked three days before, running with sweat, her arms tied and spread above her head, as the Inquisitor had taken her from behind. Even then, even after what she had been through, somehow she had remained defiant; used and abused, but ultimately in control. She was an extraordinary woman, extraordinarily beautiful and extraordinarily astute. He wondered if she might even pass the test . . .

'Well?' Stephanie prompted, mistaking his silence for reticence.

'You want to know about me?' he asked.

'I want to know what gives you satisfaction, yes. You've seen how I take my pleasure.'

'A wonderful experience.'

'And one I hope you'll enjoy again. Now I need to know about you.'

'Need?'

'Yes, need.' Stephanie's tone was insistent.

'I have very special requirements.'

'Go on.'

'As you know, I like to watch.'

Stephanie sipped the golden coloured *Eiswein* and looked at the Baron intently, sitting back in her chair, her breasts pushing against the neckline of the catsuit. She ran the fingertips of one hand over her collarbone and down into the material, lifting it slightly away from her body. She played her fingers up and down the soft flesh at the top of the dark tunnel of her cleavage.

'Go on,' she said, seeing the Baron's eyes on her fingers, almost hypnotised by their movement.

'I have a very vivid imagination.'

'You certainly have.'

'I suppose it is all part of my search.'

'Search?'

'I devised the pavilions, everything in them, everything in the Schloss.' His English accent was almost perfect but he pronounced the word 'Schloss' with full German emphasis. 'But it was not enough. I needed more. So I devised more, the ultimate pleasure.'

'Is there such a thing?'

She looked over at Devlin who sat with his fingers locked in front of him on the table, his eyes cast down at them.

'I think so,' the Baron continued. 'After many attempts I think I have devised the ultimate experience. Unfortunately . . .' his voice trailed off.

'Unfortunately?'

'It is too much. I have never found a woman capable of taking it, of withstanding it. Many have tried and failed. It is simply too much.'

'Too much?'

'Too much pleasure, too much to take. They begged me to stop or simply passed out.'

'Like I did.'

'No, that was entirely different. You passed out in the heat. You are not used to the corsets. To pass out from sheer pleasure is another matter.'

'Really?' Stephanie's imagination was already running riot. The Baron was a master of sexual fantasy, like a landscape gardener in the fertile pastures of the mind. He built on the slopes and inclines that were already there, decorating them, adding to and improving on nature, turning well-trodden byways into lush, verdant paths, transforming oft repeated dreams into vivid, elaborate realities. 'And what would happen if they did not?'

'My dear, that is what I dream about. If I could

watch a woman taking the ultimate pleasure, then I know I would at last be able to take my pleasure too.'

'Fascinating. I think I understand. It's like an electric charge; you need a very high voltage.'

'Precisely. And so far . . .'

'The lights have only burnt dimly?'

Stephanie had the key to the enigma. The Baron was an enabler, a man who had become so trapped in watching others take their pleasure, in creating scenes and settings for other's fantasies, he had, somewhere along the line, forgotten how to take his own. He had devised a method unique to him, a way he had convinced himself that would bring him enough excitement to let him share the pleasure too. Either consciously or unconsciously, he had made it too difficult. Perhaps he was afraid to do more than watch, afraid to let himself go, unconsciously creating a hurdle that he could not overcome. Or perhaps it really was impossible.

'The ultimate pleasure,' Stephanie said. 'I wonder what that might be.'

Devlin had remained silent during this whole conversation. But he was watching Stephanie and could see the look in her eyes.

'No,' he said quietly but firmly.

'No what?' Stephanie asked.

'It may be dangerous.'

'It's not dangerous, is it, Baron?'

'My dear, I was not suggesting you try it.'

'But of course I want to try it.'

'No,' Devlin repeated.

'Don't be ridiculous, Devlin,' Stephanie said. 'It's not dangerous. No one's ever been hurt, have they Baron?'

'I didn't intend that you –'

'You're right. I passed out the other night because of the heat and that damn corset. I couldn't breathe. It's not like that, is it?'

'No. But –'

'I'm fascinated.'

'I forbid it,' Devlin said.

'Devlin,' Stephanie snapped getting to her feet. 'How dare you talk to me like that. Get on your knees, Devlin, now.'

Devlin looked up into her eyes. They were cold and unyielding, staring down at him with contempt. He was trapped, trapped between his desire not to see Stephanie put herself in a situation she would regret and his need to be her absolute and devoted slave. In their relationship, since the day she had agreed to become the mistress of the castle and of him, he had never hesitated longer. He looked at the Baron and then at Stephanie again. Her dark brown eyes were flaring in defiance, her magnificent body seeming to shimmer in gold lamé, so tight it could almost have been painted on.

The slave in him won. Devlin had abrogated his authority. He slid to his knees.

'I can see I'm going to have to give you a lesson in obedience. Get your clothes off, all of them, then get back on your knees. Quickly.' Her voice was like a whiplash. 'Baron,' she said in an entirely different tone, 'let's go through to the fire.'

The Baron stood up, and Stephanie took his arm as Devlin hurriedly pulled off his clothes. His situation, his obedience, the look of contempt in her eyes and the tone of her voice had made his cock rise, and it was poking through the boxer shorts he wore as he stripped off his trousers.

The fire had been tended by the servants and burnt fiercely in the huge grate.

'I would like a glass of champagne now,' Stephanie said, 'to toast our experiment.'

'But don't you think Devlin –'

'Devlin? As you can see, Baron, Devlin's opinion does not count.'

'I did not mention my pleasure room with the intention that you should try it.'

'So you said.'

The Baron poured two glasses of champagne from the bottle of Krug still resting in the silver cooler and handed Stephanie a crystal flute.

'To the ultimate pleasure,' she said, clinking her glass against his.

'You are a remarkable young lady.'

'I hope so. I hope you think so after the test.'

'I will whatever happens.'

'You will,' she said firmly. The champagne was over-chilled, having been in the cooler for too long, but it was exactly what Stephanie needed to calm the rush of excitement she felt. It was not all to do with the thought of what the Baron had in store for her in his 'pleasure room'. It was to do with Devlin too. Their relationship was a two-way street. She had discovered his proclivity, she had formed and defined it and brought him to life sexually, but at the same time, in performing for him, she was also performing for herself. Being his mistress, the ruler of his will, was more than just a role to play: it thrilled her as fundamentally as it thrilled him to be her slave. She had seen his defiance, and the fact that his obedience to her had overcome it had her body singing with sexual energy. It was the perfect demonstration of her power.

'I would like you to make some arrangements for me, Baron,' Stephanie said, smiling to herself. She knew exactly what she wanted to do now. Devlin's behaviour, after all, could not go unpunished.

They stood in the gantry above the false ceiling to watch.

Devlin was in chains, thick, heavy chains attached to metal cuffs around his ankles and wrists. The ankle cuffs were joined by a single foot-length link, as were those at his wrists. Both were connected by a chain running between the two down the front of his body. There was a thick metal collar around his neck from which another chain ran down into the link between his wrists. More painfully, cuffs at his elbows were held together behind his back, stretching the wrist link across his lower chest and making it impossible for him to move his arms. The chain that hung down his front rubbed against his erection.

'Forward,' the woman ordered, pushing Devlin in the back and almost making him fall. He could only take diminutive steps.

They were in the Roman pavilion, the large room with the rostrum at one end, where six or seven women in short white togas all sat or lay around on cushions or Roman-style couches. At first they paid little attention to the arrival of their new slave.

'Forward,' the woman ordered again, not satisfied with Devlin's progress. The woman was the most extraordinary-looking creature. At least six feet tall, she towered above Devlin. Her naked body was black, a deep ebony, and rippled with well-defined muscles as though she regularly trained with weights. Her arms and legs were particularly developed, with muscles in bunches suggesting she was capable of considerable strength. But most extraordinary of all was her complete lack of hair. Her head was shaven and polished with oil; her belly was equally bare; the lips of her labia clearly visible. She had a long neck, its tendons stretched taut, and she held her head high. Her chest was powerful too, but her breasts were small with tiny dark nipples.

Devlin shuffled up on to the rostrum but caught his foot on the step and fell forward.

'Fool,' the woman chided, raising her hand and slapping her palm down on his rump with a smack that reverberated round the room. With one hand she picked him up bodily by the link of the cuffs at his waist, pulled him on to the rostrum and dropped him back on to the floor. 'Stay there,' she ordered in a deep rich voice as dark as her complexion. She bent over and rolled him on to his back, putting added pressure on his elbows and making him wince.

Casually, lowering herself on her big muscular haunches, she squatted over his face, her weight balanced on her feet.

'Lick me,' she said, 'and make it good.'

Devlin's cock throbbed. He wriggled his mouth into position and reached up to her nether lips. He had to raise his head, which made his unsupported neck ache, and his arms were going numb with their constriction, but he licked enthusiastically. He forced his tongue up between the smooth and large hairless labia until he could feel her liquid centre. Her sex, unlike the rest of her body, was a pale shade of pink.

'Very good, boy,' she said, dropping forward on to her knees, unable to balance any more on the soles of her feet. Devlin had to arch his head up even higher. His tongue found her hard clit.

'Yes, there, do it there,' she urged.

He tongued the little lozenge from side to side, the

way Stephanie had taught him, and felt the big black woman respond, her body trembling.

One of the other girls, a blonde who had been sitting brushing her short wavy hair, decided that Devlin was a more interesting prospect. She walked up on to the rostrum and came to stand beside him, pushing the chain that joined his wrists to his ankles out of the way of his cock with the side of her foot.

'Big, isn't he?' she said.

She stood astride his body. The black woman looked up at her. 'He's not to come. He's on punishment.'

'Don't worry, I'll just tease him a little.'

The blonde knelt with her knees either side of Devlin's hips. She held his cock in her right hand and eased her sex back on to it experimentally. She was not at all wet. Her pubic hair was thick and wiry and Devlin winced as she forced his glans into the mouth of her dry vagina. She bounced herself up and down, each time forcing the glans deeper, but producing no lubrication.

Another of the women – again a blonde, but this time with long hair – decided she wanted to join in too. She stood by the black woman, reached down and took both of her dark nipples in her fingers, pinching them and pulling them up.

'Does that feel good?' she asked.

'You know it does.'

'Is he giving you a good time?'

'He's well trained. Got his tongue right on the spot, havent you, slave?'

'Yes, mistress,' Devlin said, though the words were lost in the woman's sex.

'Don't stop,' she complained immediately, slapping his hip hard.

Suddenly Devlin felt the first blonde's sex pulse and a stream of juices flow down to envelop his cock. This time as she bounced down his cock slid deep inside her. Involuntarily he moaned against the sex pressed into his mouth.

'Is he all the way in?' the black woman asked.

'He is now.'

'Jesus, he's big. Look at that – it's still sticking out.'

'He's big all right,' the blonde said, wriggling her body on Devlin's cock and feeling herself respond.

The long-haired blonde got to her knees. She replaced her fingers on one of the black woman's nipples with her lips, and sucked the whole breast into her mouth, as the other blonde slipped her hand under her toga to feel for her sex.

Three women. And now four. A voluptuous brunette stepped up to the rostrum. She pushed the sides of the toga off her shoulders, untied the belt at her waist and allowed it to fall to the floor. Bending over the two blondes she performed the same service for them, undoing the belts and pulling the togas over their heads.

The brunette had a full, fleshy figure, her breasts large and pendulous. Her hips were equally curvaceous, and her belly was a mat of carefully trimmed black pubic hair. She knelt beside Devlin's chained body and ran her hand down over the thighs of the blonde squatting on his cock. Her fingers roamed over her labia and on to his shaft, while her other hand worked down from behind to cup his balls. She squeezed them hard and Devlin's body went rigid.

'Can't you get him all in?' the brunette asked.

'I've tried,' the blonde replied. As if to demonstrate she forced herself down on Devlin's cock, but there was no room to take any more.

'Finger me,' the brunette said, having spotted the size of Devlin's fingers. She moved so he could get his hand between her legs. There was very little room for maneouvre, chained as he was, but he managed to ease his hand up between her kneeling thighs and find the mouth of her sex.

'Yes,' she said.

Pushing against his chains, he wriggled his finger inside her.

'Oh, that's good,' she said. She relinquished her hold on his balls and concentrated instead on the blonde's clitoris. Devlin's cock had stretched her labia back and her clitoris was visible, pink and tender.

The black woman's juices were running into Devlin's mouth now and he could feel her body contracting. She was using her hand on the long-haired blonde, her finger frigging the clitoris so hard that the woman was moaning continuously. The woman leant forward to kiss her, still moaning as the black woman's mouth enveloped her, the noise muffled by the tongue that pushed between her lips.

Devlin's hand ached as he tried to push his finger to and fro in the willing sex of the brunette. He had managed to drag his hand out from his body a little but it was painful; his wrists were jammed against the metal cuffs, his elbows too. His neck muscles supporting his head stung with pain, and his tongue, stretched out to its limits to meet the black woman's demands, was in agony. His cock, by contrast, was bathed in the spring of the blonde's hot, squelching sex as it contracted around him rhythmically.

Seeing what the brunette had achieved with Devlin's finger on one side, the long-haired blonde decided she wanted the same. As the black woman continued to manipulate her clitoris, she manoeuvred herself over Devlin's hand. She didn't have to tell him what she wanted him to do. With an almost superhuman effort he pushed a finger into the mouth of her sex, fighting the cuffs again. He could get it no deeper, but it was enough.

Four women. The women were all wet, their bodies all throbbing at the same remorseless tempo, linked as they were by the same man. Their bodies bounced up and down on him, on his cock, on his tongue, on his fingers, bouncing harder and faster as the urgency of their need increased, fuelled by each other's desires. Devlin's body transmitted their feelings like radio waves from one to the other and back again and somehow multiplied them along the way.

It was not possible for them all to come together, four women as one, but they almost did. The black woman, who had started first after all, came first. Devlin felt the tunnel of her sex contract as he pushed up into it with his tongue, leaving her clitoris temporarily, and a flood of sweet hot juices ran down his chin. The black woman simultaneously locked her fingers hard into the labia of the blonde kneeling in front of her, pushing her clitoris back against the thickness of Devlin's banana-sized digit. Her fingers were perfect conductors, sending waves of orgasm from her body up into the blonde's, making her come too: a long loud moan, an almost animal noise escaped her lips.

It can have been no more than seconds before the other two women succumbed. They came together, exactly together, as the short-haired blonde, seeing the black woman convulse in front of her eyes, gave in to the feelings Devlin's cock had built up inside her, letting the dam burst and her emotions flow. The brunette felt it, felt her clitoris quivering and instantly came too, the feeling of Devlin's finger playing inside her like nothing she'd ever felt before. The sensation in one was immediately felt in the other, tossed back and forth, increasing, enhancing the delicious eruption that Devlin's size had provoked.

One by one they extracted themselves, leaving a trail of wetness on Devlin's body where they had been. His hands, thighs and face were wet, his pubic hair plastered to his body.

'Up,' the black woman said, her body glistening with a thin layer of sweat. 'You came, didn't you?'

'No, mistress,' he said, trying to indicate she should look at his cock.

'You came, you liar. Didn't he?' she asked the blonde.

'Oh yes,' she lied.

'See. How dare you lie to me!'

'I didn't, mistress.'

'Are you calling me a liar now?' the blonde said.

'No, mistress.'

'So you did come!' the black woman said conclusively. 'Do you think you could fool me? That's twice the punishment.' She bent over, grabbed him by the link between the wrist cuffs and pulled him to his feet. There was a wooden stool on the rostrum. The black woman dragged Devlin over to it. She sat down and pulled Devlin on to her lap, his cock pointing down vertically, trapped between her strong thighs. She squeezed it with her big muscles and Devlin moaned.

'Twice the punishment,' she said.

She raised her arm, her black hand out flat, its palm slightly lighter than the rest of her body, and brought it down on Devlin's buttocks. A resounding smack of flesh on flesh rang out across the big room. She felt his cock jerk between her thighs.

This will teach you,' she said.

The hand landed again, on the other buttock this time, thundering down with such power it jarred the whole of Devlin's body.

He would never be able to hold out. His cock was full of spunk, desperate for relief after what he had just experienced. He had been used by four women, bound and helpless, and now this, spanked with his cock imprisoned between black Amazon thighs.

Smack. The noise of flesh slapped against flesh was quite different from the sound of a whip. It felt different, too, the pain more diffuse, covering a wider area, not as hot as the sting of a whip but more affecting, more personal, more sexual.

His cock pulsed again against the incredibly smooth ebony flesh between her thighs.

Smack. Smack. Smack. Three in quick succession, each with just as much power. He would never be able to hold out.

Smack. Smack. She was moving off his buttocks now, down on to the top of his thighs. First one side, then the other; she covered every inch, right down to his knees, reddening the pink flesh, making his body quiver.

He saw the blonde who had sat on his cock come over.

'Poor thing,' she said.

The black woman stopped. He felt a cool hand stroking the tortured flesh, the blonde's hand, he thought. It felt wonderful: so tender, so caring.

And then he was out of control. Whether deliberately or not, the black thighs seemed to be gripping him tighter. He felt his cock spasm as the cool hand delved down between his buttocks, soothing and provoking at the same time. He felt his spunk pumping, forcing its way past the hard muscles that held his cock and jetting out on to the floor below. He had spent in mid-air, wasted his seed – the worst punishment of all. Devlin moaned. It was what he hated most, being made to come like this; though perversely, of course, because he hated it so, because it represented the ultimate contempt for what he wanted and needed, it also made him feel profoundly excited.

The black woman's hand rubbed his rump now. Unlike the blonde's her hand was hot, heated by the spanking. She rubbed cruelly, reactivating the tortured nerves, making his cock throb again, though the last drop of spunk had been extracted from his balls.

'The day after tomorrow,' Stephanie said. 'We'll release him then.'

She watched as Devlin was pulled to his feet. The brunette was attaching a chain to the link that held his elbows behind his back. The chain hung down from a pulley on the ceiling. In minutes, Devlin was hanging from it, his body bent almost double . . .

'He will be able to take that long?' the Baron asked.

'Look,' Stephanie said, indicating that Devlin's cock was already starting to sprout again.

The Baron led the way out of the pavilion.

'And what about the rest of the evening?' Stephanie asked.

'It is better if you rest, I think. I will prepare the pleasure room for tomorrow evening.'

'Not tonight?'

'No. Rest until then. Relax. The more relaxed you are, the better it will be.'

For once Stephanie didn't argue. 'All right. You're the expert.'

'My dear, I very much doubt that in these matters I am any more expert than you.'
'That,' Stephanie said, 'remains to be seen.'

Chapter Eleven

Stephanie did exactly as she was told. She had gone to bed after leaving Devlin in the Roman pavilion and slept a long and apparently dreamless sleep. She had woken feeling rested and calm and had had a long relaxing bath.

Breakfast had arrived with Mischa – no doubt on the Baron's orders – wearing a modest black dress that covered everything from the knees up. Clearly the Baron did not want to put any temptation in Stephanie's way. In fact it was a good thing that Mischa was so modestly dressed, because Stephanie's mind had began to roam and as she dried herself her body had leapt expectantly at every casual touch, thoughts of Devlin being used by the women and spanked by the hairless black Amazon stirring her feelings.

The fact that Mischa was properly dressed needn't have stopped her of course. There was nothing to say she couldn't throw her on the bed, or summon Hanna, or one of the male slaves for that matter. But it was better, she felt sure, that she save herself for whatever the Baron was going to do tonight. The prize for success was, after all, the Baron himself – a prize she valued highly.

That wasn't to say that it was easy. As she sat at the table in a white silk robe watching Mischa lay out the breakfast – coffee, blood orange juice, finely cut slices of melon – she felt her body surge in response to Mischa's proximity. She tried to see if the gold nipple rings were visible through the black cotton and wondered if Mischa was wearing lingerie. She pictured her in the thin leather straps and the full collar, her head held high, the nipple rings threaded through the thin straps like reins through a bridle, the thick crotchpiece biting into the soft yielding flesh of her thighs. She saw her in the tight leather stockings too, strapped on to her thighs, so high they brushed her labia and her wispy red pubic hair.

Her body started to churn.

'No,' she said to herself out loud.

'Madam?' Mischa said, looking puzzled.

'Not you.'

'Do you want anything else, madam?' Mischa asked, having emptied the breakfast tray.

'What I want and what I am going to allow myself to have are two different things,' Stephanie said, crossing her legs and hoping the strong black coffee would calm her.

'May I go, madam?'

'Your nipples, Mischa. Who pierced them?'

'The Baron, madam.'

'He wanted you pierced?'

'No, madam. I wanted it.'

'It was your choice?'

'Yes.'

'What does it feel like?'

'Like . . . like my nipples belong to someone else.'

Stephanie felt her own nipples throb against the white silk and decided she had better not provoke herself any more.

'You may go.'

'Thank you, madam.'

She tried not to watch as the redhead tripped back across the large bedroom but, inevitably, her eyes feasted on the young body and she remembered how it had looked before, naked and exposed.

Sipping the strong German coffee, Stephanie tried to pull herself together. Surely it was possible for her to go twenty-four hours without sex, without her body behaving as though it had had no contact for months.

She ate the melon but still found it difficult to get the images of Mischa out of her mind. Whenever she saw her, clothed or naked, her nipples puckered instantly as though she were imagining what it would be like to be pierced with cold metal permanently. That, in turn, sent signals down to her sex, and in seconds her body was churning. She knew she was wet.

Without really thinking about what she was doing, she stood up and looked at herself in the big mirror on the wall. Her dark brown eyes, pools of viscous brandy liquor, stared back at her questioningly. She slipped her robe off her shoulders, wanting to see her nakedness. The marks from the session in the medieval prison had faded completely and her unbroken tan – topped up by a visit to the Schloss's solarium during the Baron's absence – made her look fit and healthy. Her round, proud breasts, fleshy and full but with no hint of pendulousness, pointed back at her, the nipples a dark crimson red, as hard as stone. Her narrow waist emphasised the strong flare of her hips and seemed to direct the eye towards the black triangle of pubic hair at the apex of her long, sculptured thighs. She snaked her hand over her iron-flat navel, as soft as silk, and let her fingers explore the deep forest of black curls until it chanced on her labia. Her clitoris was throbbing before she touched it.

'No!' she said, tearing her hand away as if it were about to touch a poisonous snake.

Quickly she went to the chest of drawers and pulled out a black one-piece swimsuit. She pulled it over her naked body, found the white towelling robe that hung on the bathroom door and headed for the pool. Hopefully a long swim would cool her ardour and take her mind off her body.

The rest of the day she spent in this mood, playing cat and mouse with her own emotions, trying to hide from the sexual currents that would leap from the shadows on the flimsiest of pretexts.

She lunched with the Baron in the dining room overlooking the lake, a light lunch of rocket, lollo rosso and frisée tossed with lobster, and one glass – she didn't want to loosen her resolve with alcohol – of a fruity Chablis. The Baron made no mention of the plans for the evening and neither did she, but as the waiter brought tiny white cups of espresso the host did suggest they visit the pavilion to see how Devlin was getting on. Though from her point of view this was absolutely the last thing she wanted to do, Stephanie did feel responsible and decided she ought to go.

In any case, it was not a casual suggestion, she realised. The Baron had planned carefully, and taking her to the pavilions at this point was all part of that plan. He was raising her sexual temperature in stages, preparing her a step at a time. He would have rehearsed the scene in the pavilions carefully, she felt sure.

As they stepped on to the overhead gantry they saw that most of the participants in the Roman villa were 'outside', in the area by the swimming pool. Many lay on the grass, the remnants of meals scattered about the place, earthenware flagons of wine very much in evidence. The postprandial exercise was mostly sexual, and Stephanie looked down on various rather lazy couplings involving three or four people linked in numerous ways: by cock, or mouth, or both.

She tried to ignore the rush of feeling this created in her overexcited body – particularly one dark curly-haired fit young man enthusiastically pumping his glistening cock into a long-legged blonde. She lay with her legs in the air in a V-shape, while another naked woman with brown hair held the man's balls in one hand and one of the blonde's breasts in the other. Stephanie tore her gaze away with difficulty and searched for Devlin. He was nowhere to be seen.

It was the Baron who found him. Further along the gantry he was looking down into the large hall, and beckoned to Stephanie. Devlin was being 'entertained' by three women, two of whom Stephanie recognised as the blondes who had used him the previous night. His body had been strapped into an arrangement of leather bands that looked like a parachute harness and he was suspended from the ceiling. His arms were tied behind his back with leather thongs at the wrist and elbow, and his ankles, similarly bound, had been pulled up behind him and tied to his wrists. His monstrous cock stuck out in front of him, the balls beneath it bound in leather also.

Immediately in front of him one of the blondes was bending over a heavy wooden table, her buttocks raised, her legs open. The other two women, one on either side of Devlin, pushed him forward like a swing in a park so that his cock plunged into the blonde's sex, then pulled him out again. How long this had been going on Stephanie did not know, but the blonde was moaning loudly at each penetration and her knuckles were white as she grasped the top of the table.

'Yes!' she screamed. This seemed to be some sort of signal as, instead of pulling Devlin back again, the two women held him impaled on her sex while the blonde wriggled against him, moaning and coming as her vagina contracted around his massive shaft.

'Let's go.' Stephanie definitely did not want to see any more. She knew how the woman must feel, what wonderful sensations she would get in this position, filled with Devlin's cock. 'He's all right.'

The women were changing positions. The other blonde, the short-haired one, bent over the table and flaunted her buttocks in the air.

The Baron was smiling, knowing what Stephanie was feeling.

'You sure you don't want to stay? Or even join in?'

'I'll save it,' she said, walking past him back down the gantry. She heard the woman below moan for the first time as Devlin was guided into her sex. She tried not to look down at the scene by the pool, but the curly-haired man caught her eye again. He was on his knees now, a woman on all fours in front of him, as he took her from behind. The blonde was at his side, her hand cupping his balls between his open legs. He chose this moment to withdraw his long wet cock from her body and spunked, white strings of semen shooting out over her back.

'Interesting,' the Baron said, following Stephanie's eye.

'I'm going to rest,' she said weakly.

'Fine. I'll send the girls for you at seven.'

In her room Stephanie showered and tried to

ignore the feelings in her body. The temptation to touch herself – to lie on the bed with her legs open to play, her fingers over her clit while she jammed a big hard vibrator into the empty cavity of her sex – was extreme, but she was determined not to give in to it. Tonight she wanted to make sure she succeeded where every other woman had failed, and instinctively she knew that to dissipate her sexual energy at this point was a mistake – though a little voice, an evil little voice, kept asking her why and telling her it didn't matter. She just knew it did.

She knew the Baron had deliberately fed her imagination with new images, knowing they would increase the tension in her body, perhaps unconsciously wanting to tempt her because he wanted her to fail. When Mischa had come in this morning so modestly dressed Stephanie had thought it consideration on the Baron's part, but perhaps he was being more subtle, realising that, for once, modesty would provoke more than the bizarrely obscene. And he was right. If Mischa had arrived in the leather straps, Stephanie would have dismissed her immediately; as it was, she had almost been tempted.

The Baron would like her to fail. It would mean he would not have to commit himself, to cross the line he had drawn for himself in the sands of his own subconscious, thus giving up the part of the cool, detached observer. He would be required to perform and Stephanie was determined that his performance was going to be with her.

The time passed slowly. Stephanie tried to read but found her mind wandering off into musings about what the pleasure room contained. she had thought her sexual rituals at the castle were imaginative, but they were not half as elaborate as the ones the Baron had created. What the ultimate pleasure involved she could not begin to guess.

She made herself up, did her nails, brushed her hair and perfumed her body with Joy 1000, then covered herself with the white towelling robe because the silks and satins of the negligees she had brought with her rubbed against her body too sensuously.

After what seemed like a lifetime there was a knock on the bedroom door. It was exactly seven o'clock by the Patek Phillipe which she had taken off and laid on the bedside table.

Hanna lead Mischa into the room. They were dressed again as they had been on her arrival at the Schloss: Hanna in the incredibly tight leather corset that left her breasts and belly exposed, with the long leather gloves and high-heeled boots; and Mischa in the thin leather straps which ran through the nipple clips at the front and held the thick crotchpiece between her legs. Like the first time Stephanie had seen them they wore their full collars, the moulded leather covering their jaws and lips, trapping a gag in their mouths. Both walked with care in their precipitously high heels, and Mischa carried a black leather bag.

Hanna slipped the robe from Stephanie's shoulders and started pinning her long hair up on to her head while Mischa put her bag down on the bed and opened it. She extracted a silk sleeping mask and, as soon as Stephanie's hair was secured to the back of her head, slipped the elasticated mask over her eyes, plunging her into darkness.

Stephanie was glad the girls were gagged, because a hundred questions formed in her mind. Had they done this before? When was the last time? What happened? All questions she did not want answered – not now at least.

In the darkness she heard the rustle of the leather bag again. She felt hands on her arm, holding it out in front of her. Then a long leather glove being pulled up its length, up until she could feel it under her armpit, tightly gripping her flesh. The girls smoothed it on, making sure it fitted perfectly, even adjusting the stalls on the fingers so it was completely unwrinkled. They repeated the same process with the other arm.

As soon as the second glove was in place Stephanie felt hands pulling her arms behind her back. Hanna produced the lacing. Each glove was beaded along in the inner surface with a row of metal reinforced eyelets. Hanna threaded the lace through the eyelets and began to draw the two gloves together.

At the wrists it was easy, but as the lacing was pulled tighter and worked higher, up over the elbows, it forced her upper arms together, throwing her shoulders back and forcing her chest out. Stephanie moaned. But she did not resist. Hanna tugged on the lacing over and over again until she was satisfied it would go no tighter, until Stephanie's arms appeared as one, encased in a single glove. Thin leather straps were passed around the top of each shoulder to stop the glove slipping down.

Stephanie felt hands on her breasts now, and the tingle of cold metal. Small circular nipple clips were centred on each nipple. Stephanie's body surged as the spring was released and the metal bit into her corrugated flesh. She had worn nipple clips before and loved the sensation they gave her. These clips, she could feel, were joined by a thin metal chain from one to the other which hung down in a loop from her breasts.

The girls' hands were on her calves now, indicating she should raise one leg, then the other. Stephanie felt panties being drawn up her long legs – something like panties, at least. In fact it was the tiniest of G-strings, made from thick leather. Mischa pulled the waist-band around her body and adjusted it by means of a buckle so that it was tight around the top of her hips. The leather between her legs could be adjusted in the same way, by a buckle at the top of her buttocks. Hanna pulled the strap tight, the tiny triangle of leather pressing as hard as it could against Stephanie's sex, the strap biting into her labia and the cleft of her buttocks.

As the leather tightened, Stephanie could feel something cold and metallic there too. She had the sensation that the metal had given way, opening up; then she gasped out loud. Fixed into the front of the leather was another spring-loaded clip. Hanna had pulled the leather tight into her labia and it had been forced open then snapped shut, imprisoning between its metal jaws the hood of Stephanie's clitoris and the clitoris itself.

They removed the blindfold. Stephanie looked at herself in the mirror. The nipple clips and leather G-string were white, as was the single glove. Her arms were bound so far behind her back it looked almost as if they had been cut off. Her body was churning.

Pressure on her shoulders indicated that they wanted her to kneel. Stephanie complied and watched as Hanna took a white leather hood from the bag on the bed. She began pulling it over Stephanie's head; it was tight. Mischa helped smooth it over Stephanie's face, making sure the holes provided for the eyes and mouth fitted precisely, while Hanna laced up the back, pulling the leather taut until it fitted Stephanie so tightly it was possible to see the outline of her features underneath.

Satisfied that the hood was properly in place, they fitted the silk mask back over the hood. Stephanie glimpsed her bizarre appearance in the mirror – her head was like a piece of sculpture! – before she was plunged into darkness again.

In the darkness her body throbbed, the three clips on her nipples and clit making her nerves tingle.

The girls helped her to her feet. The chain on her nipples swung and she felt them surge with sensation. They were making her raise her legs again to put her feet into spiky white high heels, but this moved the clip on her labia and it bit hard against her clitoris. She shuddered.

'Oh, oh . . .' she gasped as the process was repeated with the second shoe.

They held her by the shoulders and walked her forward. Walking made her shudder again. The clip on her clit moved wonderfully from side to side, the metal round and smooth; held hard by the leather, it rolled against her body, just as the chain swinging from her breasts activated the nipple clips.

Stephanie thought she was going to come even before she got across the bedroom floor. She took a deep breath and managed to control herself, but it was not easy; the provocations of the day made her want to give in. Her shoulders ached from the constraint of the glove, so she concentrated on that feeling in an effort to overcome the waves of pleasure flooding through her body from clitoris and nipple.

Stephanie felt the coolness of the corridor. They didn't walk far. Stephanie heard a door opening after only a few yards. She was led into another room where her heels clacked on what was now a wooden floor. From the distance covered, she knew the room must be next doors to hers. Had the Baron put them in this particular bedroom because it was next to the pleasure room? Had he known all along that this is where she would end up?

The room was warm. The girls brought her to a halt.

'Good evening, my dear.' It was the Baron's voice. She did not reply. 'Bend over, please.'

She felt one of the girl's hands pushing her over and bent forward. The chain on the nipple clips swung clear of her body, her bound hands on the small of her back stuck up awkwardly, and the strap between her legs dug into the cleft of her buttocks.

She knew he was going to whip her. She wanted it. Her bottom felt cold and exposed. A hand rested on her neck, preventing her from straightening up.

She felt the draught of air and heard the whistle of the whip; then came the thwack of leather on flesh and a hot streak of pain searing into her buttock. It burnt into her, travelling like a guided missile to her imprisoned clitoris and nipples, joining the sensation they were already generating, heightening it, making her blood pound and her heart race.

Two strokes, three, four. Four red-hot welts across her buttocks. Four stripes of stinging crimson driving her to a frenzy. The pain was so hot, so sharp and acute, that she could not distinguish it from pleasure. Her body was so full of feeling already she thought she would come; in fact, she wasn't sure she hadn't already come on the metal clip that held her clit as the whip had fallen for the last time.

She might have come again when she felt a cool hand stroking the reddened flesh so softly, so tenderly, it made her surge with pleasure. She felt fingers unbuckling the leather between her legs and almost protested but, as the leather was pulled away and she felt hands pushing her back upright, the metal clip stayed where it was. This came as a great relief, as the feeling it gave her was so intense.

Hands guided her forward. She felt them making her sit, making her lie back, pulling her down on some sort of wooden padded frame.

'Do you wish to continue? This is the last time I will ask. You have to be gagged.' The Baron's voice was very solemn and serious.

'Yes,' Stephanie said without thought, her body boiling with pleasure.

'Very well.'

They were pulling her back into the middle of the frame and she suddenly felt her arms disappear down into what was obviously an aperture designed for the purpose. Her body rested not on her bound arms, which would have made it arch upwards, but on a strip of something she felt sliding in from the side of the frame, between her lowered arms and her back, so her body rested directly on its spine.

'Open your mouth,' the Baron ordered.

Stephanie obeyed. For a second she felt a finger playing at her lips. It entered her mouth and prodded her tongue. A moment later it was replaced by a big wedge of rubber, a wedge shaped exactly like a tongue but much bigger, so big it filled her mouth completely. It jammed her own tongue against the bottom of her mouth, making it impossible for her to form any sort of sound. She felt the gag being strapped in place around the white leather hood.

The blindfold was removed. Stephanie looked around but the room was so dimly lit she could hardly see anything. The walls and ceiling were all padded with thick black material, as was the frame she lay on. The board between her arms and her back made it impossible for her to raise her head more than an inch or two. She could see Hanna and Mischa on either side of the frame, but she could not see the Baron.

Hanna fastened a strap from one side of the frame over Stephanie's shoulder to the other. Mischa secured another around her waist. Then each girl took a leg and pulled it up at an angle to her body. On either side of the frame was a metal post, attached to which were small pulleys with ropes passing through them. The girls strapped leather cuffs around Stephanie's ankles, attached them by means of a D-ring to the ropes, and used the pulleys to hoist her legs higher and further apart. Her bottom was raised up off the frame, the whole of her sex exposed and vulnerable, the clip on her vulva tightened by her position.

Mischa reached up above Stephanie's body to another pulley set in the ceiling. She loosened it, brought a small hook into Stephanie's view and clipped it around the chain of the nipple clips. Stephanie watched as the chain was wound up, gradually pulling her nipples, then her breasts with it. Inured to the original pressure of the clips, her nipples suddenly started tingling at this new sensation, the delicious pain going straight to her clit. The hook appeared to be attached to some sort of elasticated rope as there was some give in the line. When Mischa had tied it off she tweaked the line with her fingers and it quivered, making Stephanie's nipples and breasts quiver in turn.

Stephanie strained her head as far up off the frame as the bondage would allow, wanting to see herself, wanting to see her breasts suspended and her legs splayed. Hanna was doing something to the clip over her labia. When she took her hand away Stephanie could see that the clip was now attached to a long thin thread, which Hanna was pulling up and attaching to the same hook that held the chain from the nipple clips. This thread too appeared to be elasticated. As soon as it was pulled tight, Hanna strummed it. It vibrated like a bow-string, transmitting a shockwave to Stephanie's clitoris and nipples. They were now all joined externally as well as by her body.

The shockwave made Stephanie close her eyes temporarily. She felt another wave when she opened them again and looked at herself, so indecently displayed, so helpless. It was too much effort to keep her head, raised, so she lowered it. The three clips seemed still to be vibrating, all to the same pulse. But then Stephanie suddenly realised this was not caused by the elasticity of the fixings. They were vibrating of their own accord. Mischa had operated a little mechanism at the point where the two lines were joined which agitated them like the strings on a musical instrument, sending vibrations along the lines and down to the clips.

The vibration got stronger. Stephanie moaned into the rubber gag but produced not a sound.

The Baron watched. He felt her wallowing in this new sensation. A lot of women had passed out even before the vibration had begun.

He reached forward and increased the vibration. Hanna tightened the pulley slightly, increasing the tension in the clips, tautening the lines. The vibration now pulsed more strongly, and Stephanie came, her orgasm erupting in her nipples and clitoris together just as they oscillated together. She came so strongly that her body fought her bondage and the feeling of helplessness, of being unable to move, increased the strength of her climax, made it go on longer. Even the fact that her cry of pleasure was drowned in her mouth somehow made her passion more acute.

She knew what the Baron meant. She knew now. As the first orgasm died another was already waiting, building, gathering in her nerves, and she knew he hadn't finished yet, that this wasn't all, that there was more. How would she stand it?

She opened her eyes and raised her head. She could see Hanna holding something in her hand but she could not tell what it was. The effort was too much however, and, as her body took control again, she dropped her head back and feeling raced between the trinity of clips that held her so tight. She came again, harder, stronger, her whole body shuddering under the impact.

She didn't think she could stand it. The Baron was right. This was the ultimate pleasure. The moment one orgasm was gone she could feel the next beginning, always bigger, always more powerful. She would have expected her body to get used to the clips, as her nipples had on the way to the pleasure room, but the vibration seemed to keep the feeling alive. She desperately tried to clear her mind but she was beginning to see things in the darkness. Images of Devlin in the Roman pavilion, images of herself in front of the forge with the Inquisitor, images of herself standing naked on the galley, whip in hand, looking down at twelve naked, erect cocks, whipping them as they started to spunk . . .

'No,' she screamed, without making a sound. The rubber wedge filled her mouth like a cock as another orgasm seized her body, shook it against its constraints, then threw it viciously aside. She thought the next time she would pass out.

Hanna inched forward. The object she held was

heavy, a metal ball with two prongs suspended from a chain just in front of the pulley that held the other lines. She manoeuvred it into place. The first of its shafts was long and curved. It was oiled and it glistened. The mouth of Stephanie's sex was open. Hanna positioned the shaft at the opening. She thought she could see it throbbing like the mouth of a fish gasping for air. The second phallus was shorter but wider. She positioned this at the puckered crater of Stephanie's anus. It too was heavily oiled. Not that it needed to be: Stephanie's juices were running out of her sex, a river of wetness.

Hanna looked at the Baron. She could see his surprise. They had never got this far before. Some women had survived the clips and the lines and the first few minutes of the vibration, but usually their first orgasm was too much for them to take. Stephanie was still going.

The Baron nodded for Hanna to continue.

Hanna pushed the two phalluses forward. They were perfectly shaped; each entered its intended passage at the same time. The shafts slid home until the metal ball rested firmly between her thighs, so heavy it held them deep inside by virtue of its weight.

Stephanie looked up. Her whole body was locked, tension in every muscle. She was penetrated front and rear. Her mouth was full too. Her nipples and clit were vibrating and now, as Hanna reached and threw the switch, the two phalluses began to vibrate too.

This new vibration doubled, trebled the feelings she had had before. The very core of her body was quivering, the two passages of her body contracting violently, out of control, invaded by thrumming dildos. She had never felt anything like it; the vibration deep inside her matched the vibration on the outside, pulsing in time. For a moment she thought she was going to pass out. There was no gap between one orgasm and the next now, just one continuous orgasm. It broke over the shafts buried in her body, making her body tremble – as if it weren't trembling enough – and her own quivering interacted with the vibration of the machines, one increasing the other, everything, every movement making her come again and again. She couldn't stand it. She squirmed her legs in the air against the leather cuffs, but this only made the phalluses move into new areas of her body, flooding new nerves with feeling, bringing the next orgasm on faster and harder. She was going to pass out.

Suddenly she felt her body change dramatically. One moment she was the victim, the helpless bound slave to the endless vibration, and the next, by what means she did not know, she was its master. Suddenly, instead of having things done to her, Stephanie was doing. She no longer lay taking her orgasms; she controlled them, caused them. She no longer absorbed the massive feelings that flooded through every nerve in her body; she started to take them over, to make them work for her. She was in control now, total control.

'I want my pleasure!' she shouted noiselessly into the gag, and began sucking the rubber as though it were a cock that could be made to spunk for her. She did the same with the phalluses, wrapping her body around them as if they were cocks, using all her muscles on them. She felt herself shape an exquisite orgasm, through her own body now, and not because of the external vibration. She could alter the focus of her feelings, make herself feel her clit or the shaft in her anus or her tortured nipples, then make herself come over one, or over all together.

She could even have stopped herself from coming, but she didn't want to do that. There was no need now. Now she could take what pleasure she wanted without being overwhelmed by it. And she had every intention of taking endless pleasure. It was wonderful, quite unlike anything she had ever experienced before. Somewhere in the back of her mind she marvelled at the Baron's ingenuity; but her main concern was her body.

She saw the two girls looking down at her in wonder and then saw the Baron, his face leaning into her line of sight, disbelief etched into every feature of his face.

She closed her eyes and allowed herself to wallow in sensation again. The lines on the clips hummed. The heavy metal ball vibrated not only the shafts inside her, but also her buttocks and thighs where it rested heavy against them. She wriggled against the ankle-cuffs again and felt the phalluses move inside. She was coming again, the waves gathering in her body while she decided where she would let them crash on the shore: over her clit or deep inside her. It didn't really matter. What mattered was that it went on, on and on, until she had had enough.

'I love it,' she said into the gag, as her body thrilled with pleasure and an orgasm rocketed through her, charging her nerves as though with electricity.

'Do exactly as I say.'

The Baron stood in front of her. His arms were laced into the leather gloves and bound behind his back, immovable. His nipples were clipped and chained together, his head covered by a white leather mask. His cock, the cock Stephanie had never seen before, was erect. It was not circumcised, and

Stephanie had pulled his foreskin back to reveal his pink glans. He had shuddered as she'd run her fingers around its tender rim.

The girls lowered him on to the frame. The board was inserted between his arms and his back, his legs raised and bound and pulled apart.

Stephanie stood between his legs and grasped his cock. The line attached to his nipples started to vibrate. He moaned. She would have loved to gag him, but she had other uses for his mouth.

She bent over and took his cock in her mouth, sucked it hard, then licked it as though it were an ice-cream, long licks up and down its whole length.

'See what you've been missing.'

She felt his cock throb.

There was plenty of time, she told herself. She moved around to his head and knelt on the frame, pushing her rump back until his face was underneath her soaking wet labia. Her sex was still tingling with excitement. He did not need to be told what to do. His tongue, hot and skilful, found her clitoris. It probed, then pushed into the mouth of her sex, extending up as far as it could. It pulled out and licked up to the bud of her anus, pushing in there, too.

He was hers now. She could do with him whatever she wanted. Today she hadn't made her mind up. She might let him spunk in her hands or in her mouth or deep inside her sex. It didn't really matter. Over the next few days he would do all three over and over again. Tomorrow she'd use a dildo on him and let it vibrate until he spunked, or perhaps she'd simply fuck him.

There were four more days to go, four days in which she would use him mercilessly, indiscriminately. She would use him and his pleasure room, him and Devlin and the girls. She might even make him pass out, as he had made so many women do on his bed of crimson joy.

Now she knew what she wanted tonight. As he'd driven his tongue into her, she'd decided what she wanted.

She had the girls lower his legs on to the frame. She stood up and walked around the frame on the padding until she could stand astride his hips. She strummed the line from his nipples as though it were a guitar string and watched as his body convulsed, his cock jerking and his mouth, still wet with her juices, open to moan. Slowly, she lowered herself on to him to take her pleasure.

This was, after all, what she'd wanted since she'd first met him, and Stephanie always got what she wanted. This was the ultimate reward; the pinnacle of Stephanie's pleasure.

NEW BOOKS

Coming up from Nexus and Black Lace

Lingering Lessons by Sarah Veitch
April 1995 Price: £4.99 ISBN: 0 352 32990 4
Leanne has just inherited an old boarding school, but she has to share it with the mysterious Adam Howard. Only one thing is certain about her new partner: he is a true devotee of corporal punishment. The last thing Leanne expects is to be drawn into his sordid yet exciting world, but the temptation proves irresistible.

The Awakening of Lydia by Philippa Masters
April 1995 Price: £4.99 ISBN: 0 352 33002 3
As the daughter of a district commissioner during the Boer War, Lydia has plenty of opportunity for excitement – and plenty of sex-starved men to pleasure her. But their skills are nothing compared to the voracious sexual appetites of the local tribesmen, who waste no time in taking the stunning sixteen-year-old captive.

Sherrie by Evelyn Culber
May 1995 Price: £4.99 ISBN: 0 352 32996 3
Chairman of an important but ailing company, Sir James is having trouble relaxing. But in Sherrie, seductive hostess on his business flight, he has found someone who might be able to help. After one of her eye-opening spanking stories and a little practical demonstration, money worries are the last thing on Sir James's mind.

House of Angels by Yvonne Strickland
May 1995 Price: £4.99 ISBN: 0 352 32995 5
In a sumptuous villa in the south of France, Sonia runs a very exclusive service. With her troupe of gorgeous and highly skilled girls, and rooms fitted out to cater for every taste, she fulfils sexual fantasies. Sonia finds herself in need of a new recruit, and the beautiful Karen seems ideal – providing she can shed a few of her inhibitions.

Crimson Buccaneer by Cleo Cordell
April 1995 Price: £4.99 ISBN: 0 352 32987 4
Cheated out of her inheritance, Carlotta Mendoza wants revenge; and with her exquisite looks and feminine wiles, there is no shortage of men willing to offer her help. She takes to the seas with a rugged buccaneer and begins systematically boarding, robbing and sexually humiliating her enemies.

La Basquaise by Angel Strand
April 1995 Price: £4.99 ISBN: 0 352 32988 2
Oruela is a modern young woman of 1920s Biarritz who seeks to join the bohemian set. Her lover, Jean, is helping her to achieve her social aspirations. But an unfortunate accident involving her father brings her under suspicion, and a sinister game of sexual blackmail throws her life into turmoil . . .

The Devil Inside by Portia da Costa
May 1995 Price: £4.99 ISBN: 0 352 32993 9
Psychic sexual intuition is a very special gift. Those who possess it can perceive other people's sexual fantasies – and are usually keen to indulge them. But as Alexa Lavelle discovers, it is a power that needs help to master. Fortunately, the doctors at her exclusive medical practice are more than willing to offer their services.

The Lure of Satyria by Cheryl Mildenhall
May 1995 Price: £4.99 ISBN: 0 352 32994 7
Welcome to Satyria: a land of debauchery and excess, where few men bother with courtship and fewer maidens deserve it. But even here, none is so bold as Princess Hedra, whose quest for sexual gratification takes her beyond the confines of her castle and deep into the wild, enchanted forest . . .

NEXUS BACKLIST

Where a month is marked on the right, this book will not be published until that month in 1994. All books are priced £4.99 unless another price is given.

CONTEMPORARY EROTICA

CONTOURS OF DARKNESS	Marco Vassi		
THE DEVIL'S ADVOCATE	Anonymous		
THE DOMINO TATTOO	Cyrian Amberlake	£4.50	
THE DOMINO ENIGMA	Cyrian Amberlake		
THE DOMINO QUEEN	Cyrian Amberlake		
ELAINE	Stephen Ferris		
EMMA'S SECRET WORLD	Hilary James		
EMMA ENSLAVED	Hilary James		
FALLEN ANGELS	Kendal Grahame		
THE FANTASIES OF JOSEPHINE SCOTT	Josephine Scott		
THE GENTLE DEGENERATES	Marco Vassi		
HEART OF DESIRE	Maria del Rey		
HELEN – A MODERN ODALISQUE	Larry Stern		
HIS MISTRESS'S VOICE	G. C. Scott		Nov
THE HOUSE OF MALDONA	Yolanda Celbridge		Dec
THE INSTITUTE	Maria del Rey		
SISTERHOOD OF THE INSTITUTE	Maria del Rey		Sep
JENNIFER'S INSTRUCTION	Cyrian Amberlake		
MELINDA AND THE MASTER	Susanna Hughes		
MELINDA AND ESMERALDA	Susanna Hughes		
MELINDA AND THE COUNTESS	Susanna Hughes		Dec
MIND BLOWER	Marco Vassi		

MS DEEDES AT HOME	Carole Andrews	£4.50	
MS DEEDES ON PARADISE ISLAND	Carole Andrews		
THE NEW STORY OF O	Anonymous		
OBSESSION	Maria del Rey		
ONE WEEK IN THE PRIVATE HOUSE	Esme Ombreux		
THE PALACE OF FANTASIES	Delver Maddingley		
THE PALACE OF HONEYMOONS	Delver Maddingley		
THE PALACE OF EROS	Delver Maddingley		
PARADISE BAY	Maria del Rey		
THE PASSIVE VOICE	G. C. Scott		
THE SALINE SOLUTION	Marco Vassi		
STEPHANIE	Susanna Hughes		
STEPHANIE'S CASTLE	Susanna Hughes		
STEPHANIE'S REVENGE	Susanna Hughes		
STEPHANIE'S DOMAIN	Susanna Hughes		
STEPHANIE'S TRIAL	Susanna Hughes		
STEPHANIE'S PLEASURE	Susanna Hughes		Sep
THE TEACHING OF FAITH	Elizabeth Bruce		
THE TRAINING GROUNDS	Sarah Veitch		

EROTIC SCIENCE FICTION

ADVENTURES IN THE PLEASUREZONE	Delaney Silver		
RETURN TO THE PLEASUREZONE	Delaney Silver		
FANTASYWORLD	Larry Stern		Oct
WANTON	Andrea Arven		

ANCIENT & FANTASY SETTINGS

CHAMPIONS OF LOVE	Anonymous		
CHAMPIONS OF PLEASURE	Anonymous		
CHAMPIONS OF DESIRE	Anonymous		
THE CLOAK OF APHRODITE	Kendal Grahame		Nov
SLAVE OF LIDIR	Aran Ashe	£4.50	
DUNGEONS OF LIDIR	Aran Ashe		
THE FOREST OF BONDAGE	Aran Ashe	£4.50	
PLEASURE ISLAND	Aran Ashe		
WITCH QUEEN OF VIXANIA	Morgana Baron		

EDWARDIAN, VICTORIAN & OLDER EROTICA

ANNIE	Evelyn Culber		
ANNIE AND THE SOCIETY	Evelyn Culber		Oct
BEATRICE	Anonymous		
CHOOSING LOVERS FOR JUSTINE	Aran Ashe		
GARDENS OF DESIRE	Roger Rougiere		
THE LASCIVIOUS MONK	Anonymous		
LURE OF THE MANOR	Barbra Baron		
MAN WITH A MAID 1	Anonymous		
MAN WITH A MAID 2	Anonymous		
MAN WITH A MAID 3	Anonymous		
MEMOIRS OF A CORNISH GOVERNESS	Yolanda Celbridge		
TIME OF HER LIFE	Josephine Scott		
VIOLETTE	Anonymous		

THE JAZZ AGE

BLUE ANGEL DAYS	Margarete von Falkensee		
BLUE ANGEL NIGHTS	Margarete von Falkensee		
BLUE ANGEL SECRETS	Margarete von Falkensee		
CONFESSIONS OF AN ENGLISH MAID	Anonymous		
PLAISIR D'AMOUR	Anne-Marie Villefranche		
FOLIES D'AMOUR	Anne-Marie Villefranche		
JOIE D'AMOUR	Anne-Marie Villefranche		
MYSTERE D'AMOUR	Anne-Marie Villefranche		
SECRETS D'AMOUR	Anne-Marie Villefranche		
SOUVENIR D'AMOUR	Anne-Marie Villefranche		
WAR IN HIGH HEELS	Piers Falconer		

SAMPLERS & COLLECTIONS

EROTICON 1	ed. J-P Spencer		
EROTICON 2	ed. J-P Spencer		
EROTICON 3	ed. J-P Spencer		
EROTICON 4	ed. J-P Spencer		
NEW EROTICA 1	ed. Esme Ombreux		
NEW EROTICA 2	ed. Esme Ombreux		
THE FIESTA LETTERS	ed. Chris Lloyd	£4.50	

NON-FICTION

FEMALE SEXUAL AWARENESS	B & E McCarthy	£5.99	
HOW TO DRIVE YOUR MAN WILD IN BED	Graham Masterton		
HOW TO DRIVE YOUR WOMAN WILD IN BED	Graham Masterton		
LETTERS TO LINZI	Linzi Drew		
LINZI DREW'S PLEASURE GUIDE	Linzi Drew		